"Were yo[u] suddenly, d[...] and gesturi[ng...]

She looked to refuse him and, really, Marcus wouldn't have been surprised. The request was beyond risqué. But she obeyed, slowly revolving until she stood with her back to him. "From what, Lord Weston?" she asked hesitantly.

"From me."

Her breath caught as he gently twisted a curl and effortlessly pinned it into place.

He reached for more pins, his fingers brushing her forearm lightly, stirring the heat low in his belly. "I apologize, Miss Tisdale, if I've offended you. Your nature seems to elicit the most unexpected behavior from me."

"Is that so?" she asked, turning back to face him.

He surveyed his handiwork, adjusting one final curl, which slid seductively near her chin. "Honestly? Yes, quite," he countered, the feel of her hair making him want to reel her in, inch by inch, and take her in his arms.

"Interesting," she said simply. "And I was not hiding from you. I was avoiding you. Two different things altogether."

He could not help himself. Her complete lack of guile was entrancing. He gently tugged until there was no more than a breath between them. "Why?"

"Because of this," she answered, then closed the distance between them with a kiss.

❧ ⚘

By Stefanie Sloane

The Devil in Disguise
The Angel in My Arms

The Angel in My Arms

A REGENCY ROGUES NOVEL

STEFANIE SLOANE

BALLANTINE BOOKS • NEW YORK

A Ballantine Books Mass Market Original

Copyright © 2011 by Stefanie Sloane
Excerpt from *The Sinner Who Seduced Me* by Stefanie Sloane copyright © 2011 by Stefanie Sloane

Published in the United States by Ballantine Books, an imprint of The Random House Publishing Group, a division of Random House, Inc., New York.

BALLANTINE and colophon are trademarks of Random House, Inc.

This book contains an excerpt from the forthcoming book *The Sinner Who Seduced Me* by Stefanie Sloane. This excerpt has been set for this edition only and may not reflect the final content of the forthcoming edition.

ISBN 978-0-345-51740-1
eBook ISBN 978-0-345-51743-2

Cover design: Lynn Andreozzi
Cover illustration: Alan Ayers

Printed in the United States of America

www.ballantinebooks.com

9 8 7 6 5 4 3 2 1

Ballantine Books mass market edition: July 2011

For my dad, Wallace "Buddy" Dyer Jr. You told me that I'd make my dreams come true—and you were right. I just wish that you'd been here to see them all. For you, Dad, and the strong will, obstinacy, and healthy sense of humor I inherited from you—required traits for any author—thank you.

1

DORSET
Summer 1811

Marcus MacInnes, the Earl of Weston, looked out over Lulworth Cove and chuckled. "Well now, Sully, you've seen it for yourself. Aye, it's my own personal Jericho. Wouldn't you agree?"

The valet's swarthy face remained unreadable, the lines around his eyes deepening as he squinted, his gaze focused on what lay below them. The cove's blue water lapped at the hulls of fishing boats. On the shore, the village dozed sleepily in the warm sunshine.

Exactly the sort of spot where a gentleman might just be sent to rusticate from a gunshot wound. Especially if the gentleman happened to be a spy.

Sully turned to look directly at his master. "It looks quiet enough, I'll give you that."

Marcus smiled wryly before turning his horse back onto the leafy path. "Indeed."

Sully followed suit, kneeing his bay gelding next to Marcus's chestnut Thoroughbred. "There *could* be smugglers."

Marcus slowed his mount just long enough to give the valet a dubious look.

"Or not," Sully admitted somewhat dejectedly.

Marcus ducked his head to dodge a low-hanging limb

and the green leaves of one of the massive whitebeam trees that lined the trail. "What a waste of time."

But there was nothing he could do about it. He'd been given an order, and he'd bloody well follow it.

Marcus was a Young Corinthian, and that meant something.

Dammit.

He and Sully continued on in silence. Their horses, Marcus thought absently, seemed thankful for the slower pace after the three-day ride from London to Lulworth, a sleepy hamlet located in Dorset along the southwestern coast of England.

The shaded lane curved and ahead of the two riders rose Lulworth Castle, Marcus's home. Originally built as a hunting lodge, the impressive structure had been expanded over the years until it was the largest home in the district.

The unentailed castle belonged to Marcus, due to his mother having been an only child. Yes, it was all his. And it was undeniably magnificent. But it was not where he wanted to be.

Marcus was a member of the Young Corinthians, a clandestine spy organization led by Henry Prescott, Viscount Carmichael. There was an unwritten rule among the Corinthians never to question an assignment. The life of a spy demanded complete loyalty and unswerving belief in your superior's judgment. Something Marcus had suddenly found particularly disagreeable.

The moment a bullet found its way into his leg during a mission this past spring, Marcus had known that his role within the elite organization would change dramatically. Until his injury healed fully, he was more a liability than an asset in the field.

Nevertheless, when Lord Carmichael suggested that Marcus investigate recent smuggling activity near his ancestral home in Dorset, Marcus nearly abandoned his well-practiced charm and told his superior exactly what he thought of the assignment.

Finding yourself with a bullet in your leg was one thing. Having your superior send you off on a fool's errand was quite another.

He couldn't deny that in all likelihood he'd made himself something of a nuisance to Carmichael as he impatiently waited for his blasted wound to heal.

And if he admitted that much, then he really could not blame Carmichael for dispatching him to the Dorset countryside when news of a possible connection between radical revolutionaries and local smugglers had the Prince Regent's drawers in a twist.

As Carmichael had informed him over plates of roast beef at their club, a string of recent robberies in London was believed to be related to the suspicious activities in Lulworth—both somehow tied to Napoleon's supporters.

Marcus had only stared at Carmichael in disbelief, a heavy goblet of brandy poised halfway to his mouth. Really, it was too much to be believed.

But still, Marcus reluctantly realized, if he were to be completely honest, his irritation with the assignment had as much to do with the location as with the smuggling investigation itself.

As a boy, when not in Inverness at his father's estate, the family had split its time between London and Lulworth. At least in London he'd been able to lose himself amid the constant thrum of social and sporting events. But the same could not be said for Lulworth. The hamlet's inhabitants had never gotten over his Scottish father's stealing away the fairest of their English roses. It hadn't helped that the elder Lord Weston embraced his role as the brutish Highlander with particular relish. His habit of donning a tartan and broadsword whenever his relatives visited the castle had only made things worse.

The locals hadn't liked the father, and as a result, they didn't like the son. And Marcus had known, from a painfully early age, that he simply did not fit in. Not in Lulworth, where everyone from the baker's son to the solicitor's daughter saw him as nothing more than the son of a thief. Not in Inverness either, where the blue English blood in his veins meant he'd never be a true Highlander.

"I've sorely missed Cook's pheasant," Sully said, pulling Marcus from his thoughts.

The stone castle stood before them with all the welcoming warmth of a midwinter snowfall.

"You're an accomplished liar, Sully, I'll give you that." Marcus's amiable tone belied his most recent grim thoughts. "But I know you too well. It's Cook that you've been looking forward to, not her creamed peas."

"Pheasant," Sully corrected him. "And it's quite a succulent bird that she cooks," he protested. "Though her creamed peas are quite delicious as well."

Marcus reined in his horse and raised a hand. "Far be it from me to intrude upon the ways of love," he said sardonically, prompting a harrumph from his valet.

With a noticeable lack of his usual ease, Marcus awkwardly swung a leg over the saddle and lowered himself to the ground, an instant stab of pain shooting up from the healing wound in his thigh. He ground his teeth together until the sensation subsided, then drew the soft leather reins over Pokey's head and handed them to Sully. "I'm going to walk off this stiffness. I'll be along shortly."

Sully gave Marcus a considering look then leaned from the saddle to take the reins. "Are you up to it?"

"Awa' an' bile yer heid!" Marcus growled, though the valet's thoughtfulness made him smile.

"Oh," Sully began, turning the two horses toward the stables, "I'll be missing that burr of yours while we're here. Can't be playing Lord of the manor sounding like one of them Jacobites though, now can we?" he teased. "I'll be in the kitchen, then."

"Oh, that's a given," Marcus shot back in a painfully perfect London accent. For as long as he could remember, he had made it a habit to hide his burr from everyone but Sully and the Scottish side of his family. There was simply no good reason to remind people of his ancestry.

"I'll send the hounds out if you've not limped your way home by dark."

"That's terribly thoughtful of you, old friend."

"Don't mention it—"

"And I do mean *old*," Marcus added with a gleam in his eye.

He could just make out another harrumph as Sully rode on, his pace quickening as he disappeared into the copse of trees that separated the expansive lawn of Lulworth from the rest of the grounds.

Marcus stretched, trying to ease the aches in his travel-weary muscles without irritating his wound further. He turned and strolled, limping slightly, toward the wood, his destination undecided. The tension that had gripped his gut when he'd first spied the castle slowly dissipated as he moved farther into the trees. He tugged at his carefully tied cravat, a low sigh escaping his lips as he yanked the length of white linen free of its intricate knot and unwound it from his throat. He mopped his brow with the dust-covered cloth before dropping it into the pocket of his deep brown riding coat.

The shade from the green-leafed canopy of oak trees provided some relief, but Marcus needed more. He stopped to orient himself, looking north, then east. Realizing that he wasn't far from the lake where he'd fished as a child, he set off at a faster clip.

A refreshing swim was precisely what he needed. The water would cool his body, clear his head, and, hopefully, tire him to the point that he no longer cared about where he was.

A high-pitched scream shattered the quiet and stopped Marcus in his tracks. A second scream followed, and Marcus ran, willing his wounded leg to keep pace with the rest of his body as he crashed through a bank of quickthorn bushes.

He fought his way through the thicket, the branches lashing his arms and legs until he broke into the open. The castle's lake lay before him, sparkling in the sunlight.

He scanned the water's surface, then the shore from left to right, but failed to find the source of the screams. Something moved suddenly in his peripheral vision. He narrowed his eyes and once more searched the lake. Water rippled in a circle too large to have been caused by a jumping trout.

He stripped off his coat and prepared to dive in. Just then, two figures broke the surface of the water. A peal of feminine laughter filled the air.

"You promised!" a young male voice whined indignantly.

Marcus squinted against the sun and made out a boy, sodden hair plastered to his skull.

"I never promised, Nigel," a woman's voice answered teasingly, "and it's very poor form of you to lie."

Marcus shielded his eyes with one hand to see the woman better. She bobbed up and down in the water, clearly amused with whatever had transpired between her and the boy.

She looked straight at him, her eyes widening in surprise. And then she smiled. A brilliant, wide smile that seemed to light up the entire world. She was soaking wet, long auburn curls in damp corkscrews atop her head and hanging to her shoulders. Her delicate skin flushed under the hot sun, a trailing frond of green water weed peeking out above the neckline of her dress.

And Marcus could not imagine a more bonny sight.

She seemed about to speak to him when her gaze shifted past him and over his shoulder. Shock and dismay filled her expression. "No, Titus!" she cried out. "No!"

Marcus turned his head just in time to make out a massive dog galloping toward him. The fawn-colored animal launched himself into the air, toppling Marcus backward onto the clay earth of the lake bank.

The weight of the beast's body settled on Marcus's chest and he planted a dinner-plate-sized paw on either side of Marcus's head. Then the dog lowered his massive face, the drool from his sharp-fanged mouth threatening to drop at any moment.

Marcus held himself completely still, knowing full well the animal had the upper hand. The dog sniffed carefully, his noxious breath hitting Marcus's nostrils with pungent force.

"Titus, get off that gentleman now. This! Very! Instant!"

The dog offered Marcus a sheepish, apologetic look before swiping his lolling tongue in friendly salute across Marcus's face.

"Now! Get off him. You bad, bad boy!"

Another apologetic look and the dog rose, allowing Marcus to sit up.

The woman leaned down to peer anxiously into Marcus's face.

"I must apologize for my dog's behavior," she began, now standing so close that Marcus felt tiny droplets of lake water hit his skin when she moved. "He is—"

"A menace to society?" the young boy at her side offered, giving Marcus a toothy grin.

"He is an enthusiastic participant in life." The woman rose to her feet to glare at the boy. "Titus is simply in need of proper instruction in manners."

"That is one way of looking at it," the boy countered, pointing at the dog, who was now a few feet away and busily tearing holes in Marcus's cast-off coat.

"Titus!" the woman protested, dashing toward the Shetland pony–sized dog. She tripped on a tree root and landed awkwardly on all fours, her nicely rounded derriere sticking up in the air.

Marcus stood with difficulty, wincing, his leg throbbing like the devil. He brushed without much success at the dirt stains on his buff-colored breeches and white linen shirt.

"Who is she?" he asked, failing to hide his stunned reaction.

The boy, whose features exactly matched the young woman's, chuckled. "Oh, no one of consequence, I assure you." He offered his hand to Marcus and shook enthusiastically. "I, on the other hand, am Nigel Edward Tisdale."

She was now engaged in a heated game of tug-of-war with the dog, her petite frame hardly a match for the big dog's superior strength.

"Marcus MacInnes, Earl of Weston," Marcus replied, hiding his burr with practiced ease. His gaze returned to the woman. "I wonder, should we assist Miss—"

"Not *the* Errant Earl?" the boy asked in wonder.

Marcus turned and looked at the lad, assuming that he had misheard. "I'm sorry, what was that you said?"

"Surely you know what people in these parts call you? I'd rather poke myself in the eye with a sharpened stick than listen to my mother and her friends gossip, but even I've heard the talk, and it's—what is the word I'm looking for?" Young Nigel paused and drummed his fingers against his lips as he thought.

" 'Unfavorable,' " Marcus offered helpfully.

"Well, I was going to say 'downright nasty,' but yes, 'unfavorable' will do."

Clearly, while the world about it had moved forward, the village of Lulworth continued to stalwartly cleave to unfounded and exaggerated assumptions. Marcus assumed that he should be offended, but honestly, he had neither the energy nor the interest at the moment.

He looked back to the woman, who was desperately attempting to maintain her foothold. "Shouldn't we . . ." he began, gesturing toward the pair.

"Oh, no, that would irritate Sarah to no end," the boy answered, watching the scene with marked delight as he wrung out his sodden shirt. "And trust me, you don't want to irritate my sister."

Marcus couldn't help but picture the woman irritated—enraged, really, as he sensed it would take very little to make her so—her auburn hair flying about her like a fiery halo, her skin heated to a delicious pink hue.

Marcus shook his head from left to right, wondering if the dog had indeed done some sort of damage to his mental faculties.

The two males watched for a moment more as the woman dug in her heels and seemed to be gaining the upper hand. But then the dog began to drag her forward, pulling her lower and closer to the ground until she collapsed with an audible expulsion of breath, facedown in the dirt.

"Sarah?" the boy queried in a mischievous tone. "Have you rescued Lord Weston's coat?"

The woman froze. Then slowly she released the torn coat and pulled herself upright, brushing lightly at the front of her wet, mud-stained gown.

"I beg your pardon, Nigel. Did you say 'Lord Weston'?"

The dog galloped to a stop beside her and dropped the coat at her feet.

"Bad dog!" she whispered vehemently, bending to snatch up the torn garment.

The boy elbowed Marcus in the ribs. "Why yes, Sarah," he said, drawing her attention back to her question. "The coat belongs to Lord Weston."

The lady's demeanor changed instantly. She leveled a cool glance at Marcus, her chin tilting slightly higher. Her diminutive shoulders squared and she attempted to unobtrusively peel the clingy gown from her fair skin.

Marcus stifled a laugh. She was covered from head to toe in dirt and God only knew what else. Any woman in her right mind would have fainted from the embarrassment of the situation. And, he realized, any man would have politely excused himself by now.

Yet, here he was.

"I do apologize for my dog's behavior, Lord Weston," she said agreeably. The trailing bit of bracken at her hemline did little to aid her dignity as she walked toward him. "And I will, of course, pay for the damages to your coat."

She thrust the ruined article of clothing toward him, avoiding his gaze.

"Mother is going to be apoplectic when she hears about this!" Nigel said with glee.

She caught Nigel's arm with some force, if the boy's pained expression was any indication. "Nigel, make yourself useful and properly introduce us, please."

"She'll be abed for days with this one—"

"Nigel!" the woman remonstrated, maintaining a polite if strained smile.

"Very well," Nigel begrudgingly agreed. "Sarah Elizabeth Tisdale, may I present Marcus MacInnes, the Earl of Weston."

The bizarre quality of the moment was not lost on Marcus. Here he stood, clothing torn and mauled by what was clearly the result of a misguided romantic encounter between a canine and large bear. The female standing in front of him was in absolute and, not to put too fine a point on it, scandalous disarray. And a devilish sprite was performing polite introductions in the middle of the wood.

It was of Shakespearean proportions. A farce, to be sure.

He should be appalled. Any man of his standing would be.

But he was delighted.

And he couldn't remember a time that he'd been so thankful for the ache in his leg and the need of a walk.

"Miss Tisdale," he said, offering her a respectful bow.

She executed an awkward curtsy. "Lord Weston, I'm delighted to make your acquaintance."

Marcus found it oddly amusing, their mutual adherence to the proprieties despite the clearly *improper* circumstances of this encounter. "And I yours."

She looked at him then, a blush settling on her ivory skin. "We were not aware you were in residence at the castle."

"Do you always make use of the lake in my absence?" he asked teasingly, his charm returning.

"I can assure you, sir, that we do not make a habit of trespassing on your—"

"We most certainly do," Nigel interrupted indignantly. "It's the best fishing in the county."

Miss Tisdale looked as if she might spontaneously combust. The flush of heat traveling from her neck upward would certainly erupt in flames among her fiery auburn curls.

She took a deep breath, an impish grin coming to rest on her lips. "Oh, all right, then. We do. Now, Nigel," she paused, looking about as if searching for something, and then whistling in a most unladylike fashion. "Do secure Titus's leash."

The earth shook as the huge dog ran toward them. Marcus braced himself as Titus came to a sliding stop mere inches from his legs.

Nigel retrieved a leather lead, coiled in a serpentine pile near the bank. "I don't know why we bother with this. It would hardly keep him—"

Miss Tisdale daintily cleared her throat and shot Nigel a murderous look. "The lead, Nigel."

No sooner had the boy obeyed when Titus lifted his massive head and caught the scent of something on the wind. He bounded off with Nigel in tow, leaving Marcus and Miss Tisdale quite alone.

Miss Tisdale watched as Titus dragged her brother along, a small smile forming on her mouth. "Serves him right," she said under her breath.

Marcus pretended not to hear her, as it was the polite thing to do. Still, he smiled.

He could not look away. The sun had begun to dry her auburn hair so that it gleamed. He wanted to reach out and touch it, to measure the weight of it in his hands.

Her profile enthralled him. Her pert nose—sprinkled with freckles, no less—was the ideal accompaniment to her high cheekbones and that perfect mouth.

"I apologize, Lord Weston," she offered quietly, without looking at him.

Marcus abruptly ended his cataloging of her features. "For trespassing or for Titus?" he quipped.

"Both, actually," she answered, turning to look at him, a charming smirk lighting up her face. "And the mud. I'm really quite sorry for the mud."

And just like that, she ran from the lake bank and disappeared into the shrubbery, her long hair swaying behind her as she went.

"What in bloody hell just happened?" Marcus said aloud, not sure what to do next.

"Ouch!" Nigel cried, rubbing at his head. A moment before, Sarah's knuckles had come in all-too-enthusiastic contact with his scalp. "What was that for?"

Sarah took Titus's leather lead from Nigel and yanked the dog to a slower pace. "Do not play innocent with me, young man."

Nigel gave her a mystified look. "Honestly, Sarah, I've no idea what you're talking about. Oh, wait," he offered, "is this about me calling Lord Weston the Errant Earl?"

"You did what?" Sarah shrieked.

Nigel scurried ahead. "It's not as if I lied to the man. I've heard Mother and her friends call him by that name plenty of times."

So had Sarah, but she wasn't about to validate Nigel's point. Besides, she'd always thought it rather presumptuous of the women to label him as such. If he'd spent so little time in the district, then it was surely impossible for anyone to know the man well enough to judge.

"No, not that—though it was rather rude. I'm referring to the fact that you all but admitted that we trespass upon Lord Weston's land on a regular basis."

"Actually, I did admit to that."

"Exactly!"

Nigel kicked at a rock in his path. "Is not honesty the best policy?" he queried, using his sister's words against her.

"This is hardly the time to become virtuous, Nigel," she answered, her words laced with amusement.

Titus lunged for the rolling rock and grasped it within his powerful jaws.

"Lord Weston seemed a reasonable man." Nigel leaned over to pry the rock out of Titus's mouth, with little success. "I hardly think he'll alert the parish constable."

Sarah was loath to tell Nigel precisely what was needling her about the interlude with Lord Weston. Though any human being with a modicum of sense could have guessed that the entirety of their introduction was beyond acceptable.

She was speaking to Nigel, though, she reminded herself. Twelve-year-old boys, in her experience, embraced a different view of the world and the niceties of society's rules.

Actually, more often than not, Sarah seemed to agree with Nigel on this very topic. But in the short amount of time she'd spent in Lord Weston's company, Sarah had recognized that he was . . . Well, Lord Weston was different, though she could not put her finger on exactly why.

"I do not fear our arrest," she began, pulling upon the lead until Titus protested with a loud whine. "It's simply that as introductions go—"

Titus gagged loudly. The rock flew out of his mouth, landing in the grass just beyond the path.

"Well," she continued as if there had been no interruption, "it was hardly ideal."

Titus instantly recovered and pulled Sarah forward.

"Oh, I don't know about that," Nigel replied, running to catch up. "I'd say that we made quite an impression."

Sarah shook her head. But Nigel's smile had a way of warming her heart.

And, in truth, she couldn't tell him why she was so upset.

Because she herself didn't precisely know the cause.

Making "quite an impression" was nothing new to Sarah Tisdale. Since leaving childhood behind, she'd suffered through countless introductions to eligible bachelors. Her physical clumsiness and alarming tendency to say whatever might be on her mind had resulted in a profound lack of interest on the part of said bachelors.

At first, their reactions had upset and saddened her. And then, they angered her. And now? Well, now she simply did not care. Or did she?

Sarah attempted to rein Titus in as they approached Tisdale Manor.

Marcus MacInnes, the Earl of Weston, had, beyond a shadow of a doubt, met Sarah at her worst. She had to give him credit for exhibiting only mild horror at her appearance and disarray.

Sarah released Titus from the lead and allowed him to run into the yard of Tisdale Manor, his enthusiastic barking alerting the entire household to their return.

"No hiding from Mother now," Nigel declared, nudging Sarah in the ribs before loping after Titus.

Sarah squared her shoulders and sighed. Lord Weston was remarkably handsome, even when covered in mud. His golden hair brought to mind long, lazy summer days spent out-of-doors. Titus's attack had helped to outline the man's physique, his sodden shirt and breeches molding to an expansive set of shoulders that tapered to a trim waist and well-muscled legs.

Yet, she reminded herself, despite his good looks, he was a man, and as such, could only be relied upon for one thing: disappointment.

If trespassing on his grounds had not been enough to drive him off, surely her tripping over the tree root must have convinced him that the opinion held by the entirety of England's male population had been correct: Sarah

Tisdale was simply more than any man should—or could—take on.

"Bollocks," Sarah muttered.

She delighted in swearing. Borrowing from Nigel's supply of inappropriate terms secretly thrilled her.

And putting Marcus MacInnes, the Earl of Weston, in his place, if only in her mind, was endlessly satisfying.

He was handsome. And charming. And he'd failed to lose his temper and take a stick to Titus, even though most men in his position would have done so.

And the heat of his gaze lingering on her damp skin had nearly done her in. Her toes had curled, she was sure of it.

But curled toes or no, Sarah would not entertain any further thoughts of Lord Weston.

"Sarah!" Her mother's hysterical shriek carried from inside the house. Titus howled and ran to hide in an outbuilding.

"Coward," Sarah grumbled at the dog, walking reluctantly into the house. Nigel must have already shared the news of Lord Weston's arrival with the family.

"Sa-Rah!"

She sighed with resignation.

This would not end well.

Sarah entered the sun-filled foyer and hesitated, closing her eyes for a moment to enjoy the midday heat.

"Do not keep me waiting, child."

Sarah's eyes popped open at the demand. One more moment of delay and she'd have to sacrifice Titus to appease her mother.

Pulling a twig from her curls, Sarah walked down the hall, her ruined kid boots leaving mud in her wake.

Think, Sarah, think.

She'd bested her mother in less time before, though her current state of disrepair would prove an impediment.

She turned into the parlor, her mother's appalled gasp too loud to ignore.

"Really, Sarah, do you wish to frighten me to death?" Lenora Tisdale exclaimed, gesturing for her daughter to come nearer.

Sarah looked across the room. Nigel stood at the tall windows, fidgeting with the umber drapery sash. His guilt-ridden expression told her without words that their mother already knew of Lord Weston's presence in the district.

She gave Nigel a reassuring look and one quick wink before answering. "Come now, Mother, it would take far more than fright to fell the likes of you," she answered, the sarcasm in her voice nearly hidden.

Her mother eyed her with reproach, clearing her throat. "Sarah, am I to understand that you—"

"Though, I am sorry to say," Sarah continued over her mother's words, "there is a bit of news that you, in all likelihood, will find most distressing."

Managing the direction of a conversation was a maneuver that usually worked well with Lenora Tisdale. The myriad disparate bits of information residing in her brain were easily toppled and confused by the lure of interesting news.

"What are you telling me, girl?" her mother asked, her brows knitting together briefly as she smoothed the skirt of her primrose-patterned day dress.

Sarah drew nearer, sinking to her knees and settling herself on the Aubusson carpet with her damp muslin skirts pooling about her. "Oh, yes, Mother. Quite distressing indeed," she answered with a foreboding tone. "The Earl of Weston has returned to Lulworth Castle," she proclaimed with dramatic effect.

Lenora faltered, and then found her footing. "Am I to understand that Nigel speaks the truth? You have met the Errant Earl? In such a state?" she asked, her eyebrows rising to meet her hairline.

"Can you imagine the impertinence of such a man?" Sarah answered, schooling her countenance into offended lines. "He has returned to Lulworth Castle unannounced—a social faux pas, if there ever was one. And as if that were not bad enough, he insisted on an introduction when I was clearly neither prepared nor inclined to acknowledge him! The presumptuousness of the man knows no bounds!"

"Indeed. He is no gentleman—but we knew this already," Lenora agreed quietly. Her eyes narrowed, her mind clearly working to rearrange the facts of the situation so as to suit her needs.

Sarah held her breath as she watched the emotions play across her mother's face. The truth was quite simple: Since being put on the shelf at the age of two-and-twenty, Sarah had enjoyed an uncomplicated life, relatively free from the machinations of her mother. The moment her last remaining prospect, Sir Reginald Busby, proposed to Lilith Mackam nearly three years before, it was as if she no longer existed, at least to Lenora.

It had been, in a word, bliss.

Lord Weston's return could ruin everything. The gossip over the years had made it clear enough that the Errant Earl held no special place in the villagers' hearts, including her mother's. But Sarah suspected that his title and all that came with it would give Lenora cause to reconsider.

Sarah believed with grim certainty that she was not meant to be the wife of an earl, as well the entire county knew. Men did not want a woman. They wanted a wife who would fawn over them. And a mother to bear their children. And a dressmaker's dummy to look the loveliest at social events. But not a woman with a mind. Or spirit. Or independent tendencies. And especially not one who could hardly manage walking—never mind dancing—without maiming herself.

In short, not her.

Was it too much to hope that Lenora would agree?

"Yes indeed. Not a gentleman," Lenora repeated, though this time with markedly more enthusiasm and disdain. "Really, one should be able to expect more of a titled man, though Weston has proven himself in the past to be quite undeserving of his station, so I do not know why I would hope for improvement."

Sarah wanted to point out that Lenora had not even met the earl, at least not since he'd been in short pants. But she curbed the desire to do so and instead nodded in solemn agreement, then rose from the carpet. "Yes, quite," she offered, slowly backing toward the door.

"Just let the man attempt to make amends. I will give him the cut direct."

"Of course."

"And if he thinks for one moment that we may be obliging," Lenora continued, indignation rising. "Really, to force an introduction with you looking like *that*—"

"Absurd!" Sarah nodded before exiting the room, breaking into a run the moment she was out of sight in the hall and dashing toward the stairs.

Brava, Sarah, she commended herself with a satisfied smile, though she'd failed to include Nigel in her escape, she realized. *Ah, well, serves him right. He is the one who wanted to go fishing.*

"Did you capture the smugglers all on your own, then?" Sully asked, regarding Marcus's appearance with a raised eyebrow.

Marcus tossed his ruined coat at the valet, hitting him squarely in the head. "I applaud your restraint, Sully. We've walked the length of Lulworth Castle to reach my rooms and you've kept your gob shut until now."

"Is the leg bothering you?" Sully inquired, pulling the coat from atop his head and dropping the sodden garment to the floor.

Marcus eased himself into an armchair near a large window. "Don't go changing the subject." His leg throbbed and he winced, shifting to ease it.

"Bloody martyr," Sully said under his breath as he knelt and carefully pulled off Marcus's boot. "The doctor ordered you to rest."

"This was hardly of my doing," Marcus informed him.

"Why do I find that hard to believe?" Sully asked, eyeing the muddy Hessians with disgust.

"I've absolutely no idea," Marcus replied.

Sully turned to drop the pair of dirty boots by the door. "I was right to begin with, was I? The smugglers surrendered after a brief but doomed resistance?" He returned to stand by the window, eyeing Marcus with interest.

"Hardly, though I suspect a boatload of smugglers would be far easier to catch than Miss Tisdale."

"Miss Tisdale? A woman did that to you?" Sully asked, not bothering to smother a laugh.

"Not precisely," Marcus began, but the discomfort caused by his wet breeches urged him upright. "No, it was her mongrel."

Sully laughed out loud. "A lady's lapdog did that—to you!"

"Hardly a lapdog. The thing was a mass of fur and claws. And the slobber. Oh God, the slobber. I assure you," Marcus answered, unbuttoning his linen shirt, "the size of a full-grown man and just as strong."

"Of course, my lord," Sully replied, attempting to rein in his mirth. "And his name? Precious? Or Lord Knicker-bottom, perhaps?"

Marcus balled up the shirt, tossed it, and hit Sully in the chest. "Titus." He walked to the chest of drawers, where a porcelain bowl and a pitcher of warm water sat. Sluicing his fingers first, he cupped both hands and lowered his head, dousing his face and hair.

"And the woman? Was she a mass of muscles and claws as well?"

Marcus almost answered in the affirmative. Sarah Tisdale certainly possessed canine qualities, though one would not know it to look at her.

The epitome of an English rose, Miss Tisdale sprang to Marcus's mind immediately, despite the fact that he'd never before been intrigued with such countryside offerings. Her fresh complexion perfectly complemented her mass of auburn hair. That hair had swung seductively back and forth as she walked, the length of it nearly reaching her rounded backside.

And those green eyes. The color of the lush banks of Loch Ness. They spoke of wildness. Of passion as yet unrealized.

Marcus splashed himself again and let the water drip down his neck and bare chest.

His tastes had always run toward the polished. He supposed that had everything to do with Lulworth and, to a lesser extent, Inverness. The local girls in both towns had feigned interest only when their mamas had thought of his titles and financial worth, leaving Marcus with the feeling that he fit neither in their world nor his.

London, with its capricious rules of polite society that were easily bent with the right amount of money or charm, had given Marcus the opportunity for advancement after his time at Oxbridge. So had his affiliation with the titled men of the Young Corinthians. Carmichael had recruited the solitary youth after witnessing his skills in a fencing match, though Marcus learned later that the man had been following his progress for some time.

The secret arm of England's royal forces, the Corinthians counted among their numbers many of the ton's most prominent members. Associating with powerful men who were stars in the ton's firmament had done wonders for Marcus's reputation.

"Did she slobber then?"

His mind still absorbed in the past, Sully's question surprised him. "I'm sorry?"

The valet handed Marcus a linen towel. "Miss Tisdale. Was she as terrifying as her hound from hell?"

Marcus wiped his face and neck with the length of linen. "Oddly enough, she was."

"Missing teeth and as round as a carriage wheel, then?"

Marcus chuckled. "No, not at all. Quite attractive, actually." He dropped the damp towel on the bureau and crossed to the armoire. "No, I'm referring to her demeanor. Not that she was rude. There's just . . . something."

Something good. She'd been flustered by the situation, that much had been clear. But despite this, the woman had treated him as though he were any other male of her acquaintance—English, Scottish, canine, or otherwise.

Sully followed at a leisurely pace. "Lust, my lord. The girl's a mere country bumpkin. When a woman such as she is presented with a dashing London gentleman, well, what else was she to do?"

Marcus did not have to turn and look at Sully to know he was smiling. "No, it was most decidedly not lust, though I'll have you know," he paused, flexing his well-honed arms for effect, "I am, indeed, a fine specimen, even with the limp."

"That you are, my lord, that you are," Sully answered with amusement. "Which ought to be helpful at your dance tomorrow night."

Marcus ceased perusing the linen shirts and turned to look at his valet. "*My* dance?" he asked, a hint of irritation lacing his question.

"Oh, yes, my lord," Sully answered firmly, moving past Marcus to choose a shirt. "We've discussed this. You'll need to do the pretty with the locals if there's any hope of gathering information on the smugglers."

Marcus ground his teeth together at the mention of the investigation. "You're assuming that there's a shred of truth to Carmichael's suspicions?"

"I'm assuming we might as well get on about our business," Sully answered succinctly. "Carmichael's not about to forget why he sent you here."

Marcus knew Sully was right. Though the likelihood of any real nefarious goings-on was slim, he had a job to do. "What makes you think the local gentry will bother to come?" Marcus pressed, "especially with such short notice?"

Sully reached for one of the dozen folded shirts and handed it to Marcus. "Come now, my lord. You know as well as I that they'll overcome any misgivings they may have for the opportunity to step foot in the castle. Especially with you here—you're a curiosity. Only half an Englishman you may be, but your titles are complete enough and there's no arguing on that point."

Sully spoke the truth, and it only made him loathe the locals more. He could almost admire them for holding a grudge against his family for so long, such an undertaking surely requiring single-minded strength and dedication. But to put aside their convictions for quality claret and a view of the brutish Scot? That was deplorable, plain and simple.

He dropped one arm into the shirtsleeve and then the other, moving on to the buttons. "Fair enough."

"Really, quite beyond the pale," Lenora exclaimed, her statement nearly lost under the methodical rattle of the carriage wheels. "Really. Quite."

Sarah's father, Sir Arthur Tisdale, pretended to doze in the corner, though his breathing pattern told otherwise.

"If it is beyond the pale—which I most certainly do agree with—then why do we find ourselves in a carriage bound for a dance at Lulworth Castle?" Sarah asked pointedly, in no mood to encourage her mother. She'd started out strong in her quest to throw Lenora off the earl's scent, yet here they were. Not good. Not good at all.

Lenora rolled her eyes and huffed as if she'd never heard a more ridiculous question in her life. "Sarah, the earl's hastily planned party shows arrogance and the assumption that the village will simply jump to his bidding, I'll give you that," she began, pausing to pick a piece of lint from Sarah's pomona green gown. "But what are we to do? Nearly everyone of our acquaintance will be there. Would you have us not attend?"

"And would you have me ask the earl exactly how high I should jump?" Sarah replied, perfectly aware of how dangerous this game could be, yet unable to stop herself. "I do wonder if I'll be able to perform to his standards in these slippers. I should have worn my more serviceable boots. Far easier to jump—"

"Sarah Elizabeth Tisdale!" Lenora twisted her fingers together in her lap, apparently to restrain herself lest she reach out and throttle her offspring. "You are impertinent and—"

"Did I nod off?" Sarah's father interrupted, his large, strong hand covering his wife's.

Lenora visibly calmed at his touch. "Of course you did, Arthur. You always do."

"Pity, that," he replied, looking out the carriage window. "Well, if my descent into slumber was ill-timed, it looks as if my awakening could not have been more timely."

Sarah and her mother followed Sir Arthur's gaze out the carriage window. The walls of Lulworth Castle loomed nearer, the stone exterior softened and made more welcoming by the gathering of the county's polite society as the coaches delivered them to the front door.

The Tisdale carriage rolled to a slow stop and Sir Arthur released Lenora's hand. "The earl awaits," he urged, alighting from the carriage and reaching for his wife.

Her mother gave Sarah *the* look, adjusted the silk shawl about her shoulders, and then stepped gracefully from the coach on her husband's arm. Her clear voice called a greeting to Mrs. Rathbone as she joined a number of acquaintances chatting together on the castle steps.

"If I'm not mistaken," Sarah's father began, looking after Lenora as she walked away, "that was your mother's 'Please do behave or I'll be forced to lecture you into an early grave' look. Am I correct?"

Sarah laughed lightly at the statement. "I would be careful if I were you, Father. She's not above delivering such discipline to you," she warned, rising to step down from the coach and into the warm night air.

Sarah took her father's offered arm, allowing him to escort her to the castle steps.

"No need to remind me," he answered, wiggling his bushy eyebrows.

The two entered the castle and mounted the stairs, the soft sound of stringed instruments just audible above the jovial din of the gathering.

"Is this why we're here, then?" Sarah asked her father, taking in the impressive surroundings. "To get a look at the castle and the Errant Earl?"

Arthur lovingly tucked Sarah closer to his side and patted her hand with his own. "Well, the way I see it, the man needs at least one ally. And with both of us here, he has two. A good start, wouldn't you agree?"

"You are a dear man, you know that, don't you?" Sarah said warmly, her father's sensibilities calming her jangled nerves.

Sir Arthur emitted a low grumble of approval. "Or extraordinarily lazy and loath to apply myself to the business of forming opinions about one I've yet to meet. But I do prefer your reasoning to mine."

The two paused to look behind them, searching the faces in the line that reached all the way to the entry. Lenora appeared suddenly, walking toward them as quickly as was seemly.

"There you are," Sir Arthur said as his wife neared. "You nearly missed our announcement."

Her look of complete and utter horror at violating the strict rules governing the introduction of guests had Sarah stifling a laugh.

"Really, Arthur," Lenora protested.

He patted her arm and steered her toward the entry to the room.

The trio stepped in front of the majordomo, who held a tall black lacquered stick topped with a gold lion's head in his right hand.

"Sir Arthur Tisdale, Lady Tisdale, and Miss Tisdale," Sir Arthur told the man in his authoritative but kind tone.

The majordomo bowed his head, then turned, striking the Axminster carpet with the stick three times before announcing their names.

As Sarah looked out over the crowd, she noticed her dear friend Lady Bennington waving to catch her attention, smiling brightly at her. Sarah smiled and offered an enthusiastic wave in return.

"I'm going to say hello to Claire and the marquess," she told her parents, avoiding her mother's second admonishing look of the evening.

Her father kissed her on the cheek. "Do give them our best, dear."

"Of course, Father." Sarah nodded before turning to thread her way across the crowded room to reach her friend.

"My dear," Claire said, pulling Sarah to her in a warm embrace. "I'm so pleased to see you. But I must say I'm somewhat surprised to find you here."

"No more surprised than I," Sarah answered, smiling at Claire's husband, Gregory Crawford, the Marquess of Bennington, over her friend's shoulder. "And you, my lord, are you surprised?"

Bennington gave Sarah a wry smile. "Miss Tisdale, if I've learned anything about my wife's dearest friend, it is that surprise over your actions is a waste of time."

"Not a day goes by that I do not thank the heavens you married such a perceptive man," Sarah whispered in Claire's ear before releasing her. "Let us pray that your child inherits the trait," she added, patting Claire's growing midsection affectionately.

"Now, can you, for even one fleeting moment, fathom the audacity of Lord Weston?" Sarah asked, her eyes widening with disbelief.

"Am I to assume that a certain woman is—or shall be soon—in search of an earl?" Claire asked, her expression solemn.

"As if she could help herself!"

Claire nodded.

Bennington broke.

"Ladies, I'm afraid my curiosity has gotten the best of me. What are you talking about?"

Claire looped her arm through his and leaned in. "It is the sad tale of a life most assuredly about to be ruined—" she began in a murmur.

"*My* life, Claire," Sarah added. "Do not forget what is assuredly a key point in this most heart-wrenching of tales."

Claire reached out and squeezed Sarah's shoulder in mock sympathy. "Of course. Now, where was I?"

"A life in ruins," Bennington put in.

"Thank you, dear." Claire's smile was brilliant and adoring as she met her husband's gaze. "A life soon to be ruined by the most uncharitable treatment of Marcus MacInnes, the Earl of Weston."

"What could Weston have done to ruin Sarah's life? He's only just arrived in the district," Bennington queried, looking confused. "We were at Oxbridge together. A bit of a solitary chap to be sure, but a good enough man."

"Oh, he's not ruined my life *yet*. After all," Sarah paused, leaning in conspiratorially, "he has yet to meet my mother."

Bennington's face lit with dawning understanding. "Ah, I see. Had I known of Lady Tisdale's involvement in this particular ruination, I would have had a far easier time following the conversation."

"Oh, quite. She's full of contempt for the man one moment, and the other? Here we are, in his home, awaiting an introduction. I'd bet a year's worth of pin money that she'll soon set about making a match. And that is where my simple life will end," Sarah lamented.

"Is that so?" Bennington asked. His gaze moved past the two women to the entryway. "And am I to understand that we would prefer to avoid Weston this evening?"

Sarah rolled her eyes. "Oh, yes, though I hardly think the earl will seek me out after our last meeting."

"Sarah?" Claire asked, clearly curious.

"It's hardly worth mentioning. And it involved mud, so really—"

"Is that so?" Bennington interrupted.

Sarah tilted her head. "My lord, you repeat yourself."

"Yes," he answered distractedly, his gaze still fixed. "Well, it's just that Lord Weston is coming this way—despite your assurances that he would do no such thing."

Sarah whipped around, nearly knocking into the pianoforte. "Dammit," she whispered as the earl strode confidently toward her.

"Oh. My," Claire whispered in her ear, slipping her arm about Sarah's waist.

"Remember, you're a married woman, Claire," Sarah hissed. "And with child!" she added, though she could not help but agree. Lord Weston looked even more handsome than he had at the lake, his black coat perfectly complemented by his white neckcloth tied trône d'amour. Sarah could not bring herself to examine anything below the man's waist, for fear of where her mind might wander.

Claire gave her a squeeze before releasing her. "Married and with child, Sarah, but not dead. Perhaps we should not forget the earl so hastily," she answered with a laugh.

Sarah straightened her spine and squared her shoulders. This was not good at all. She was a guest in the earl's home and thus was required to behave in a polite manner despite the fact that the man had . . . Well, he'd . . .

Well, he'd chastised her for setting foot on his land. And he'd had the audacity to see her when she was most assuredly not presentable. It was good material, to be sure, but Sarah could not quite bring herself to believe it. Nevertheless, she just *knew* the man was exceedingly dislikable.

Sarah wondered if anyone would notice if she suddenly dropped to the floor and crawled out of sight. There were a fair number of people in the room, after all. Though she'd have to avoid—

"Miss Tisdale. A pleasure to see you again."

Sarah blinked once, then twice, realizing with a start that the earl was standing right in front of her. And addressing her. "Drat."

"I beg your pardon?" he asked.

"Delightful," Sarah spat out, "to see you as well, my lord," Sarah continued, recovering. The earl looked at her with an intensity that Sarah found alarming. "Is something amiss, my lord?"

"No," he said unconvincingly, pausing for a moment, then turning to look at Claire and Bennington. "Bennington, it's been quite some time."

He offered his hand to Claire's husband, a friendly smile breaking across his face.

Bennington gripped Weston's hand enthusiastically, and then turned to his wife. "Claire, may I present Lord Weston."

Weston bowed before Claire, brushing a kiss against her fingers.

Claire's eyes danced with amusement. "It is truly a pleasure, Lord Weston."

Sarah rolled her eyes. "Really?"

The three turned at once to stare at her.

"Um . . . that is," Sarah began, looking frantically

about the room for an acceptable excuse. Lady Farnsworth and her niece Constance Shaw, who was visiting from Norwich, hovered nearby conversing with a small set of women. Sarah had met Constance only a few weeks before. The girl was agreeable enough. Lady Farnsworth, on the other hand, was absolutely dreadful. But there was little that could be done about it now.

"Lady Farnsworth, Miss Shaw, how extraordinary to see you," Sarah blurted out at the two women.

They turned at the sound of their names. "Miss Tisdale, it is indeed," Constance beamed, genuinely delighted to see her. Lady Farnsworth took in their small group, smiling approvingly at Claire and Gregory, nodding politely at Sarah, and freezing at the sight of Lord Weston.

Oddly enough, the awkward silence that fell over the six was worse than if Sarah had simply stood her ground and conversed with Lord Weston to begin with. *Bugger.*

Gregory cleared his throat and smiled at the women. "Lady Farnsworth, Miss Shaw, may I introduce our host, Marcus MacInnes, the Earl of Weston."

Lady Farnsworth omitted the obligatory curtsy, but fractionally inclined her feathered turban in acknowledgment. "Lord Weston, I knew your mother—and your father, of course," she added peevishly, reluctantly extending her hand as if forced to do so.

Lord Weston smiled serenely at the woman and took her hand in his, kissing it gently. "Lady Farnsworth, it is a pleasure to meet you. Perhaps one day you can regale me with stories of my mother's youth. I do adore a good tale."

"Oh, will you be staying in Lulworth much longer?" Lady Farnsworth asked acerbically. "Silly question, I suppose. You've been here all of two days now, so of course you'll be off—"

"With such charming neighbors as yourself," Lord Weston interrupted, his tone silken smooth though a dangerous gleam showed in his eyes, "why would I ever leave Lulworth?"

Lady Farnsworth compressed her lips into a tight line of indignation. "Indeed," she replied, reluctantly recognizing that she was no match for the man.

Sarah struggled to keep her mouth shut, but a tiny giggle of delight escaped her lips.

"Are you quite all right, Miss Tisdale?" Lady Farnsworth asked testily, still smarting from Lord Weston's subtle set-down.

As she'd done many times before in similar situations, Sarah forced herself to think of Theodore, a beloved spaniel she'd owned as a child. "Actually, I do believe I could not be better," she answered, the deceased canine having come to her assistance yet again.

"Lord Weston, do address Constance before she faints from her efforts," Sarah said hastily, looking at the girl as she held a perfect curtsy.

He bowed expertly and captured Constance's hand in his, pressing a firm and lingering kiss on her kidskin glove. "My dear Miss Shaw, it is a distinct pleasure to make your acquaintance."

Constance looked at Lord Weston—or rather, the top of his head as he kissed her hand. If she had been delighted to see Sarah again, then the girl was absolutely enraptured over the earl. She blushed from her neckline to the top of her pale blonde head.

Lady Farnsworth cleared her throat and looked to be making ready to forcibly remove her niece's hand from Lord Weston's lips.

And just like that, the earl released the girl's hand and rose, looking into Constance's eyes and smiling as if she were the only woman in the room.

"Come, Constance," Lady Farnsworth barked, nodding to the group and ushering her niece away.

Sarah nearly applauded. "Brilliant," she whispered in awe.

Claire gasped, Gregory laughed . . . and Lord Weston? Sarah could have sworn he winked at her.

Claire nodded serenely at the earl. "Gentlemen, I've need of Miss Tisdale's attention at the moment. Do excuse us, won't you?"

They hardly waited for anyone to reply. Sarah bolted for an alcove while Claire sailed slowly behind, stopping a servant on the way and relieving him of two glasses of punch.

"That was indelicate, even for you," Claire professed, handing a glass to Sarah and taking a sip from her own.

Sarah took one small drink and followed it up with another. "The woman is like a viper—rather more round, mind you, but still, very snakelike. That tongue of hers is deadly. I would not be at all surprised to discover it is forked. And he trounced her—wait, is that what one would do to a viper? Or would one obliterate, perhaps crush?"

"I would run," Claire offered, demurely sipping from her cup.

Sarah rolled her eyes in response. "Tell me that Lord Weston's skewering of Lady Farnsworth was not a thing of beauty."

"I most assuredly would not skewer—"

"Claire!"

"Oh, all right," her dear friend relented. "It was most definitely a sight to behold. I don't remember the last time Lady Farnsworth retreated from a fight, especially one that she started."

Sarah wanted to ask just what the Errant Earl was guilty of that made her fellow residents so emboldened as to eat his food, drink his wine, then thank him with slights. But she could hardly do so without seeming interested in the earl—which she obviously was not.

"What is it?" Claire asked knowingly.

Sarah feigned innocence. "What is what?"

"You want to ask me something but are holding yourself back."

Sarah had never had any luck keeping her thoughts from Claire and wasn't quite sure why she even bothered to try at all. "The thing is, I can't imagine what Lord Weston could have done to deserve such treatment."

Both looked to where Weston and Bennington stood engaged comfortably in conversation.

"You know as much as I," Claire began. "His absence from the county has been a hardship for the farmers who work his land."

"I suppose," Sarah answered distractedly.

Claire delicately sighed. "Sarah dear, do explain to me why you are acting as though you've lost your senses."

"Lost my senses? Why, I am the only one here with any reasonable—"

"Take a breath."

Sarah filled her lungs with air, and then expelled the breath with a huff, the act restoring her equilibrium. "Thank you."

"Of course," Claire said reassuringly, taking Sarah's hand in hers. "Now tell me what is the matter."

"Don't you see? I've spent the last several years most happily avoiding any nonsense concerning marriage."

"What of Mr. Dixon?" Claire interrupted, her mouth pursing as if she'd eaten a particularly disgusting bug.

"Come now, Claire," Sarah protested. "You know as well as I that the Honorable Ambrose Dixon is so monumentally unpleasant a person that even Mother cannot wholeheartedly recommend him as a husband."

Claire nodded in agreement. "Proceed."

"Well," Sarah continued, "Weston's return will have Mother thinking on marriage."

"True, though she's not made any attempts since Lord Reginald Busby," Claire pointed out.

Sarah huffed. "Which means she's out of practice. She was dreadful at it before. Just imagine what I'll be asked to endure—what Lord Weston will be forced to endure—in the interest of a fortuitous match. And Bennington's befriending him will only encourage her. To say nothing of your acceptance."

Claire's face fell. "Oh."

"Oh indeed," Sarah said gloomily.

"He is quite handsome, though."

"Claire!"

Her friend giggled. "I'm only trying to find the bright spot in all of this."

"Fine. He is handsome and charming."

"Quite awful, to be sure," Claire affirmed.

Sarah smiled at her, though her heart ached just a little from the effort. "Claire, when was the last time a man such as Weston courted me?"

"What of Blackwood? Or Thorpe?"

"Let me rephrase the question: Claire, when was the last time a man such as Weston pursued the courtship once he'd come to know me?"

Claire squeezed Sarah's hand. "Most disagreeable chap, that Weston. Certainly not the sort that Gregory nor I would endeavor to form a connection with. But my dear, it's Weston's loss. Any man should be so lucky to have you."

"Thank you," Sarah said softly.

Claire placed a gentle kiss on Sarah's forehead. "You are most welcome. Now," she said, turning back toward the crowd, "let us rejoin the festivities before Gregory sends out a search party."

"Yes, let's," Sarah agreed. After all, one could not hide in an alcove for the entirety of a party. She'd tried before, with no measure of success.

"They seem to have returned," Marcus commented.

Bennington's gaze followed Marcus's and found his wife and Miss Tisdale, strolling arm in arm on the far side of the room. "Yes, it's what women do—disappear for apparently no reason, then reappear out of thin air. Much like cats, I suppose."

As Marcus watched the two women, their heads bent toward each other as they whispered, their affection caused him to pause. "Is it a habit of theirs?"

"Oh, yes, thick as thieves, those two."

Marcus nodded. "I suppose our rather unorthodox meeting at the lake is the subject of their whispering."

Bennington watched his wife, his love for the woman written across his face. "I know nothing of a lake, but Lady Tisdale's impending attack is quite enough to keep them chattering for ages."

Marcus wondered if he should pretend to understand, but really could not see the point. "I'm afraid I do not follow."

Bennington turned back to face Weston, his demeanor changing abruptly. "Sorry about that, Weston. I should not be allowed to speak while looking at my wife."

Marcus was beginning to suspect that all things having to do with Miss Sarah Tisdale, no matter how trivial, were to prove exhausting and utterly confusing. "No apology necessary, though I am curious as to the nature of your statement. Does this by chance have anything to do with the dog?" he asked, trying to untangle Bennington's words.

Now Bennington looked just as confused as Marcus felt. "I'm sorry? Did you say 'dog'?"

Clearly the dog did not come into play. Surely no one could possibly forget Titus. "It's nothing."

Yet Marcus could not help but wonder if the interlude at the lake was the reason for Lady Tisdale's "impending attack." True, Miss Tisdale may as well have stood there in her chemise for all the concealment her sodden gown had provided. But he'd made no advances whatsoever. And her brother was present the whole time. Not to mention the mighty-sized mongrel.

"I am mystified," he said frankly, watching as the two women left the room.

"You're not alone," Bennington commiserated, punching him lightly on the arm. "Nothing about Miss Tisdale is ever straightforward. Or my wife for that matter. Women," he finished, his eyes softening yet again as he watched his wife leave.

"Is Miss Tisdale such a trial, then?" Marcus asked, unable to leave well enough alone.

"Well," Bennington began, turning back to Marcus, his brows furrowing a fraction of an inch. "She's a lovely girl, don't misunderstand me. It's just that . . . How shall I put this?"

Marcus resisted the urge to grab him by the shoulders and shake the words from his mouth.

Bennington pondered a bit more, then finally spoke. "She's exceedingly bright and knows not how to hide it, which has proven to be an impediment to retaining suitors in the past."

"A bluestocking, then?" Marcus queried, sure that Miss Tisdale could not be categorized so easily, but anxious to discover the details about her just the same.

"I suppose that such a term is useful when speaking of her," Bennington replied, flagging down a servant. "She was not always so—well, the intelligence was always there, of course. But early on, I've been told, she was able to hide it better."

Marcus watched the man toss back the bubbling, pale gold contents of the flute. "I suppose the same can be said of any of her ilk."

"Perhaps," Bennington answered, placing the glass on a passing servant's tray. "I can't say that I possess any real experience with such women. But Miss Tisdale seems . . . I don't know . . . Different somehow."

The understatement of the century, Marcus thought to himself while murmuring his agreement aloud. If there was ever an excuse to not further an acquaintance with a woman, Bennington had just handed it to him on a silver jewel-encrusted platter.

"I suppose I should extend my apologies for mine and Miss Tisdale's introduction all the same."

Bennington coughed loudly. "God, no. Best to let sleeping dogs lie. Besides, you'd have a devil of a time trying to catch her alone long enough to do so."

Oh, but what fun it would be to try. "And why is that?" he asked, distracted.

"The mother."

Bennington's tone was so ominous that Marcus's attention shifted instantly from the lusty image in his mind. "Lady Tisdale?"

Bennington gestured for Marcus to follow him. The two made their way across the small crowd to a turned railing that overlooked the room where a merry country dance was under way. "Do you see the woman in the purple gown, near the gentleman whose hair matches Miss Tisdale's?"

Marcus searched the crowd, looking past the dancers to a group of men and women conversing. He caught sight of the woman, her countenance pleasant enough, though a hint of something severe could be seen just beneath. "Yes."

"That is Lady Lenora Tisdale. A force of nature, that one. And the only person Sarah fears."

Marcus studied the woman. "I can't imagine Miss Tisdale being afraid of anyone."

Bennington folded his arms and leaned back against the railing. "Perhaps 'fear' is the wrong word. Lenora will not mortally wound you physically, but if one could kill by vexation—well, that's the woman to do it. No, you'll want to keep a goodly amount of distance between you and Lenora Tisdale, which means avoiding Sarah at all cost."

Marcus chuckled. "You've so little faith in my ability to elude the woman?"

"Oh, it's not that," Bennington began. "I simply have more faith in Lady Tisdale."

"Where is Gregory?" Claire wondered aloud, looking about for her husband.

Sarah stood as close to the wall as she could without weakening its structural integrity. "Never fear. Bennington knows you adore dancing. He'll not let you down."

She watched the couples as they trotted through the steps of a country dance. It was so graceful that she almost—almost—found herself tapping her toes.

"At last!" Claire exclaimed.

Sarah followed Claire's gaze and saw Bennington, his compact form making quick work of the distance between them. "Ah, your knight hath come!"

"And he is not alone," Claire replied, her mouth forming an O of surprise.

Sarah spotted Weston just behind, his presence drawing morbidly curious glances from everyone in the room. "But why?" she asked, puzzled. Only yesterday she'd made his acquaintance covered in mud and dog slobber. This evening she'd bumbled her way through their earlier conversation, all but running from him in the end. She'd assumed the man would keep his distance. He'd struck her as intelligent, after all.

"I can't say that I blame him," Claire replied hastily. "With the likes of Lady Farnsworth in attendance this evening, I dare say, if I were the earl, I'd spend the majority of my time with Gregory as well."

Bennington appeared at his wife's side and smiled with besotted affection. "My dear, I believe you promised me this dance."

"That I did," Claire answered, offering her hand to her husband. "Lord Weston, do join us," she added politely, cheerily looking about the room for his potential partner.

Lord Weston followed Claire's lead, his gaze skimming the crowd. Most wore looks of mild boredom—a few boldly displaying their outright disgust with the earl.

"Miss Tisdale, may I have the honor?"

"No," Sarah answered quickly, her earnestness clear.

"That is to say," Claire interrupted in a smooth tone, "Sarah prefers to observe rather than participate."

Sarah snorted lightly. "What Claire is trying to tell you, Lord Weston, is that I cannot dance without causing injury to myself or my partner. I am utterly hopeless and destined to remain so."

Lord Weston quirked an eyebrow, his mouth curving with male amusement. "Come now, you can't be as bad as all that."

Sarah looked expectantly at Claire and Bennington, the two nodding in agreement. "You see," she waved a hand at the couple. "Even my dearest friends support the claim."

"Are you afraid to dance?" he asked, his eyes narrowed, challenging her.

"Please," Sarah ground out, never one to back down. "There's nothing to be afraid of." Her skin tingled with what felt oddly like anticipation.

"Prove it."

Sarah had never been prone to violence; in fact, she abhorred the very idea. But she wanted to slap him. And then tell him in a most impolite manner why she had nothing to prove to him.

And then slap him a second time.

Dammit all.

"Fine," she said through clenched teeth, her eyes shooting daggers at him. "On your head be it—don't say I didn't warn you."

He bowed and held out his arm. She laid her hand on his sleeve and he smiled, cocking his head toward the dance floor. "Shall we?"

They joined a group and lined up with the other couples, clasping hands to form a circle. Priscilla Willit, the woman next to Lord Weston, visibly tensed at his touch.

Lord Weston only smiled at her, his lips turning up at the corners in an irresistible fashion. "I'm so glad you were able to attend this evening," he began.

Priscilla's demeanor changed, the coldness melted instantly by the earl's charm. She hesitated, then offered him a small smile.

For her part, Sarah could not help but glare at Priscilla. How the earl had managed to keep from throttling the girl for such boorish behavior was beyond her.

The music began and Sarah looked worriedly from the musicians to Lord Weston. "La Boulangere?" she whispered to the earl.

"Yes," he answered, offering her a reassuring look. "Only a simple country dance."

Sarah rolled her eyes and swallowed a whimper of protest.

"I am the one with an injured leg," he said in response to her silent objection. "If either of us had cause for trepidation at such a task, I would think it was me."

Of course Sarah had taken note of the earl's slight

limp almost immediately, but she had possessed the sense to hold her tongue.

"I'm sorry, but why, exactly, would you put us through such torture, especially in light of your infirmity?"

Lord Weston looked somewhat shocked at Sarah's indelicate question, and then he let out a shout of laughter, the sound drowned out by the two violins beginning a lively air.

Unable to avoid it, they moved with the dance, the circle traveling right with a simple enough step, then left. "Do you always say exactly what is on your mind, Miss Tisdale?"

Sarah was concentrating on her feet so closely that she very nearly missed the earl's question. "Well, yes," she answered matter-of-factly. "Don't you?"

"Good God, no," he answered emphatically before he joined the men in a separate circle while the women twirled.

Sarah counted time to the music, her gaze fixed on the polished oaken floor and the graceful movements of the other women. She looked up just in time to rejoin Lord Weston. "So, you make a habit of concealing your true thoughts, then?"

Weston was amazingly graceful for a man with a limp. He clapped in time and completed a full turn with impeccable precision. "I suppose it depends on the situation," he answered, arching an eyebrow.

He was making it difficult for Sarah to concentrate. And the seductive curve of his mouth as he smiled at her did little to help. "Lord Weston, why did you ask me to dance?"

He looked at her incredulously, as if for the first time in a long while he wasn't sure what to say. "Why does any man ask a woman to dance?"

"Come now, Lord Weston," Sarah said. "There's no

need to be mysterious. I assure you, no matter the truth, I'm hearty and hale enough to hear it."

It used to be that men would ask Sarah to dance in order to inquire after Claire. But that was obviously not the case now.

The circle broke and couples joined hands together, the step bringing Lord Weston face-to-face with Sarah. "Miss Tisdale, have I done something to offend you . . . or perhaps your mother?"

Sarah gripped the earl's hands reflexively, his bluntness most unexpected. "Where would you have heard . . . ? I'm sorry, but who . . . ?" she asked, struggling to complete the sentence. "Bennington," she hissed, searching the dancers for the traitor's face.

"Miss Tisdale," Lord Weston pressed, squeezing her clenched hands in his. "Bennington did not intend to betray your confidence, I assure you. He was caught off guard—"

"You queried while he was pining after Claire, didn't you?"

Marcus nodded, a mixture of guilt and resignation on his face.

She could hardly lie now. He knew the truth of it and she wasn't about to be caught in a falsehood. "He talks too much," she said lightly, hoping that he would simply laugh and let it go.

"Miss Tisdale, please," he replied, his face taking on a determined set.

Really, she thought, as if being made to dance was not enough. "You'll not drop it, then?" Sarah asked hopefully.

"Not a chance."

The dance was winding down and Sarah desperately needed to be free of the earl. Especially his hands, which held hers in a most distracting way—too large, too . . . male. "Very well, then. I fear that your return to the district will pique my mother's interest in matrimony—mine, to be more specific."

Lord Weston's forehead wrinkled slightly. "And the thought of marrying me is what's troubling you?"

"Not exactly," Sarah replied, flustered. "Did Gregory tell you anything of my mother?"

"He mentioned a few things."

Sarah winced at the thought of their conversation, though she could hardly blame herself for her mother being, well, her mother. "Then you might understand why I'm loath to undertake a courtship—doomed to fail, no less—with Lenora Tisdale at the helm. I am perfectly content on my own and have no reason to assume that I'll ever feel otherwise."

Sarah watched the earl take in the information with a purposeful detachment, as if she'd shared a trifle from the morning's newspaper. It was humiliating, which only made everything worse.

"So this has nothing to do with our encounter at the lake?" he asked, slowing as the music floated to a halt.

"Not at all," Sarah replied, pointedly retrieving her hands from his.

He looked relieved as they walked from the dance floor, which only made Sarah feel more humiliated. "Thank you for the dance, my lord. And good night."

"Miss Tisdale, wait—"

But Sarah could not. She'd noticed that his limp was now slightly more pronounced. She knew she could outrun him if she had to. And she desperately needed to be away from the man, though she could not explain why.

3

Marcus sat on the edge of the cliff overlooking the cove. Moonlight illuminated the craggy rocks and beyond, to where the channel lay, its waters black beneath the night sky. As a boy, he'd made a habit of sneaking out at night and settling in the very same spot, the cool summer air soothing his restless thoughts then much as it did now.

Lulworth society had changed little in the past twenty years. His position and wealth could not be denied now that he was a man and marriageable, but the thinly veiled repudiation was still there.

Marcus supposed he could have done more throughout the years to endear himself to the village. Made more of an effort to guide the goings-on at the castle, as most landowners did. But his pride had been stung, and if there was one truth he'd walked away with, it was that someone such as he would never find where he belonged, no matter how hard he might try.

He'd learned in his time with the Corinthians that his charm, when applied evenly, was enough to smooth his way in most situations. That was all he could hope for in the way of acceptance. Not that he'd hoped for anything in quite some time.

He stretched out his leg and swore, the pounding throb of pain in his healing wound hitting him. He should not have danced with Miss Tisdale.

"Miss Tisdale," he said aloud, the words carried off in

a rush by the wind. She was a mismatched puzzle of right and wrong, the pieces fitting into place only when coaxed with a considerable amount of strength. Nothing like any other woman of his acquaintance. God, the woman was charming for the very reason that she tried so hard *not* to be charming.

"And tae mak' matters worse, th' lassie is bonnie and braw," he said to the sky, his burr appearing as if it had never left. Part of Marcus wondered that no man had wedded her for the great pleasure of bedding such a creature.

The other part of him completely understood why she'd been put so firmly on the shelf.

Marcus retrieved a rock from the ground and turned it between his fingers, the cool smooth surface slowing his thoughts. He was not himself around her. His reliable charm and easy wit were compromised in the presence of Miss Tisdale.

And he could not say why. Shock, perhaps? He dropped the rock into his other hand and repeated the pattern. How could anyone find themselves at ease with Miss Tisdale? One never knew what to expect, which, in Marcus's experience, was most *unexpected* when it came to women. Bennington's comment concerning the woman's unease had spurred him on. After all, any man worthy of calling himself a gentleman would have done the same.

The true nature of her complaint had surprised Marcus. Not that he would have expected any woman within the county to have willingly jumped at the opportunity to be courted by him. If there had ever been doubt, the evening's party had proven him correct on this point.

But Miss Tisdale had been so bloody honest about the whole thing. No contempt, nor arrogance. Just the simple fact that his presence could disrupt her life. And she liked her life—loved her life, actually, from what he'd seen so far. Marcus couldn't help but envy the woman, just a little.

Her mother? She was entirely what one would assume of a prying country mama with nothing more to do than meddle in the lives of those around her. Marcus had been introduced to the Tisdales by Bennington toward the end of the evening. Lady Tisdale had been stiff, though polite, her air of superiority somewhat quelled by her undeniable fascination with him and his titles. She'd made it clear, though, that she would not be making a match between her daughter and the Errant Earl. The woman obviously disliked him.

Sir Arthur had welcomed Marcus with a hearty pat on the back, his easy, friendly style in stark contrast to that of his wife.

Miss Tisdale's father had gone so far as to invite Marcus to their home for a glass of "the choicest brandy to be had in all of England." His accompanying wink had not been lost on the entire group standing about, their conspiratorial nods piquing Marcus's interest.

He slowly stood, stretching as he rose. He could hardly believe that a man as well-respected locally as Sir Arthur Tisdale was involved in a plot to extend Napoleon's empire.

He lobbed the rock into the air, losing sight of it as it disappeared against the blackness.

"Strange lot, those Tisdales," he mumbled to himself, turning back toward the castle.

Sarah knew the way by heart, even in the dark. The winding path leading through the woods just beyond the gardens of her family's home was one she routinely traversed.

Filtered moonlight appeared here and there as she

walked, the distant lapping of the Channel's waves against the rocky shore the only sound for miles.

Save for Titus's panting behind her, she realized. The dog's massive head bumped Sarah's backside as he dutifully followed after her.

She reached down and patted his soft fur and he responded with a stealthy swipe of his tongue on her wrist. He'd been none too pleased when she'd risen from bed, tripping over him in the process. But he'd wearily accompanied her out into the night, familiar enough with Sarah's habits.

She'd begun sneaking out of the manor house at the age of eight. Despite being clumsy, Sarah's need for motion was undeniable, especially when something was on her mind.

Her father had noted on more than one occasion that even in the womb, Sarah's preference had been clear. Lady Tisdale had hardly been able to lie down without a stout kick from their unborn child.

Sarah reached the edge of the wood, stepping out into the open and the gentle wind that blew in from the Channel beyond the cliffs below. Titus walked to an outcropping of rocks and threw himself down on the cool dirt, a huff escaping his wet muzzle.

"You came of your own accord, Titus," Sarah chided the giant, walking to where he lay. She crouched down beside him, slipped off her clogs, and ran her fingers through his smooth, short fur. "Though I am happy for the company."

She lifted her white cotton night rail slightly, and then collected as many pebbles as she could settle into the fabric. She rose, climbed a large flat rock, and stood, her bare feet tingling from the porous, faintly abrasive surface.

She carefully poured the rocks onto the boulder's surface, then picked a smooth, oblong pebble from the pile and flung it with force over the cliff, hardly pausing before choosing a second one and sending it on its way.

She tilted forward, the feel of the grainy rock beneath her toes a welcome distraction. Walking alone at night in the woods was hardly troublesome. Well, to her anyway. Sarah could not imagine what her mother would do were she to discover her daughter's solitary and certainly quite scandalous behavior.

Sarah bent down and retrieved a large, rough rock, gripped it tightly, then hurled it into the ever-increasing wind. No, it was not *what* she was doing that was troublesome, but *why*.

A gust of wind caught her unbound hair, strands blowing every which way and obscuring Sarah's vision. She reached up and captured the mass and quickly plaited it before tossing the braid back over her shoulder.

Why had Lord Weston returned to Lulworth Castle? She picked up two pebbles and sent them quickly after the others.

Surely he knew the villagers' feelings toward him? It was plain that those who attended his party were there to drink his wine, eat his food, and stare at the man as though he were one of the horrid animal attractions in London that Claire had told her about. If she were in Lord Weston's shoes, Titus could not have dragged her back to Lulworth.

At least now Sarah had a *good* reason for not liking the man. She'd been painfully embarrassed by their conversation during the dance. She cringed as she recalled her mother's icy demeanor upon meeting Lord Weston, though, upon reflection, she really should have known that her silly mother would be unable to look past her dislike for the earl.

Her face grew hot as she thought back to how Lord Weston had turned to look at her, one eyebrow raised and a question in his eyes. All she'd been able to manage was a mouthed "I was wrong" before hurriedly walking away to find Claire. A coward's way out for sure. But at least she was safe from her mother's machinations. And now she could return to her life before Lord Weston.

Sarah grabbed a pebble and aimed for Ursa Major. Unsurprisingly, the rock fell short of its destination.

She had to admit that Lord Weston *was* handsome. And charming.

There was an intensity that seemed to lie just beneath his lightly tanned skin, though Sarah found she could not get far beyond thoughts of the skin itself. The vee of it visible beneath his unbuttoned shirt when he'd thought to jump in the lake was similarly colored. Sarah wondered just how far the tan continued down Lord Weston's torso.

She had a spectacular imagination, one that easily removed the earl's fine lawn shirt and traveled lower to where it had been tucked into his snug breeches.

A trickle of sweat ran between Sarah's breasts and she rubbed at it distractedly.

The earl was making her perspire. No, the mere *thought* of the man was making her perspire.

She reached for the remaining pile of pebbles and gathered them together, standing and lobbing them over the cliff with force.

She would not let Lord Weston capture her fancy. At best, such folly would be distracting. At worst, disastrous. And Sarah had experienced too much of both in her life to volunteer for such a fool's errand.

She undid her hair and shook it out about her, the long tendrils blowing wildly in the wind, tugging at her scalp.

She lifted the hem of her night rail and jumped from the rock, landing in the soft dirt near Titus. "To bed," she said simply, stepping into her clogs then cluck-ing at the dog as she walked toward the woods.

Titus heaved himself up with a second sigh and fol-lowed his mistress home.

Marcus awoke stiff and sore from the past evening's events. Despite the short distance to Tisdale Manor and the balmy afternoon weather, his aching leg wouldn't allow him to walk there.

Pokey, Marcus's chestnut character of a Thorough-bred, had been enlisted for the trip, his champion bloodlines surely recoiling at the thought of such an in-consequential task, while his lazy disposition clearly rel-ished the briefness of the short ride.

The horse plodded up the private lane toward Tis-dale Manor. Marcus idly scanned the grounds, noting the beech trees neatly lining the earthen track and the rhododendron bushes along the edge of the grassy lawn beyond.

And a curvaceous backside, low to the ground as its owner crawled somewhat awkwardly from bush to bush. A muslin dress, the very faintest of moss greens nearly lost against the color of the grass, pulled tight over the swell of buttocks as the woman moved, knee to knee, the fabric straining to contain the ripe, round—

Marcus squeezed his eyelids shut and swallowed hard. "Miss Tisdale, have you lost something?" he asked, adding "such as your mind," under his breath.

She stopped suddenly, frozen, obviously unaware that Marcus had approached.

"Bugger."

Or at least that was what he *thought* he heard her say. "I beg your pardon?" he queried.

She sat back on her heels and twisted to look over her shoulder at him. "Is that what it looks like?"

Oh, the lass was clearly trouble, but so entertaining.

"May I be of assistance?" he asked, turning Pokey from the path and onto the lawn.

"No!" she vehemently whispered, her eyes darting toward the manor. "That is to say," she paused, regaining her composure, "thank you for the kind offer."

She was breathing a bit harder now, her breasts moving up and down with the effort. "I'm glad to offer my services," Marcus pressed, noting that each step Pokey took toward her made Miss Tisdale's breath that much more labored. Marcus wondered if he urged Pokey closer whether Miss Tisdale's delectable bosom would heave itself right out of the green gown.

On second thought—

"Miss Sarah!" a servant's voice rang out, the loud call coming from the general vicinity of the manor.

She muttered something under her breath. He couldn't make out the exact words, but the tone was anything but ladylike.

"Is it that you've lost something, Miss Tisdale, or that something—or someone, rather—has lost you?" Marcus asked, enjoying this far more than he should.

She looked as if she were contemplating something of great importance, her brow furrowing as she looked first at the manor house and then back to Marcus. Finally, in a very defeated tone, she muttered, "The Honorable Ambrose Dixon."

"Dixon has lost you?"

She rose up on her knees, arms akimbo. "I am not the man's to lose, on that point you may be sure."

"Miss Sarah!" the cry came again, this time markedly closer than before.

Miss Tisdale threw herself to the ground, apparently attempting to become one with the lawn.

"I see," Marcus replied, stifling a laugh. Clearly, for all of her heat and fire, Miss Tisdale was very neatly stuck. "Well then, it appears you do require my aid, after all."

She ceased clutching the large blossoms in a vain attempt at concealment and looked him squarely in the eye. "In what way, my lord?"

Marcus turned Pokey back toward the drive. "I'll keep your location a secret, for a price."

Her emerald eyes grew as round as saucers, and she seemed on the verge of an apoplectic fit. "Are you implying that should I not agree to this price, you will reveal my hiding place?"

Marcus was discovering the benefits of angering Miss Tisdale. Color flooded her cheeks and spread down the graceful arch of her neck and below, disappearing beneath the neckline of the green gown. *Do not play games* he told himself, but something about Miss Tisdale urged him on. "Exactly."

"You cannot be serious!" she whispered angrily, her hands balling into fists at her sides.

"Is there a servant about?" Marcus yelled, causing Miss Tisdale to gasp.

"Name your price," she said through gritted teeth.

Marcus's brain practically spun with the possibilities, but the sound of approaching footsteps forced him to cut short the most enjoyable mental parade. "I fear there is not sufficient time at the present. Let me think on it."

Her mouth opened and closed with outrage. "Within reason, my lord. The price must be within reason."

"Of course," Marcus answered with a telling grin, turning Pokey to intercept the approaching servant.

"Tell Sir Arthur that Lord Weston has come," he said authoritatively, and watched the servant hie himself to the house before he turned Pokey toward the stables and into a slow trot.

He looked back only once to where Miss Tisdale lay.

He could swear he saw the heat of anger wafting up from her in waves.

Within reason indeed.

Marcus had known the Honorable Ambrose Dixon as a boy, though he'd forgotten most of the details, save for one: He'd disliked him immensely. The man had always been snide, despite the fact that they were not equals in rank. Dixon was the second son of the Earl of Swaton, pushed further down the line of inheritance by the arrival some three years before of the current earl's twin boys.

Comfortably ensconced in a sturdy brown leather armchair, which time and several generations of Tisdale males had worn soft on the cushioned seat and along the rounded arms, Marcus studied both Dixon and Tisdale while drinking what was arguably the best brandy he'd ever had the good fortune to swallow.

Dixon was tall, and while slight of build, he possessed something in the way of looks that Marcus was sure women might find appealing. He also drank his brandy with gusto and spoke in a firm, condescending tone.

It was not until he inquired after Miss Tisdale that Marcus truly began to understand her hesitancy.

"Really, Tisdale, this business of allowing the girl to wander about the property must end," Dixon pronounced with barely concealed annoyance, swirling the last of his brandy about in the cut glass before finishing it off. "After all, it's not as if we're in the Highlands of Scotland, where women run barefoot through the heather. Isn't that right, Weston?" he baited.

Yes, that look of distaste on Miss Tisdale's face when she'd uttered Dixon's name made so much more sense now, Marcus thought.

Marcus looked about the room for a broadsword with which to clout the bastard. Finding none, he took a long pull of brandy and drank.

"Perhaps she saw you coming?" Marcus queried innocently, enjoying the slow heat of the superior brandy.

Dixon discarded his glass on the window ledge then eased back into his leather chair. "You always were quite the clown," he answered, clearly irritated.

"I'm sure that's not the case," Sir Arthur added hastily, finishing his brandy. He winked at Marcus then picked up the Waterford decanter and offered Dixon a second glass. "For your efforts, my lord."

Dixon gestured toward a fresh glass that accompanied the decanter and nodded. "It's the least you can do, I suppose," he said jokingly, though it was clear he would have expected no less.

Sir Arthur poured the man's second glass and settled back in his chair. "Now, Weston, tell me, is this not the finest brandy?"

"Without a doubt," Marcus answered, giving Tisdale a genuine smile. "You are a man of your word."

Tisdale looked terribly pleased with himself. "A fine compliment indeed."

"And where might one secure a supply of his own?" Marcus asked, adding, "Theoretically, of course."

Sir Arthur let out a bark of laughter, and Dixon cringed. "Jolly good fun, you are, Weston. Jolly good." His host leaned in, dropping his elbows to the broad mahogany desk topped in gilt-tooled leather. "How much, theoretically speaking," he said with emphasis, "might you like to acquire?"

Dixon set his glass down with a heavy clunk. "Really, Tisdale, I don't know that this is something—"

"Come now, Dixon. Everyone through the length and whole of Weymouth knows of such things. The brandy's origins are hardly a secret. And Weston is—"

"Be that as it may," Dixon interrupted, his gaze narrowing in on Marcus with barely concealed suspicion. "I can hardly allow a family with whom I hope to be intimately connected to take such chances. Surely you can part with a bottle or two for the earl?"

Sir Arthur understood the simplicity of the matter, answering in the affirmative and turning to retrieve a bottle of the brandy from the cabinet behind him.

Did Dixon think Marcus so inept that he'd not seen something was amiss? The question was, which of the men was suspect? The amiable and intelligent Sir Arthur or the arrogant Dixon?

Marcus was inclined to assume it was Dixon, but he could not be sure so early in the investigation.

"It cannot be easy to part with such drink," Marcus said as Sir Arthur handed him the bottle.

He nodded in the affirmative, though his lips spread into a smile. "Let it be in honor of our new friendship, my lord."

"Yes," Dixon added, "to friendship."

That broadsword came to Marcus's mind yet again as he downed the last of his brandy in reply.

"Within reason, my arse," Sarah said to Percival. The peacock eyed her with a weary look, as though he completely disapproved of her language. The bird had found his way to Tisdale Manor after the death of his mate. Well, in all honesty, it was not the death of his dear Penelope but rather Percival's grieving—which had taken the form of endless crowing without regard to either time nor day—that had landed him in his current situation.

His owner, Lord Such and Such from two counties beyond Dorset, threatened to turn him loose—a death sentence, to be sure. Which was when Sarah had stepped in. Percival had been transported to Tisdale House posthaste, where he'd settled in quite comfortably, though the lack of a peahen did trouble him now and again.

Sarah sighed deeply and looked about the wood, the roof of the manor house visible between the trees. "I promised to give up the use of such colorful language when I married, did I not?" she asked the bird, careful to keep her distance. She adored Percival in all of his sumptuous finery, but he could be a bit testy at times.

Percival looked off to the right, his exquisite blue breast and head shining with brilliant color, even in the shadows of the forest.

"And I am, to the best of my knowledge, not as yet married," Sarah added succinctly.

Percival let out a plaintive caw, and then looked back at Sarah.

The sound of approaching hoofbeats drew near and Sarah looked to the section of the drive visible from her hidden vantage point. Mr. Dixon trotted by on his bay, not bothering to lift his mount into a canter, but rather digging his spurs into the horse to force the gait.

Sarah very nearly cried out for him to stop, the bay visibly flinching at the act. But she held her tongue, knowing that it would, in the end, be of no use.

Mr. Dixon never abused his animals in a way that his peers would find objectionable. He was gifted in the art of nuanced cruelty, as the bay could attest. There were many aspects of Mr. Dixon's personality that made him utterly repellant as a suitor or potential husband, but his treatment of his animals was the worst by far.

She'd endured his attention all these years for one reason and one reason alone: She'd made Mr. Dixon promise that she could give his animals a home once they'd reached the end of their usefulness to him.

It had been easy enough to convince such a vain man to release a five-year-old Thoroughbred based on his coloring or a two-year-old mastiff due to his slobber. One word from John Fairweather, Dixon's farm manager and Sarah's true friend, and the man was convinced the animals had reached a shocking level of unworthiness.

"I do believe that it appears bay horses are frightfully out of fashion this season, Percival," Sarah said to the bird, getting to her feet. "I'm sure that Mr. Fairweather will agree."

"Caw," Percival offered in return, his gorgeous head turning alertly at the sound of yet another rider.

Sarah instantly backed up against a massive tree trunk and stood stock-still, nearly groaning aloud as Lord Weston rounded the corner on his impressive chestnut. The earl lazily held the reins in his hands, the horse meandering along as if they were enjoying the scenery.

A reluctant smile tugged at Sarah's lips. The pair's obvious affection for each other was endearing. She knew enough about Thoroughbreds to know they could be fiery and fierce, yet here strode the chestnut, as gentle as a lamb in his owner's capable hands.

Sarah looked yet again at the leather reins in Weston's hands, looped loosely about his long, sun-kissed fingers as they rested on his thighs. She'd not noticed earlier how his fawn breeches fit so snugly, the contours of the muscles visible even from the considerable distance.

"I was a bit preoccupied with hiding at the time," she whispered absentmindedly to Percival, who blinked in response.

The rhythmic thud of Pokey's hoofbeats held Sarah's attention as she watched Lord Weston's leg muscles flex and release as the horse walked on. Flex and release. Flex and release.

"Caw!"

Pokey stopped abruptly, tossing his head anxiously at the sound of Percival's ear-piercing cry.

Lord Weston swung the horse in a circle to keep Pokey from rearing. "Easy, boy." He patted the big chestnut's neck while scanning the woods, his gaze stopping scant inches from where Sarah stood.

"Miss Tisdale, is that you?" he called.

Sarah held her breath, her eyes widening with fear, certain she was about to be discovered. Percival appeared ready to caw at any moment.

"No? All right, then—only a bird, Pokey." Weston clucked, urging the horse forward. The chestnut complied, apparently eager to move on and away from the cawing woods. The earl looked back, a small smile on his lips.

Sarah waited what felt to be nearly a quarter of an hour before moving, her limbs stiff from the effort. Percival had strutted over to a rotten log and was currently nibbling at bugs.

"This is entirely your fault, you know," she said accusingly, wincing as she stretched complaining muscles. "If you could have only kept quiet."

Thankfully, Titus had trotted after Nigel and a group of village boys earlier in the day. Lord only knew what disaster would have transpired had the mastiff been in attendance.

"Caw?" Percival replied, then bent back to his meal.

"Precisely!" Sarah answered resolutely, in truth not entirely sure how her need to hide in the first place had been Percival's fault, but hardly willing to argue the point.

"Caw."

The Boot Inn had changed little in the century since its door first opened to the thirsty fishermen and townsfolk of Lulworth. Marcus had visited a time or two on past trips, usually dressed in homespun and waiting until the patrons were sufficiently in their cups before making his way to the simple and unassuming tavern. Drunks were easily persuaded by rough clothing and the offer to purchase a round for all.

Tonight was no different. A raucous tune spilling from the open windows of the inn greeted Marcus as he handed Pokey's reins to an ostler.

He'd gone home after visiting Tisdale Manor, consulting with Sully on the little he'd been able to glean from his conversation with Tisdale and Dixon.

The valet had arranged for a fellow Corinthian agent to meet Marcus at the Boot with information from Carmichael.

A blast of warm air and the pungent odor of hops hit Marcus as he pushed open the Boot's door.

Come all you young sailormen, listen to me
I'll sing you a song of the fish in the sea

The patrons' lusty singing was infectious. When a portly man, a thin scar running the length of his face from forehead to chin, clapped Marcus on the back, he could not help but join in the chanty's chorus as the song made its way back around for the second time.

"Jolly sou'wester, boys, steady she goes!" the men sang in unison, Scar Face taking a heavy drink from his pewter cup.

"You've a fine voice, lad," the man growled to Marcus before staggering off to join his friends.

Marcus continued on to the back of the room, where an ancient oaken bar took up the length of the cramped tavern. A tavernkeeper stood behind the counter, wiping down tankards with a rough cloth.

"The high and mighty Lord Weston, in the Boot, then?" the man said by way of introduction, twirling his drying rag over his head and sketching a sardonic bow.

Marcus remained silent, quirking his eyebrow as if to suggest the man had misspoke.

The tavernkeeper dropped the rag on his shoulder and placed his large, rough hands on the ale-stained bar.

"Don't bother, your lordship. I never forget a face—specially one that belongs to a swell that stole from me."

Marcus's eyes narrowed as he looked more closely at the man. "I've no idea what you're talking about."

"Fish, three of 'em, and caught by my own hand."

The summer of Marcus's twelfth year came into his mind's eye. He'd gone to swim at the lake and found a boy fishing. The youth had uttered filthy insults until Marcus could take no more. Two solid punches to the boy's face had knocked him flat. Then Marcus had gathered up the fish and thrown them back into the lake.

The man grunted. "Has it come back now?" he asked, his crooked nose making Marcus smirk.

He reached into his pocket and pulled out a handful of coins, dropping a guinea on the bar. "For the fish and something to quench my thirst," he replied, knowing full well the man would hardly say no to such a sum.

He hesitated, one beefy hand finally reaching out to claim the coin. "What'll you have?" he asked in a no-nonsense tone. "Ale?"

"No brandy, then?" Marcus asked.

"We've no brandy here, as well the two customs officials over there in the corner can tell ya," he replied, jerking his chin in the men's direction.

Marcus did not bother to look. "And what makes you think I'm not one of them?"

"I hear tell you've a taste for brandy, Lord Weston. And any man with a taste for brandy in Lulworth is not bloody likely to be a customs official. Besides, quality like you have no need for the work."

Marcus couldn't argue with the man's logic. Nor was he surprised that news of his visit to Tisdale Manor for a tasting of the fine drink had traveled so quickly. There was, after all, very little to do in towns the size of Lulworth, and gossip spread fast.

He reached into his pocket again and threw down several more coins. "And what would a man have to do to get a decent drink?"

The tavernkeeper was smart enough to know that a thirsty man, with the ready in his pocket—even one with Scottish blood—was, at the end of the day, a thirsty man. He pocketed the coin. "Did you see the ship lamp when you came in?" the man asked, filling the newly dried tankard with ale and setting it in front of Marcus.

Marcus wondered at the man's line of inquiry but nodded his head.

"When it shines you'll find what you're looking for."

Marcus thought back to his view of the Boot just before entering. The ship's lamp was dark—a ship lamp that could easily be seen by smugglers waiting for a sign of safety in order to deliver their goods. "The customs officials don't much like the lamplight, then?"

"You're a smart man, Lord Weston—smarter than they say," he replied. "Enjoy your ale."

Come list on ye, landsmen, all to me,
To tell the truth I'm bound . . .

Marcus managed to avoid being pulled into service for the second song as he carried his ale to a small table near the front.

So the Boot was intimately involved in Lulworth's smuggling? Hardly surprising, Marcus thought to himself, sipping the thick mixture from his tankard. A tavern would have good reason to serve more than ale.

Oh, I had not long scurried out,
When close alongside the ocean . . .

Scar Face had staggered up to dance with a number of his friends. They were getting louder and more raucous. And their dancing skills left quite a bit to be desired.

A man walked toward Marcus, his appearance mirroring that of Scar Face and his cohorts: rough and faded clothing with the brine of the sea still on his boots. "Don't mind Simon and the boys. They're only having a spot of fun." He pulled the chair out opposite Marcus and sat.

Marcus took another pull from his tankard. "If not in Lulworth, then where else?" he asked, the words learned from Sully only hours before.

"From sunup to sundown, a man can never go wrong in Lulworth, 'tis true," the man replied, recounting word for word what the Corinthians had told Marcus to accept.

. . . This crocodile I could plainly see
Was none of the common race . . .

"James Marlowe," the man said by way of introduction, "or Jamie, as my new friends seem so fond of calling me."

Marcus knew enough of the peerage to connect Marlowe with the House of Richmond, though he could not remember the man's rank. Not that it would have mattered, as he looked like a native Dorset fisherman. "Weston."

. . . I lost my hold and away I flew
Right into the crocodile's mouth.

"Do tell Carmichael of the singing, won't you? Particularly this ballad, which I'm sure he'll find of great importance to the case," Marcus said sarcastically.

Marlowe laughed heartily. "You're not of a mind to believe the Weymouth coast activities bear a connection to the London robberies?"

"Are you?" Marcus countered, draining his tankard. "Or are you inclined to believe the more plausible explanation?" he asked, patting his thigh very near the bullet wound.

Marlowe rubbed at his beard-roughened jaw. "I'll admit as much, though the news from London does make one wonder."

"Do tell," Marcus urged, more than eager to turn his pathetic excuse for a holiday into something far meatier.

"Another robbery in Mayfair. Sheffield, just as our informant told us," Marlowe offered, his tone remaining casual.

Scar Face trundled across the tavern and embraced Marcus, pulling him to his feet.

So now I'm safe on earth once more,
Resolved no more to roam . . .

"A golden voice, this one," the drunken Scar Face assured Marlowe before returning to his friends.

Marcus sat back down, the ditty having given him time to think. "Sheffield seems an obvious enough mark, don't you think?"

"True enough, though the thieves took only what our informant said they would—one of the Orlov emeralds."

Marcus absorbed the information with particular interest, though his gaze remained neutral.

"These Orlov emeralds, what do you know of them?" Marcus asked, having, in true Corinthian style, received only the necessary information when Carmichael and he had spoken of the smuggling.

Marlowe took a swig of his ale. "Well, there's eight emeralds in all—egg-sized, from what I've been told. They were originally fashioned into a necklace for Empress Catherine nearly fifty years ago. The piece was stolen and the jewels were split up and sold. Most of them found their way here, to England."

Marcus wondered at the name. "Orlov? Surely not named for Alexei Orlov?"

Marlowe paused, applauding Scar Face's jig. "No, not for the man who murdered Catherine's husband—for his brother, Gregory, rumored to be her lover. From what we've learned, the Empress was outraged when she learned of the theft. Seems the emeralds had been in the Orlov family for generations—bore mystical qualities or some such nonsense. Whether they do or don't is of no consequence. They're worth a fortune, and every emperor since has attempted to recover them."

"And what does Napoleon have to do with these particular emeralds?" Marcus pressed.

"Emperor Alexander promised to behave and maintain the trade embargo against Britain if Napoleon finds and returns the emeralds," Marlowe replied. "And that means one fewer war on his hands, which many say even Boney could not win."

It was plausible, Marcus realized ruefully. "And how many are in French possession?"

"Six."

Marcus nodded. "Any villagers of interest?"

"Beyond the common smugglers? Not that I've found."

"Have you met the Honorable Ambrose Dixon?" he asked, taking one last drink then pushing his tankard aside.

Marlowe smiled. "Not Dixon himself, but I've made the acquaintance of some of the female servants."

"I'm sure that you have," Marcus scoffed, remembering Marlowe's reputation with women. "Do endeavor to remain on friendly terms with them, won't you? There's something about Dixon. I can't put my finger on it just yet."

"Always happy to be of help," Marlowe answered knowingly.

"Keep me informed," Marcus said simply, rising.

"That I'll do," Marlowe replied, "that I'll do."

4

Claire Crawford was everything that Sarah was not. Her impeccable style, irreproachable demeanor, and innate ability to charm the horns off a disgruntled ram made her the envy of the entire female population of Dorset.

Save for Sarah.

For Claire made Sarah feel just as special, and not because she was kind or thoughtful or any of those things that women are supposed to be.

Though she was.

No, Claire treated Sarah as though she were special because Claire believed it to be so.

"Six events, Sarah, and I'll not take one less," Claire insisted, holding a lovely blue gown up for approval.

"Beautiful. It matches your eyes," Sarah answered, twisting a lock of stray hair around her finger as she reclined on Claire's bed. "One event," she bargained.

Claire smiled at the compliment, then flung the dress onto the end of the bed and reached for another. "Five. And I'll not budge." She held the pale yellow gown up to her body, emphasizing the low neckline that would accentuate her growing bosom with an arching of her eyebrow.

"Oh yes, please," Sarah confirmed with a giggle. "Two events, and that's my limit."

The yellow gown joined the blue one in the colorful

pile of silk and lace on the bed. "Really, Sarah, stub-bornness is not an attractive quality. Four."

"Two."

"Three or I'll . . ." Claire paused, obviously attempt-ing to conjure the vilest of threats. "Or I'll . . . Bad dog!"

Sarah sat up just in time to see Claire retrieve what was left of a badly chewed pale brown kid boot from Titus's mouth.

"Or I'll banish your beast from my house. Forever!"

"Really, Claire, it was not the most attractive shoe to begin—"

"Forever, Sarah!" Claire repeated, running her finger through a hole in the toe of the boot and glaring threat-eningly at her.

Sarah gave Titus the most scolding look she could muster, and then flopped back on the bed. "Oh, all right. I will attend three events at your house party, but they will be of my choosing and will most certainly not include dancing. Of any kind," she emphasized with a severe look. "Agreed?"

"Agreed," Claire confirmed with a winning smile be-fore rubbing her lower back and joining Sarah on the bed.

The mattress suddenly sagged in the middle as Titus hefted himself up onto the cream-curtained bed and thrust himself between the two women. He rested his head on Sarah's thigh and heaved a huge sigh of content-ment.

"You bribed him, didn't you?"

"I most certainly did not!" Claire answered resolutely. "Titus needs little convincing on matters involving de-struction, as you well know."

The dog lifted his head, looked from Sarah to Claire, then back again, before a leather-scented huff escaped from between his enormous jowls. Then he lowered his head once more, closed his eyes, and immediately began to snore.

"Speaking of which, did you ever see fit to reimburse Lord Weston for the dogged demise of his coat?"

"Oh, Lord Weston."

Claire carefully positioned herself so that she was facing Sarah. "I'm sorry, was that a dreamily uttered 'oh' or one laced with irritation?"

"Really, Claire, I thought that I'd made my position as regards Lord Weston clear," Sarah answered. "Besides, I can't imagine what he must think of me after that whole disaster with my mother."

"I know—it's just that, well, he is quite handsome. And perhaps his attentions would dissuade Dixon from pursuing you quite so vigorously."

Sarah turned to face her friend, upsetting Titus's nap. "Do you propose I use him for my own nefarious plans? Is that an honorable act?"

Sarah watched the expressions flit across Claire's features as the woman struggled with her conscience. Claire could no more urge her friend to do such a thing than she could do it herself.

"Did I mention that he's quite handsome?"

Sarah laughed. "Yes, yes, you did."

And really, Claire needn't remind her of Lord Weston's physical attributes. The thorough perusal she'd made of him while hiding in the woods still weighed heavily on her mind.

And other more intimate places of her person, if she were being completely honest.

"Besides, I highly doubt the earl will want anything more to do with me at this point," Sarah continued, brushing a lock of stray hair from her cheek.

"I doubt the coat was of such significance to him—"

"Oh, no, this has nothing to do with the coat," Sarah interrupted. "No, he found me hiding on the lawn."

Claire's lips pursed as she thought through the statement.

"Actually, I was crawling toward the rhododendron bush," Sarah elaborated. "So, really, he found me in the act of—"

"Your lawn?" Claire queried, her lips continuing to purse.

Sarah gently tugged on the errant strand of hair and brushed it against her lips. "Well, I'd hardly be hiding on *his* lawn, now, would I?"

Claire rolled her eyes. "Sarah," she said, in the long, drawn-out way she always did when it was clear more details were needed.

"I was hiding from Mr. Dixon, as I am known to do," Sarah began.

"True."

"Only this particular situation required quick thinking on my part, as Mr. Dixon arrived much earlier than expected. I'd just begun to cross the lawn when I heard his horse. So I ran."

"Quite rude of him, I must say. Making you run," Claire interjected.

"Precisely!" Sarah agreed with relish. She dropped the curl and reached for Claire's hand. "I found myself in the middle of the lawn with only bushes and fronds for cover. Which, I must say, actually worked quite well until Lord Weston arrived."

"Why on earth did you leave the safety of the bush?"

Sarah smiled as Titus began to snore. "Well, I could hardly spend the rest of my life in a rhododendron bush, and besides, I'd no idea that Lord Weston was coming to call."

Claire nodded. "I see. Then what happened?"

"I made a bargain with Lord Weston, and then crawled my way to the wood. So you see, the earl will surely have no need of me now that he's witnessed—"

"A bargain?" Claire asked, gently pulling her hand from Sarah's. "What sort of bargain?"

Sarah grimaced. "I can't say."

"You can't or you won't?" Claire pressed, worry in her tone.

"Good heavens, Claire, nothing as coarse as what your tone implies. Lord Weston simply required a price for his failure to make my whereabouts known and I agreed."

"The price, then?" Claire probed again.

Sarah cleared her throat. "There was hardly time to discuss such matters—"

"You agreed without knowing what you promised?" Claire squeaked, her eyes growing slightly wild.

"I could hardly argue, Claire. There I was, covered in grass and the good Lord only knows what else, embarrassed and, quite frankly, desperate to be done with the matter. If Lord Weston has any sense he'll demand that I promise to not come within a league of him or his home."

Claire's face fell. "Oh, Sarah. I'm sorry. I didn't realize."

"What, that one could hardly decide upon a price while astride a horse whose nose is dangerously close to a certain woman's derri—"

"Sarah."

" . . . ere. Really Claire, I adore you, but must you always interrupt—"

Claire rolled onto her back. "You fancy Lord Weston."

Sarah let out the breath she'd surely been holding in all day. "Is that what's wrong with me?"

"I believe so."

"Bollocks."

The two laughed softly as only the best of friends could.

Sarah snuggled in closer to Claire. "He makes me perspire. Is that to be expected?"

"Oh, yes," Claire answered furtively. "It's to be hoped for, actually."

"And angry."

"You would not be you if he did not."

"It's hopeless, of course."

Claire slowly sat up and patted Titus on the head. "Do not assume anything, Sarah." She dropped her feet to the polished oaken floor and carefully stood, pulling the crushed gowns from under Titus's weight with annoyance.

"I do adore you—you know I do," Sarah continued, pushing herself up and settling next to Titus reassuringly. "But your positive outlook can be a tad irritating."

"Positive outlook or not, I saw how Weston looked at you while you danced together. For once, can you not simply let things unfold as they may?" Claire countered, setting the gowns on the gilt-edged upholstered chair near the window. "Can you do that for me?" Claire asked, turning to face Sarah. "Right now."

Sarah hesitated. "As in this very moment?"

"If not sooner," Claire answered, walking toward the bed. "Lord Weston is here."

Sarah's hand stopped midair over Titus's wrinkled head. "Here? At Bennington House?"

"Yes. Gregory asked him to aid in the plans for tomorrow's hunt."

Titus batted at Sarah with his gigantic paw until she resumed petting him. "And you only just now thought to tell me?"

"I'm sorry, I truly am, but I honestly didn't realize that his presence would be a problem. There's little time to dwell on such things now," Claire said apologetically, pulling Sarah to stand. "You've only a few moments to compose yourself before he arrives and we must go downstairs and join the men."

"I'll do no such thing," Sarah answered, her sharp tone causing Titus to bark.

"But you only just confirmed that you would try—"

"I'd no idea you meant immediately. Claire, I've only just . . . That is, my feelings for Lord Weston—"

"—to let things unfold—"

"Claire!" Sarah yelped. "I am not accustomed to such a cacophony of emotion. You must give me time!"

Titus began to howl.

And Sarah ran for her life.

"Howling, Bennington?" Marcus asked as the two men jointly peered upward at the striking Adam-style ceiling, its delicate details painted in shades of blue appearing to quiver with fright from the sound.

Bennington smiled. "Have you met Titus, Miss Tisdale's dog?"

"In a manner of speaking, yes," Marcus confirmed, following Bennington out of the drawing room and into the long hall that ran the length of the stately country mansion.

Bennington paused, the rumbling from the floor above them marking Titus's progress toward the stairs. "He's a brute, but Sarah adores him—and he, her. We attempted to tie him up outside during her visits, but—"

"He chewed through the rope? Ate the cook for an appetizer, and then demolished the east wing?" Marcus asked jokingly.

"Howled. For the entire length of Sarah's visit. Do you have any idea how irritating one dog can make himself?" Bennington asked, flinching as the floorboards seemingly began to sway from the dog's lumbering.

"An inkling," Marcus answered, though he couldn't help but smile as he listened to the dog. A brute, indeed, but a loyal and, quite honestly, humorous one. "Will your wife and Miss Tisdale be joining us?"

The thunder of paws grew softer and softer until one could hear a howl only now and again. "I'm sure that the ladies will want to say hello, but beyond that they'll be of little help with the cub hunt," Bennington answered casually. "Sherry will be served on the terrace. Please go on ahead," he suggested, gesturing down the hall to where a set of glass-paned doors stood ajar. "I'll just check in on the ladies—make sure that Titus hasn't swallowed a servant. Or worse. I'll be but a moment."

Marcus threw him an amused smile before Bennington took the stairs two at a time, disappearing onto the upper floor.

He walked slowly down the hall, peering in several open doorways as he went. The house was well appointed and in perfect order, nary a speck of dust to be found in sight. He reached the open terrace doors, noting the expanse of manicured lawn and gardens that lay just beyond.

There was something lighter—airier—about Bennington's home than his own, though Marcus couldn't be sure what precisely caused him to think such a thing. Bennington himself, perhaps, whose good nature was infectious. Or maybe it was the man's pregnant wife.

"Woof!"

Titus's deep bark echoed through the house. Marcus noted the sound wasn't coming from the front, where the stairs were, but somewhere off to his right.

He wandered in the general direction of the noise, passing through several rooms until he found himself at the foot of the servants' stairs.

"Please, Titus. Do behave yourself," a female voice urgently whispered.

"Woof."

Clumsy footsteps sounded on the stairs, followed immediately by the loud, untidy gait of one enormous dog.

"Titus!" the voice implored in another loud whisper, followed quickly by "Bad dog!" as the footfalls turned to a rhythmic bumping.

"Woof!"

"Drat!"

Marcus jumped back as Titus slipped, tumbled, and crashed down the stairs, Miss Tisdale sliding down closely behind.

"A pleasure to see you, Miss Tisdale," Marcus said with amusement, hiding a smile at the surprise on Miss Tisdale's face.

She'd clearly slid nearly the entire length of the staircase on her bottom, landing with her printed walking dress pushed to her knees. Her attempt to stop herself before crashing into the rear of the big dog had her stretched out on the stair treads so that her head now rested on the fifth step from the bottom. Hairpins were scattered on the upper steps. What once was surely a presentable chignon was now reduced to a cascade of long shining auburn curls.

Marcus could not recollect ever witnessing a lady in such a state.

Nor could he recall being quite so aroused.

Her eyes went round as saucers as she surveyed the damage. "Lord Weston?!"

He bent to assist with her dress, though he secretly hoped to accidentally skim the creamy expanse of her leg in the process. "Is that a question, Miss Tisdale, or a proclamation?"

"My limbs!" she choked out, apparently in shock.

Marcus bent down so that they were face-to-face. "Miss Tisdale, is there something wrong with your legs?"

She reached for her skirt and awkwardly attempted to

cover herself. "I cannot imagine what you must be thinking. I really—"

Marcus impulsively reached out and touched his forefinger to her lips, quieting her instantly. "Miss Tisdale, my only thought is for your safety."

Her eyes, no longer saucers, had gone all dewy, and Marcus feared his ability to control his body's urging. He took his finger from her soft mouth and held out his arm.

"Seems a rather dangerous way to amuse oneself, wouldn't you agree?" he asked mildly as she grasped his arm and allowed him to pull her upright.

The moment she was on her feet, Miss Tisdale snatched her fingers away from Marcus's arm and set about straightening her attire and hair. "You'd do better to ask Titus, Lord Weston, as I had very little to say in the matter. I typically make use of my feet when leaving Bennington House, rather than my—" She halted, her brow furrowing as she searched for the right word.

"Were you hiding again, Miss Tisdale?" Marcus asked suddenly, deftly taking a hairpin from her hand and gesturing for her to turn.

She looked to refuse him and, really, Marcus wouldn't have been surprised. The request was completely improper. But she obeyed, slowly revolving until she stood with her back to him. "From what, Lord Weston?" she asked hesitantly.

"From me."

Her breath caught as he gently twisted a curl and effortlessly pinned it into place.

He reached for more pins, his fingers brushing her forearm lightly, stirring the heat low in his belly. "I apologize, Miss Tisdale, if I've offended you. Your nature seems to elicit the most unexpected behavior from me."

"Is that so?" she asked, turning back to face him.

He surveyed his handiwork, adjusting one final curl,

which slid seductively near her chin. "Honestly? Yes, quite," he countered, the feel of her hair making him want to reel her in, inch by inch, and take her in his arms.

"Interesting," she said simply. "And I was not hiding from you. I was avoiding you. Two different things altogether."

He could not help himself. Her complete lack of guile was entrancing. He gently tugged until there was no more than a breath between them. "Why?"

"Because of this," she answered, then closed the distance between them with a kiss.

She was unschooled in the ways of sensuality, that much was obvious. But her innocent boldness captured Marcus instantly, the feel of her lips against his—so eager, so true—urged him on, his arm wrapping around her waist with instinctive possession.

She murmured incoherently and pressed closer, her breasts tight against his chest.

"Weston?" Bennington's voice echoed from the front of the house, breaking the spell.

Miss Tisdale pulled back, shock and surprise in her eyes. "And I do not hide, Lord Weston. I run, and it just so happens that no one to date has been able to keep up."

And with that she turned quickly and fled, Titus galloping behind.

It was a lovely day to be out-of-doors, though Sarah suspected the quick clip of her escape from Bennington House would be felt ever so sorely by her muscles in the morning.

It was just that: an escape. But from what—or, perhaps more accurately, from whom?

Sarah forced herself to slow to a walk, Titus bumping her with his head in approval.

She'd kissed him. There was no point in denying the fact. He'd in turn pulled her close until her breasts pressed up against his chest in a most delicious manner. And deepened the kiss in an expert fashion. And nearly coaxed a moan of pleasure from her throat that would have, in all likelihood, set Titus to barking.

But she'd started it all.

Sarah anxiously pulled the pins from her hair that Lord Weston had carefully put back into place. If experience had taught her anything, it was that following through on sudden desires almost always ended badly.

Suggesting that Lord Blackwood find a hat that housed both his head and his enormous ears, if only to keep them from the sun. Advising Lord Bishop as to the miraculous effects of peppermints on noxious breath. Both said with the utmost of care, yet taken, well, in a word, badly.

She touched her lips, still tingling with sensitivity. Sarah could not classify the kiss itself as bad—quite the opposite, actually. And Lord Weston's willing participation surely was a good sign. Wasn't it?

She forcefully ran her fingers through her mussed locks, the sensation so stimulating as to be nearly painful. "What do you want, Sarah Tisdale?" she asked herself out loud, kicking viciously at a rock in the path.

And what does Lord Weston want? she thought, kicking the rock a second time and sending it skittering off into the trees.

True, the man had not been deterred by Titus at the lake. Nor by Sarah's flight from Dixon. Even her fall down the stairs barely elicited a response from the man—well, a negative one anyway. And he'd failed to mention her silly blunder with regards to her mother's intentions—which Sarah was immensely grateful for.

Any other suitor would have run for his life somewhere in between the first and second incident.

Titus retrieved the rock and loped back onto the path, proudly dropping the treasure at Sarah's feet.

But Lord Weston is no suitor, she reminded herself. There had been no declaration of interest. Only fleeting moments. And though one of those had involved a kiss, it was hardly a proposal for something more.

Something more? Sarah stared down at the rock, Titus's panting the only sound she could hear.

"Bloodiest of bloody hells."

She kicked the rock with all of her might and watched as it flew down the path.

What did she know of Lord Weston, really? That he was handsome and wealthy, with—one must assume of such a man—some experience in the ways of love. Sarah had lived a sheltered life. But she'd heard enough gossip to know that men of Lord Weston's ilk did not, as a general rule, wait for their wedding night to dip their wicks.

What had she gotten herself into?

Feeling dizzy, Sarah bent at the waist and dropped her torso, closing her eyes tightly.

"We'll lighten you of your jewels now, mademoiselle," a voice said in a low tone, the feigned French accent more comical than frightening.

Sarah opened her eyes to discover the dusty toes of a familiar pair of boots in front of her. She rose slowly, taking in the faded breeches and untucked linen shirt, then finally the endearing face of her brother.

Sarah smiled and planted a kiss on the boy's forehead. "Nigel, dear, I've no jewels to be taken, as you well know."

"Ew."

"Blimey."

Sarah smiled sweetly at Nigel, whose cheeks were turning red before her eyes, then looked behind him. Jasper Wilmington and Clive Burroughs, Nigel's fellow highwaymen, stood in aghast wonder at the kiss their poor friend had just endured.

"Boys, do any of you wish to lighten me of my belongings?" Sarah asked, taking a step toward them.

Nigel and Clive leapt back in fear.

"You wouldn't," Jasper asserted, holding steady, though he looked to be wavering.

Sarah took another step forward. "Wouldn't I?"

"Oh, hell, it's not worth it," Jasper said before lunging out of Sarah's way just as she began to pucker her lips.

The other boys broke out in laughter until all three were wrestling good-naturedly on the dirt path.

Sarah watched them for a moment, wondering at the way in which the males of her species seemed to so easily be taken off course.

"Boys?" she asked, the sound of grunts and such drowning out her voice.

"Boys?" she shouted, this time capturing their collective attention.

One by one they stopped, until the dust settled around them. "What is it, Sarah?" Nigel asked, clearly having forgotten that it was he who had sought her attention in the first place.

"Did you come looking for me or was your attack purely serendipity?"

All three of the boys uttered a forgetful "Oh" in unison, Nigel standing first then lending a hand to the rest. "Right. We've come for Titus, actually."

The dog, who until this point had been happily rolling in the remains of a dead animal, stopped what he was doing at the sound of his name and came running to Sarah.

Sarah pinched her nose with two fingers and began to breathe out of her mouth. "You won't be getting up to no good, will you?"

All of the boys in Lulworth—and most of the grown

men as well—had dealings with the smugglers who ran goods from France across the Channel. It was more of a game to them than anything else and, as far as Sarah could tell, it was a harmless one at that.

Her own father bought vast quantities of fine French brandy from the men, many of whom made their homes up and down the Weymouth coast.

No one had been taken into custody for smuggling in as long as anyone could remember. And Sarah hardly wished for Nigel to be the first.

"Titus will see to that, Sarah," Nigel assured, making to pat the brute on the head, then, as the wind shifted, thinking twice and pinching his nose instead.

Sarah rolled her eyes. "Remember, he's a colossal coward. He'll be the first to run at any sign of danger," she warned, looking down at the slobbering dog.

"I know, Sarah. It's his size that matters," Nigel replied, adding "Though I think the stench will serve him well today."

"Come on then, we'll be late," Jasper pressed, turning to head south. Clive followed him, but Nigel hesitated.

"You're going straight home, aren't you?" he asked, looking toward the setting sun.

Sarah shooed him off teasingly. "Of course. And if anyone dares bother me I'll simply threaten to kiss him."

Nigel made a disgusted face then loped off after his friends, calling for Titus to join him.

The big dog licked Sarah's hand then took off down the path toward adventure.

Leaving Sarah to wonder at the irony to be found in a kiss.

Marcus had never enjoyed the hunt. Be it stag or fox, the Highlands of Scotland or the coast of England, the excitement that most men found in the act left Marcus cold.

Trips with his uncle Calum, where he'd learned the nuances of tracking and cleanly killing the beast—well, that had been altogether different. Of course, it had just been the two of them, and he'd not been on assignment.

As he surveyed his fellow hunters from his saddle, Marcus wondered what would be revealed today. People tended to let down their guards in a hunt, all sorts of unsavory aspects of their personalities tumbling out amid the noise and action of the event.

"Sizing up the competition, Lord Weston?"

Marcus peered over his right shoulder to where Lady Bennington approached. "Should I be?" he asked, nodding in greeting.

"No, not really," she answered with a mischievous smile. She lovingly petted Pokey's neck, cooing to the Thoroughbred as if he were a puppy.

"And how will the ladies be spending their day?" Marcus asked, looking to where the female houseguests milled about on the expansive lawn just beyond.

Claire gave Pokey one last pat then turned her attention to Marcus. "Far from the hunt, my lord. It's a fine day for a bit of watercolor painting, I believe."

"And do all the ladies of Lulworth share your opinion?"

"Oh, no, my lord," Claire answered, adding, "only the truly enlightened among us."

Marcus laughed. "And Miss Tisdale, is she counted among your ranks?"

Claire looked surprised at the mention of her friend, though whether she was pleased Marcus could not say.

"You could not find a more enlightened individual, Lord Weston. I'm sure she is at this very moment conversing with the fox concerning strategy."

He made to refute such a notion, but thought better of it.

After all, it would not be out of character for Miss Tisdale to be doing just such a thing. Which he found both odd and utterly adorable.

"She'll not be joining you today, then?"

"Unfortunately not," Claire replied. "She'll attend three events. No more, no less. It is the agreement we struck."

"Agreement?" Marcus pressed, wondering at the woman's statement. "Every female of my acquaintance would no more not attend a house party's entirety than they would refuse the Prince Regent a dance."

"Have you not discovered the truth yet, my lord?" she asked, adjusting her bonnet to better shade her face from the morning sun.

"What's that, Lady Bennington?"

"Miss Tisdale is unlike any other woman you've ever met."

She pinned him with her gaze, and even beneath the broad brim of her bonnet, Marcus could see the depth of her words as they played upon her face.

"I do believe you're quite right, Lady Bennington," Marcus quietly replied, wondering at the nature of their conversation.

Did she mean to drive him away or pull him in on Miss Tisdale's behalf?

"Besides, have you danced with the Prince? Hardly worth the effort," she said, breaking the peculiar spell that had been cast over their exchange.

The horn sounded just then, Pokey's ears pricking forward with eagerness. "I believe it is time," Marcus offered in farewell.

"Happy hunting, Lord Weston," Claire finished, slapping Pokey on the rump as they trotted off.

* * *

Pokey was slow for a regally bred Thoroughbred, hence his telling soubriquet. But as compared to most of the fine yet lesser-known stock ridden by Marcus's fellow hunters, he was a whirlwind who could quite literally run circles around them.

Which he very much wanted to do, despite Marcus's urgings otherwise. Finally, Marcus gave up and allowed the horse free rein, taking off at a clip that no one save Bennington's horse could hope to match.

They'd been riding some time with nary a growl from the pack of dogs. Marcus thought it as good a time as any to engage Bennington in conversation. Though he continued to doubt the merit of Carmichael's concern, he was still obligated to do his duty.

And James Marlowe's information concerning the London business still niggled at the back of his mind. He pulled gently at the reins, and Pokey abandoned his canter for a trot.

"I apologize, Weston," Bennington offered as he pulled his bay alongside Pokey. "I don't know what has become of the fox today."

Marcus smiled, thinking back on Claire's comment. "Perhaps Miss Tisdale did warn him of the hunt, after all."

"Ha!" Bennington laughed out loud, slapping his thigh. "I wouldn't put it past her."

They slowed to a walk and continued on in companionable silence, the other men still some distance behind. Marcus could not help but like the man, Bennington's utter lack of concern for Marcus's heritage seemingly as real as his love for his bonny wife.

Bennington would have invited him to hunt whether he liked Marcus or not, that much could be assumed. But he wouldn't have asked for his help in planning the day's events, nor listened to Marcus's advice in the end.

There were Young Corinthians whom Marcus trusted

with his life, even a few whom he counted as friends. But he'd always assumed they were the exception.

"I had the good fortune to call upon Sir Arthur—and his exquisite brandy—the other day," Marcus remarked conversationally, hopeful that Bennington would pick up the thread.

"Ah, yes, his brandy. The finest in the county—some say in the entire country."

Marcus curbed his eagerness to continue and waited the appropriate amount of time before pressing further.

"Do all of Lulworth's residents so heartily support smuggling, then?"

Bennington nodded. "In a word? Yes. Even his son plays at smuggling, acting as a courier now and again. Nothing dangerous, mind you . . ."

He stopped, the troubled look on his face confirming that he realized what he'd shared. "The Tisdales, for all their eccentricities, are a fine family, Weston. I would not want my words to lead you to believe otherwise."

Weston gave the man a reassuring nod. "Of course. You've in no way dissuaded me from believing the Tisdales to be anything but what you claim."

Marcus knew he was good at lying, and Bennington's look of relief only underscored his talent.

Still, in all likelihood he'd use the man's words against him, and not without pain.

The sudden cry of the pack as they shot off toward a copse of trees to the north caught both men by surprise, the unexpected appearance of Dixon as he raced past irritating to both.

"We cannot leave Dixon to win," Bennington announced, spurring his bay into a gallop.

Marcus allowed Pokey his reins, the giant chestnut catching up to Bennington's in no time. "On that we are united."

5

"Cricket?" Sarah's voice rose in disbelief as she and Claire took seats near the edge of the grassy lawn.

"Come now, I've seen you play. Those men could not hold a candle to your skill with a bat."

Sarah pinned Claire with a testy glare. "Not that I'll be allowed to play."

Claire smiled at the bevy of ladies as they took their seats before turning her attention back to Sarah. "The game today has something to do with a school rivalry. Which"— she lowered her voice to a confidential murmur—"if you ask me is complete poppycock. But after yesterday's failed hunt I could hardly tell my husband no."

"Why," Sarah began through gritted teeth, "must their pride be tied to such ridiculous pursuits?"

"Because they are men, my dear. Now, smile and pretend to enjoy yourself. This is one of but three activities that you agreed to, remember?"

"I agreed to archery, not cricket," Sarah reminded Claire, watching with lukewarm interest as the men took the field.

Sarah searched the crowd of men for Lord Weston, but could not find him.

"Lady Bennington, Miss Tisdale." The deep male voice was polite, a thread of amusement faintly discernible.

Disoriented, Sarah wondered for a moment where the voice, so rich in tone and seductive in manner, could have come from. Her gaze quickly cataloged the men on the field for a second time, but failed to find him.

"Lord Weston," Claire answered politely, looking across and slightly behind Sarah.

Sarah turned slowly, finding a pair of well-muscled thighs clothed in fawn-colored breeches directly in her line of sight. Her gaze continued upward, noting a coat of dark blue superfine and a white linen shirt covering what she could now state with conviction to be a granite-hard chest. And finally, her gaze reached his tanned face and those deep green eyes that turned nearly black when he was aroused.

She swallowed, her mouth suddenly dry. "Why are you not on the field, my lord?"

Claire coughed and jabbed her in the ribs with an elbow.

Lord Weston settled into the chair next to Sarah, sprawling negligently and allowing a footman to place a stool beneath his feet. "I'm afraid yesterday's hunt proved too strenuous for my leg."

Try as she might, Sarah could think of nothing but when the expertly formed limb pressed deliciously against her own. "Were you shot? A duel perhaps?" she blurted out.

Claire's elbow landed a second blow. Sarah couldn't suppress a wince but found if she continued to speak, she didn't have time to worry about what Lord Weston might be thinking.

"I'm sorry," Sarah offered halfheartedly for Claire's benefit. "I should not inquire after your—"

Lord Weston laid his hand on the arm of her chair, perilously close to Sarah's bare arm. "I applaud your curiosity, though I fear the truth would only bore you. So yes, let us say it was a duel of great consequence."

Sarah turned to give Claire a smug smile, then examined Weston's words more closely. Curiosity? What sort of curiosity might he be referring to? Intellectual? Physical?

Bugger.

The entire situation was distressing indeed. Sarah didn't know whether to be thrilled at his presence, as her body seemed inclined to be, or terrified.

"Who is winning?" she rattled off, her vision blurring as she attempted to watch the field.

Claire beamed. "Gregory's team."

Lord Weston shifted in his chair. "Miss Tisdale, I thought to call upon you and your family tomorrow afternoon. Will you be at home?"

Sarah looked at Claire pleadingly. She wanted to ask just what his intentions were, but knew that, well, she'd make a fool of herself if she did.

It was much more complicated than she'd ever imagined—had she *ever* before considered the problem. One simply could not go about kissing men and expect that all would be just as it had been before.

Or maybe one could. Perhaps if she simply took Lord Weston aside and asked his intentions, all would be made clear.

Or she could rely on her baser instincts and attack the man again.

Bugger.

She stood abruptly, needing to do anything but sit for one more moment.

"Brava, Sarah!" Bennington yelled from across the field, running toward her with cricket bat in hand.

He thrust the bat at her. "I'd thought to call a footman to bat for Weston, but you'll do splendidly."

Sarah eyed Bennington then turned to look at Claire and Lord Weston.

She'd bungled her way into ridiculous situations before, but this was a new low. Of course the proper thing was to refuse, though if she agreed she'd have no choice but to concentrate on hitting the life out of an innocent ball.

It took only a second to choose. She'd take her chances with the bat. "Tell the boys to move back, Bennington. I'm known for my distance hitting."

"Sarah," Claire began, but her voice was soon drowned out by applause.

Lord Weston said nothing, simply clapped, a smile making his features even more rakish.

Whether that smile was a reflection of admiration or horror, Sarah could not say.

Nor did she want to.

She gripped the bat with one hand and marched onto the field, walking to the pitch and taking her place.

Mr. Dixon stood stock-still with the ball in his hand, as though he thought to deny her.

"Come, Mr. Dixon, or are you afraid?" Sarah teased.

The men on the field responded with hoots, while the women tutted with satisfaction.

Mr. Dixon looked angry enough to strike someone, but he reined in his pride and prepared to bowl.

Sarah did not doubt that she could hit the ball, having played cricket with Nigel and his friends more times than she could remember.

But she wanted to hit it hard. And far. And she didn't want to think why.

Mr. Dixon rolled the ball in his hands once, then twice, then took his run up and lobbed the ball toward Sarah with force.

He attempted to deceive Sarah by adding spin to the ball, typical of a leg bowler such as Mr. Dixon.

Sarah waited for the precise moment then swung, the crack of the bat against the ball deafening.

She didn't bother to look to where it may have landed, but simply picked up the skirts of her floral print muslin gown and ran. Ran for her life down the length of the pitch while all around her chaos ensued. Men chased after the ball while women screamed with sheer delight. Bennington, her fellow batsman, shouted with glee as he passed on his way to the opposite end of the pitch.

Sarah rounded the wicket and headed back toward Bennington, skidding to an awkward stop upon reaching the end of the pitch.

"Splendid, Sarah!"

Bennington and the rest of her team gathered around, cheering.

Sarah lost herself for a moment in the pure, unadulterated joy. Laughing, she allowed each man to kiss her hand and may have, in her enthusiasm, even accepted a marriage proposal.

And then she looked across the field to where Lord Weston sat, the same small smile affixed to his face, undecipherable as ever.

She was unique, he had to give the lass that. Marcus hadn't bothered to entertain thoughts of just what Miss Tisdale might do or say after their brief kiss at Bennington House.

Her surprise at his presence amused him—or, more specifically, pleased him. For once, he had surprised her, rather than the other way around.

And he'd been honest enough. His leg did throb from the prolonged ride yesterday, followed by attending the excellent, if tedious dinner with the rest of the party that evening.

Nothing of interest had come up in the stilted conversations he'd endured during the meal, and God knew Marcus had tried nearly every trick in the book. His reputation as the Errant Earl was getting in the way. Not even when the women left the dining room did talk turn to anything that might lead Marcus to believe the noblemen present were tied to the Orlov emeralds.

Save for Dixon. The man had guardedly underscored what Marcus had already guessed: Sir Arthur loved his brandy so dearly that he'd do almost anything for it.

Marcus watched as Dixon made ready to pitch Miss Tisdale's ball. He wondered if his suspicions concerning the man were valid. Marlowe had yet to discover anything that tied Dixon to the smugglers or the burglaries.

Perhaps his suspicions had everything to do with Dixon's obvious designs on Miss Tisdale.

And if it was the latter, what in the name of all that was holy was Marcus thinking?

Dixon threw the ball, a bit of spin adding to its speed.

Miss Tisdale appeared to desire the quick demise of the ball, sending it whistling through the air with all the force her slender body could muster. And then she ran as if her life depended upon it.

Marcus caught a glimpse of Lady Bennington beaming with pride.

He laughed out loud as Miss Tisdale gleefully accepted the thanks of her teammates.

She was unique, to be sure. But that was not reason enough for Marcus to risk his heart.

His uncle Calum had long ago promised there would be a woman for him—one woman whose heart beat only for Marcus. One woman whose soul completed his own.

Marcus had shuddered at the description but kept it tucked away in his heart for safekeeping. It was those words that had kept Marcus carrying on through every vicious attack and bitter tongue he'd encountered over the years.

It was foolish and absurd.

True, at times he'd lost hope of ever finding such a woman. But not completely, at least not yet.

His kiss with Miss Tisdale had gotten him to thinking, but that was all.

The risk was too high, the timing impossible. When he gave his heart it would be forever, and he could not see forever in her eyes.

Bennington marched across the field with Miss Tisdale in tow, finally reaching his wife and bowing with a flourish.

Claire nodded in acknowledgment, graciously holding out her hand for her husband's kiss. "My dear Lord Bennington, congratulations on the win."

Bennington scoffed at her hand and instead leaned in to kiss her full on the mouth. "My dear Lady Bennington, I thank you."

Marcus dropped his feet from the stool and stood, offering his hand to Bennington. "Congratulations."

Bennington took his hand and shook it enthusiastically. "Thank you, Weston. Now, let us retire to the house for refreshment, shall we?"

Claire accepted Bennington's help and stood. The two set off at a slow pace, following the rest of the party as they made their way back to Bennington House.

Leaving Marcus and Miss Tisdale alone.

Marcus offered his arm to her. "Shall we?"

Miss Tisdale looked at the chattering party trailing toward the house, then back at Marcus, as though judging the distance. "We shall," she answered, slipping her hand through the crook of his arm.

Marcus could feel the nervous energy coursing through her slim body. She nearly hummed with it.

"Where did you learn to play cricket?"

She flexed her fingers once, then twice. "Well, here, of course, in Lulworth. Nigel and his friends used to beg me to play."

"Until?"

"Until I got better than them," she answered simply. "Do you find that hard to believe, Lord Weston?"

"Not at all," he said, chuckling.

"Why are you laughing?" she demanded, stopping to pull her arm from his.

She was angry, though Marcus truly could not understand why. "Miss Tisdale, have I done something to offend you?"

"You're laughing at me," she declared forcefully, her cheeks faintly flushed with pink.

God, he loved that. She was fiery and damned confusing, but she drew him to her like a moth to the flame.

And she didn't even know it.

She wasn't the one for him, her comfortable life in Lulworth having guaranteed she'd never understand a man so at odds with his world. But she was damn close.

"I'm not laughing at you, Miss Tisdale. I simply find it delightful—and, on my word, completely believable—that you've bested your brother at cricket."

Her breath slowed slightly but she still looked capable of exploding. "You're not scandalized by my participation in today's game?"

"No," Marcus answered, "on the contrary."

"Oh," she answered quietly, her ire dissipating. She slipped her arm through his once again and they set off.

He chuckled. "Come now, of all people, did you truly expect the Errant Earl to judge you?"

"Lord Weston, do not use that ridiculous name," she scolded.

"But why ever not?" Marcus countered teasingly, though her reaction secretly touched his heart.

"Because it's not true," she answered, looking at him earnestly. "Besides, it's hardly creative enough for a man such as yourself," she added, breaking into a gorgeous giggle.

Marcus could not help but join her, the two drawing questionable looks from the party up ahead.

"You are not like every other gentleman, are you, Lord Weston?" Miss Tisdale asked, clearly regretting the words once they'd slipped from her mouth.

Marcus whispered conspiratorially in her ear. "I am not. Nor are you like every other gentleman's daughter."

He could see from the quick rise and fall of her breasts that the lady liked him near.

He straightened, and instantly missed the scent of her skin. "Miss Tisdale, I believe I asked earlier whether you will be at home tomorrow but you've yet to respond."

Her fingers drummed a nervous tattoo on his coat sleeve. "Do you remember my mother, Lord Weston?"

"Yes."

"And yet you would pay us a visit—of your own accord," she pressed, the tattoo now resembling a fast reel.

Marcus covered her fingers with his own, regretting the white gloves that kept him from feeling her warm, silky skin. "Miss Tisdale, you are aware of my heritage, are you not?"

She nodded, her brows furrowing with confusion.

"We Highlanders have faced markedly rougher foes than your mother."

"With all due respect, my lord," she began, leaning in toward Marcus, "you've more of the London dandy about you than the Scottish warrior."

Marcus didn't know whether to chastise her for saying such a thing or commend her, his own misgivings about his place in the world having led him to ponder the very same conundrum on more than one occasion. "You do say whatever comes to mind, don't you?"

She smiled insecurely. "It is who I am, my lord."

"Yes, it is," Marcus agreed.

He would find it easy enough to play this game.

But stopping? That was an altogether different matter.

*   *   *

Sarah could hardly breathe. The dress that Claire had insisted she borrow for dinner was beautiful, to be sure. The subtle peach hue perfectly complemented her coloring, just as Claire had said it would.

The cut, on the other hand, was a touch constricting, even with the alterations that had been made to accomodate Claire's growing figure. Sarah wiggled in her seat at the table, to no avail. Her hips were encased in the fabric with nary an inch to spare.

And her breasts! Sarah peered down at them, now rising toward her chin. Claire had gone on at some length the previous summer about the Scafells in the Lake District where she'd spent her honeymoon. The mountains were said to be the tallest in all of England.

Sarah tilted her chin slightly, testing just how little movement was required to spy the Tisdale Range.

"I suspect that you two would fare well against the Scafells," she murmured under her breath.

"I'm sorry?"

Sarah snapped her head to the right and answered Sir Hugh Darlington. "Oh, it's nothing. Simply thinking aloud."

Sarah had known Hugh for years. Born less than a year apart, they'd spent many an hour together as children, racing through the forest, playing smuggler and customs official, and talking their way out of many scoldings. And despite Lenora's best efforts, they'd never moved past viewing each other more as playmates than romantic interests.

"Talking to yourself again, then?" Hugh teased, wiggling his thick black eyebrows.

Sarah rolled her eyes. "Hugh, we're adults now and really should behave as such," she chided, adding, "besides, it was only the one time—and, need I remind you, we were all of eight. So really, a conversation with oneself was hardly outside the realm of acceptable behavior."

A servant set a Wedgewood china bowl of turtle soup in front of Hugh, though his attention was now turned to the woman sitting across the table. "Quite."

"Hugh, are you speaking to me or to Lottie Dunworth?" Sarah asked, accepting her soup with a nod and admiring the delicate crest and bands of interlacing gold that adorned the otherwise white bowl.

Hugh continued to stare dreamily at Lottie, while Lottie continued to stare dreamily elsewhere.

Sarah followed the woman's line of vision down the length of the expansive rosewood table. It was beautifully set, with artfully arranged flowers from the Bennington gardens lining the center, along with shimmering silver candelabras holding the finest of wax tapers. A snowy white tablecloth provided the perfect contrast for the heavy silver cutlery and fine glassware. It was, in a word, perfection—hardly surprising considering Claire's domestic skills. But the masterfully laid table was not what held Lottie's attention.

Sarah looked to the end of the table, where Lord Weston sat, just to the right of Claire. He leaned in and whispered something, making her laugh.

"What, exactly, does she see in that man?" Hugh pondered, taking up his spoon begrudgingly.

Sarah turned her gaze to her own bowl and brought a spoonful of the flavorful soup to her lips. *He's desperately handsome, quietly charming, and mysterious in a most delicious manner. And seems to care not a fig whether a woman plays cricket or not.*

"Lucky for the lot of us he's an abysmal landowner or there wouldn't be a single eligible chit left."

Sarah swallowed hard. "Hugh, what are you talking about?"

Hugh brought a second spoonful to his mouth,

slurped softly, and swallowed. "Come now, Sarah. His family's bad enough—what with his barbarous father storming down from Scotland and stealing Lord Steele's only daughter away—"

"Really, Hugh," Sarah interrupted, stopping short of voicing her own opinion on the matter—which was that it seemed all rather romantic to her. She'd never met Lord Weston's parents, but in her mind his father wore a colorful kilt and his mother an even brighter smile.

He set the spoon down and reached for his claret. "Oh, all right, complete and utter balderdash, but enough to put off a fair number of our neighbors," he replied, glancing at their fellow diners, many of whom were clearly engaged in gossip, pausing only to cast a critical eye in Lord Weston's direction.

"And the rest?" Sarah pressed, anger warming in her belly.

"You know as well as I that a titled landowner has certain responsibilities to the community," Hugh began, returning his glass to its place and taking up his spoon again. "Especially to those who work his land. Weston's turned his back on the lot of us—from the farmers to the big landowners. It's as if he thinks himself too good for the likes of Lulworth."

The anger in Sarah's belly began to grow, the flames licking at her throat. "Did no one ever stop to wonder whether Lord Weston's absence from Lulworth had anything to do with the treatment he's received while in residence?"

Hugh lifted a brow. "Really, Sarah, what difference does it make?"

"Let me ask you this, then," Sarah replied, gripping her silver spoon as though it would fly from her hand at any moment. "Mr. Dixon," she began, looking to where the insufferable man sat near the head of the table. "He's of 'pure English blood' and an extremely involved landowner—some would say too involved, actually."

She paused, turning to look at Hugh in an effort to underscore her meaning.

Every last inhabitant of Lulworth knew of Dixon's efforts to cheat the very men who worked his land, yet the snake was far too slippery to ever be caught.

"Do you mean to tell me that Mr. Dixon is a better man than Lord Weston?" she finished, only to discover that she was pointing her spoon toward Hugh in an accusatory manner.

Hugh eyed the spoon warily. "What is Weston to you, Sarah?"

"That's hardly the point, Hugh," Sarah replied in a heated tone, lowering her spoon awkwardly.

Hugh looked to those who'd turned their gaze in hopes of capturing the two in an argument. He smiled, then laughed. "All right," he began in a nonconsequential manner, "you have a point, I suppose. But the situation is what it is. Common sense will hardly change history, my dear."

Sarah reached for her own glass of claret and raised it in Hugh's general direction. "Do not be so sure, Hugh," she said, and then laughed gaily before taking a robust sip of the deep red liquid.

"God help us all," Hugh replied, reaching for his own glass and finishing it in one fell swoop.

"What of Dixon? He seems a nasty piece of work, if you ask me."

It was well past midnight, and while Marcus suspected that Sully would rather be warming Cook's bed than sharing a drink in the study with him, he needed to talk through the case.

At least he was able to offer his valet the best brandy this side of the English Channel, Tisdale having sent four more bottles for Marcus's drinking pleasure.

Marcus admired the deep sheen of the brandy in the candlelight. "Nasty enough to turn traitor?"

"More than enough—I feel it in my bones," Sully offered, taking a drink from his own glass.

Marcus nodded thoughtfully then reached to refill Sully's glass. "I've tasked Marlowe with keeping an eye on the man. He's yet to unearth anything useful, but that doesn't mean nothing is there."

Sully leaned forward from his mahogany chair and propped his elbows on his knees. "And Sir Arthur?"

"The man is liked and admired by his neighbors, loved by his family. Hardly a nasty streak in him such as the one to be found in Dixon. So the problem is motive."

"For money?" Sully offered, taking a long pull from his glass.

Marcus mentally pictured Tisdale Manor. The home was on the small side, with few servants and slightly shabby, though this could all be attributed to Tisdale's preferences as much as a lack of coin. "I think not, though it never hurts to be thorough. Ask around after the family's financial state."

"For the love of brandy?" Sully paused and drained the glass. "It is damn good drink," he finished, smiling widely.

"True enough," Marcus agreed. "And I suppose men have done many a foolish thing for love of one sort or another."

"At least the daughter's making it easy enough on you."

"Your meaning?" Marcus asked, nearly sighing with relief as the potent alcohol loosened his tight muscles.

Sully set down his glass then let out a low chuckle. "Well, she's pretty enough, which always makes the job . . . how shall I put it, more pleasurable. Wouldn't you agree?"

The brandy's effect suddenly lessened, the muscles in Marcus's neck tightening. "She's not a common whore, nor will I have you talking as if she is, Sully. Do I make myself clear?"

Sully's eyes widened in surprise at Marcus's growled words, and he rubbed his face with both hands. "It's late, my lord. I should be to bed."

Marcus had not meant to snap at Sully. His swift defense of Miss Tisdale had been unplanned and unexpected. "I apologize, Sully."

The valet shook his fist in mock outrage, a wide smile filling his face.

"And whose bed might you be referring to?" Marcus continued with his own grin.

Sully let out a throaty laugh and stood. "I'm a gentleman through and through. I'd no more kiss and tell than—"

"Ach, be on with ya', then," Marcus interrupted, his burr thickening as the brandy took its hold.

He watched Sully go, then turned his attention to the silver candelabra on his desk. The light from the six candles glowed, the flames flickering in the occasional draft through the open window.

Marcus licked his thumb and forefinger and put out the first three beeswax candles, dampening their flame with quick, precise movements.

Sir Arthur would be a fool to put his family in the path of danger. The Prince Regent was a buffoon, but he'd hardly allow a citizen of his realm to take part in such a scheme and live to tell about it.

Marcus reached for the fourth and fifth tapers, extinguishing them as quickly as the first three.

But if there was one thing Marcus had learned in his work with the Corinthians, it was that at times even seemingly ordinary men went out of their way to do the wrong thing.

He stared into the light of the last lit candle, contemplatively. *Do not play the fool,* he thought to himself. *You cannot afford to.*

6

"Thank you," Lord Weston offered, smiling at Sarah's mother as she offered him a cup of tea.

Lenora accepted his words with frosty politeness, and then readied a second cup.

Sarah fingered the corded edge of a burgundy velvet pillow and watched as Lord Weston ignored her mother's rudeness, choosing instead to savor his first sip.

"Perfectly brewed," he commented, taking a second sip.

Lenora stiffened, nearly spilling the tea as she handed a cup to her husband. "You're too kind."

When news of Lord Weston's impending visit had reached Lenora's ears she'd been visibly upset, the blossoming friendship between her husband and the earl quite a predicament indeed.

After all, he was the Errant Earl, which meant, of course, that Lenora was obligated to loathe the man. Yet, the deliciousness of sharing Lord Weston's visit with her friends was a treat she could already taste. Sarah would have been mortified were she not too busy examining Lord Weston's behavior. He was aware of Lenora's dislike, yet he ignored it.

She took a cup from her mother and settled back into her favorite chair, eyeing Lord Weston over the rim. No, she'd been wrong in her assessment. He did not ignore, but rather pressed his advantage where he could.

The conversation flowed, occasionally demanding

Sarah's attention. But she held back in an attempt to further study Lord Weston.

Much as he would in a game of chess, Sarah realized, Lord Weston thought five turns ahead of Lenora, reminding her of his extensive wealth when she dared to trot out something to do with Dixon, or dropping names of such influential London families that she was left speechless.

Sarah could not say whether or not Lord Weston found Lenora's treatment of him to be hurtful. She tried to discern something from his manner, but blast it, she could not.

Regardless, he'd not sought escape—something Sarah was quite adept at doing.

He finessed and quietly charmed, making it so that Lenora could not deny all that there was to recommend him.

Quietly charming. Sarah sipped her tea and remembered that she'd thought the very same thing while watching Lord Weston at the Bennington dinner.

In fact, she'd thought the very same thing when she'd leaned in and kissed him at Bennington House.

The swift mental image of the moment flashed uninvited into Sarah's mind. Her palms itched with eagerness. She dropped her cup, sending tea sloshing over the rim to pool upon the saucer.

She pasted a smile on her face and willed her breathing to slow as she accepted a linen serviette from her mother.

If only she knew what to do with the delicate linen square.

An image of Lord Weston appeared yet again in her mind's eye, only this time he was naked and reclining on a bed made up entirely in scarlet silk.

Scarlet silk? Sarah rolled her eyes at such a garish image.

Oh, he was tan everywhere. Down to—

"Miss Tisdale?"

"Oh!" She abruptly realized that Lord Weston was staring at her.

He beckoned to her with one finger, crooking it in a most seductive manner.

"Stop," Sarah said suddenly, squeezing her eyes shut and willing the man to depart from her clearly feverish mind.

Lenora's clipped voice echoed in her ears "Are you quite all right? Perhaps you should rest, Sarah."

"I am perfectly fine," Sarah replied, opening one eye and then the other, peering apprehensively at Lord Weston. He was fully dressed. Well, she thought with relief, that was a start anyway. "I simply forgot . . ."

My mind? No, that won't do.

She peered about the room and down the hall, noting, with some relief, a discarded riding crop near the entryway.

"Buckingham."

"Really, Sarah, hardly seems the time to mention—" Nigel began.

"Buckingham?" Sarah's mother and Lord Weston asked in unison, interupting the boy. Their faces held matching expressions of confusion.

Sarah carefully set the cup and saucer down on the silver tray and rose from her chair. "Yes, Mr. Dixon's bay. He arrived today and I want to be sure he's settled in."

Lenora arched an eyebrow so forbiddingly that Sarah feared it might never again find its natural place on her mother's face. "Another horse?"

Oh, dear. Sarah had been so caught up in her brilliant plan to escape that she'd failed to remember one small, yet infinitely important detail.

Bugger.

Sir Arthur cleared his throat and stepped into the

awful silence. "Yes, my dear, I feel certain I told you of Buckingham. Apparently Dixon suddenly decided he wanted nothing to do with the horse. It had nowhere else to go—"

"It was my understanding that the enormous dog was the last of Mr. Dixon's castoffs we would accept, was he not?" Lenora replied with a tight smile.

Without realizing what she did, Sarah slowly backed out of the room, an action so natural in such situations that her body undertook it of its own accord.

Only Lord Weston followed suit, the two stealthily creeping away as Sir Arthur searched for a reply.

They'd very nearly reached the front door when Nigel noticed them. "Sarah, you can't mean to drag Lord Weston to the barn?"

Bloody bugger.

"My leg is in need of a good stretch," Lord Weston said in a normal tone, leaning ever so slightly to the right and rubbing carefully at his thigh. "I thought to accompany Miss Tisdale to check on Buckingham and ease my leg in the process."

Sir Arthur's brow cleared as he ceased racking his brain for a rebuttal to his wife. He exhaled deeply and smiled his thanks at Marcus. "How kind of you, Lord Weston."

"And I'll act as chaperone," Nigel added with a wink, quickly crossing the entryway to stand next to Lord Weston.

"Thank you, my boy," Sir Arthur said hastily before disappearing toward his study.

Lenora continued to stand in the same spot, as though trying to grasp what had just occurred. "Sarah . . . Sir Arthur . . ."

But Sarah had already seized the opportunity and disappeared out the door, taking Nigel and Lord Weston with her.

"It will be getting dark·soon enough," Lord Weston said warily as the three made their way across the lawn that separated the manor house from the outbuildings.

"Sarah wanders about in the dark all the time—don't you, Sarah?" Nigel stated in an utterly innocent tone.

Sarah's palm smacked him lightly on the back of the head. "Do behave, Nigel," she replied, matching her irksome brother's angelic voice.

Nigel smiled beatifically at Sarah then promptly loped off toward the barn, leaving them to follow.

Sarah huffed irritably. "I apologize for my brother, Lord Weston. He is . . ." She paused, thinking over all of the possible adjectives at her disposal.

"A twelve-year-old boy," Lord Weston finished for her.

"Precisely."

His voice, deep and throaty, with a subtle hint of Scottish burr, was dangerous to Sarah's peace of mind.

Especially, she thought, the small piece of her mind that had taken up the habit of picturing the man naked.

"May I beg your indulgence, Miss Tisdale," he said, his hard, warm fingers closing over her bare wrist. "I could do with some support. Would you mind leading me?"

To bed?

To—

This had to stop.

Did he perspire at the sight of her? Was he struck dumb by the scent of her skin? Did he picture her naked on sheets of questionable origin?

"Lord Weston," she began, turning to face him.

He was beautiful. And while Sarah had yet to puzzle out what her hopes were with regards to Lord Weston, she felt sure she most decidedly did not want her acquaintance with him to end with him running away.

As it had with Sir Rupert Westmont.

And Lord Chase.

And Sir—*Oh, bother,* she chided herself, realizing that it was hardly worth tallying.

"I would be happy to do so." And with that, she took his arm in hers, turned toward the barn, and shut her mouth.

"Welcome to the Tisdale Menagerie, my lord."

Nigel, accompanied by a tongue-lolling Titus, bowed low to Marcus, a mischievous grin lighting his face. "Chickens, pigs, a donkey, four horses, too many cats to count, three cows—"

"That's quite enough, Nigel," his sister admonished with little heat. She walked toward the back of the barn, where the latest addition to the collection peered at them over his stall door.

"So this is where you keep the brute," Marcus teased, scratching Titus's head. The stables where they stood were redolent with the scents of hay and leather. Several lanterns were burning, lighting the space with a golden glow. "I thought he most likely slept at the foot of your bed."

Nigel laughed good-naturedly. "The foot of the bed? If she's lucky. Titus rather prefers Sarah's bed."

"Nigel," Sarah ground out. "Honestly, Lord Weston will think you're telling the truth."

Marcus walked slowly down the center aisle, half expecting to encounter Noah himself. Indeed, chickens, pigs, an ancient donkey, three cows—

"Good Lord, is that a peacock?" he asked, stopping to look at the large, colorful bird in the stall next to Buckingham's.

Sarah joined him, peering over the stall door at the bird sitting in the straw. "Yes, that's Percival."

"Percival?"

The bird rose as though responding to Marcus's call. "Caw."

Marcus leaned forward. "What is he doing?"

"Saying hello, I suppose," Sarah answered, leaning in to get a better look.

Percival regally walked toward the two, and then all of a sudden, in a flash of brilliant jeweled tones, he spread his tail feathers in a glorious fan.

"Oh," Sarah breathed.

"What does *that* mean?" Marcus asked, turning to look at Sarah.

Her eyes were wide. "I think he fancies you."

Nigel ran up to the stall door, pushing in between Marcus and Sarah. "He's never done that before."

"I know!"

"Does it mean what I think—"

"What?" Marcus said, growing more confused by the moment. "Would someone please tell me what's going on?"

Percival was now strutting back and forth across the stall. "Caw."

"*Now,*" Marcus growled.

Sarah cleared her throat. "Have you never seen a peacock before, Lord Weston?"

"Only on my plate, Miss Tisdale," he answered truthfully, and he could have sworn that Percival flinched at his statement.

"Peacocks display their feathers only for mating purposes," she said simply. Nigel chuckled, Sarah smacked him, and the sound startled the bird.

"Caw!"

"Percival has not seen fit to show his feathers to anyone since his arrival nearly three months ago," Nigel said, his mirth under control. For the moment.

"I'm honored, I think," Marcus replied skeptically, regarding the bird with a wary eye.

Sarah smiled before turning back toward Buckingham. The warmth of her curving mouth and amused eyes struck him speechless for a moment.

"And where do you think you're off to?" Sarah asked.

Marcus gathered his wits, looking over his shoulder in time to witness Nigel creeping toward the door.

"Answer your sister," Marcus pressed.

Nigel turned back to face the two. "Not you as well," he said to Marcus, looking utterly betrayed.

"You laughed at the bird," Marcus offered in explanation. "I owe you one. Now, I believe you also owe your sister an answer."

"Just a spot of fun with the boys, Sarah," he replied sheepishly.

Marcus looked at Sarah, whose lips were pursed adorably, though he suspected the effect was unintentional.

"Fun?"

"Oh, all right," Nigel responded, waggling his eyebrows. "It's dangerous, bloodcurdling fun," he said dramatically, "the details of which are hardly appropriate for such delicate ears."

His sister rolled her eyes. "Off with you, then." She made a shooing gesture, using both hands. "Take Titus with you."

"I'll just lighten the kitchen of Cook's apple turnovers, then be on my way." Nigel sketched an awkward bow and sped away, disappearing out the barn door with Titus on his heels.

"What was that all about?" Marcus asked, disguising his interest with mild amusement.

Sarah patted Buckingham's large head. "Nothing, really. Nigel and his friends fancy themselves smugglers."

Marcus adopted a look of disinterest and joined her at the bay's stall. "Smugglers?"

"Yes. It's all far less romantic than they make it out to be."

The horse sniffed cautiously at Marcus's fingers when he held out his hand. "A bit dangerous, wouldn't you agree?" Marcus asked casually.

"Oh, I don't know about that," she said distractedly as she watched Buckingham slowly accept Marcus. "From what I gather, Charles only employs the boys for minor errands and such."

"You know the smugglers by name?" Marcus asked, his years as a Corinthian allowing him to make the interrogation seem as innocent as casual conversation.

Sarah held out her hand, palm flat, for the horse's perusal. "Let us just say that Nigel is not the most tight-lipped of smugglers," she replied, an affectionate smile curving her lips.

Marcus nodded. "He won't be rising in the ranks, then—supplanting Charles then taking hold of the operation from . . ." He paused, as though searching for something. "I'm sorry, what was the ringleader's name again?"

"I have no idea who the local smugglers report to," Sarah answered simply, rubbing Buckingham's nose. "I'm not even sure if Nigel does. It's all become rather secretive over the last few months."

"I wonder why," Marcus mused, his tone carefully idle.

She patted the bay one last time before turning away, gesturing toward the exit. "I don't know. Smuggling has always been a part of our coastal life—nearly an accepted vocation, much like fishing or trade. Perhaps the customs officials have grown weary with boredom and have finally decided to make inquiries."

Marcus followed her down the aisle, cutting a wide swath when they passed Percival's stall.

Charles, though not the man in charge, was a start. And perhaps Nigel knew more than he realized, Marcus thought. Following the boy might be worthwhile.

Sarah paused to blow out one of the lanterns, and then moved on before halting abruptly. She turned, her green gaze questioning as she searched Marcus's face. "You seem keenly interested in the smuggling business, Lord Weston."

"Caw."

"It was Percival calling in the woods that day, wasn't it?" Marcus asked, the bird's call suddenly clicking in his mind, and not a moment too soon. He needed to distract her from her questions about his interest in smuggling.

"Yes, it was," she answered. She frowned, clearly not swayed. "About the smuggling—" she continued.

"And you were in the woods as well?" he interrupted.

She blinked rapidly, her cheeks slowly pinkening as she stared at him. Then she turned on her heels and nearly ran toward the door. She barely paused to snuff out two more lanterns before hurrying on.

"Miss Tisdale, do you recall our bargain?" he said lazily, strolling in her wake.

She lifted a lantern from its spot on the broad windowsill.

"Our bargain?" she asked, retreating until her back was pressed against the rough, whitewashed wall.

"Yes," Marcus confirmed, stalking slowly nearer. "The one we struck when I found you hiding from Mr. Dixon that day on the lawn."

"I told you, Lord Weston, I do not hide."

"Yes, well, in any case," Marcus continued, enjoying himself far more than he should, "we made a bargain, whereby you are to grant me one wish, within reason."

Only one lantern continued to glow, leaving them

standing in a pool of golden light, the stable beyond cast in shadows. "Oh, yes, that bargain. Now I remember."

Marcus halted in front of her. "I'd like to collect."

He could see her pulse beating wildly at the base of her throat, her breasts moving with her quick breaths beneath her charming striped gown. She licked her lips and he thought she was going to answer.

And then she blew out the remaining lantern.

"Were you in the woods with Percival that day?" Marcus asked, leaning in so that his lips brushed the shell of her ear as he whispered.

"Is that all? I answer honestly and the debt is paid?" she countered, relief in her voice. "Why then, yes, it was I—and Percival, of course."

Marcus threaded his fingers into the silky strands of her hair. "That was too easy," he murmured.

"I know," she agreed, then bit her lip. "That is, I'd assumed you would ask for more."

"Such as . . ." Marcus licked her earlobe and nearly growled. "This?"

"Oh."

"Or this . . ." He ran the tip of his tongue down her soft, warm throat and over the faint upper swell of her breasts just above the neckline of her gown. He tugged at the fabric with his teeth.

She dropped the lantern.

"Oh," she whispered, voice dazed. "Um, yes, something like that."

"Pity I've used my one wish." His voice was deeper, rasping with arousal as he tested the frantic, pounding pulse at the base of her throat with his tongue, then brushed tender, damp kisses up the inward curve of her throat and the vulnerable, soft underside of her firm little chin. Unable to resist tasting her, he took her mouth with his in a searing, purely carnal kiss.

She moaned, wrapping her arms around his waist beneath Marcus's coat and pulling him tighter until the cove of her hips cradled the harder angle of his.

"Sarah," Nigel's voice called across the lawn.

She stiffened, her mouth going still beneath Marcus's before she pushed back, taking her lips from his.

"Hurry," she hissed, grabbing his hand to tug him with her out of the darkened stables.

"There you are," the boy said, running up to meet them. "Mother caught me sneaking in and insisted that I fetch you at once." Nigel gestured wildly. "Come along. Before she accuses Lord Weston of compromising you and insists on a wedding in the morn," he joked.

"Really, Nigel," Sarah chastened as the three approached the house. "You've quite the imagination."

If this was the current state of smuggling, Marcus found himself thinking as he followed the three boys through the moonlit wood later that night, then Napoleon hadn't a prayer of succeeding.

Pokey picked his way along the path quietly, obeying Marcus's slightest cue. But his habitual stealth was wasted on the boys—Marcus doubted they would have noticed a Highland clan painted for war.

The three were far too busy contemplating the excitement of the night and Charles's promise of a task much more worthy of their ability—if they proved themselves ready.

The conversation dissolved into stories of amazing feats, each boy attempting to outdo the other.

Marcus had said his good-byes to the Tisdales and mounted Pokey, following the drive as far as the bend, then doubling back and waiting for the boy near the quiet stables. He'd been rewarded for his patience when Nigel finally appeared, running as fast as his lanky legs would carry him across the lawn, past the stables, and deep into the wood, where his two friends waited.

But now the memory of Sarah Tisdale's sweet, hot mouth beneath his tormented Marcus. The feel of her soft curves against him when she pulled him close. The scent and taste of her skin beneath his tongue—God, the woman made him as randy as a youth.

And that made her dangerous. She threatened the very aspects of his personality that he'd fought to hide for so long—and won.

The ton had wondered at his self-control when he'd first arrived in London, as though every Scotsman worthy to wear a tartan was a ravenous animal waiting for the opportunity to strike.

He'd proven them wrong with his accomplished charm and self-control.

But Miss Tisdale, whether she intended to or not, was systematically destroying years of hard-won control.

In the barn, earlier, he'd wanted nothing more than to raise her skirts and bury himself deep within her.

And sensing that she'd wanted the same had only made him burn hotter.

A woman had never pushed him to the brink of control like Miss Sarah Tisdale.

He'd seduced before in the interest of the Corinthians, and he'd do it again, of that Marcus was sure.

He had to be. He was a Corinthian.

Marcus watched as the boys walked into a clearing, the sound of the sea informing him they'd arrived at the cove. The three ceased talking, the light from Nigel's lantern suddenly disappearing from view.

Marcus waited for a few minutes until the boys moved out of sight, then he urged Pokey slowly forward. They were next to the cliffs, the smell of salt and seaweed filling Marcus's nostrils as he peered down.

He eased himself from Pokey's back, landing silently on the hard-packed earth, and tied him in a concealing copse of green brush and woods. Stealthily, he moved from the shelter of one tree trunk to the next until he could peer out into the clearing where he'd last seen the boys.

A crude path was cut into the side of the cliff, and Marcus located the light of Nigel's lantern as it bobbed up and down in the distance, marking the boys' progress as they wound their way down the path to the beach.

A small fire burned on the shore, and the low voices of men traveled over the sound of the waves, the rough murmur reaching Marcus's ears.

He craved a closer look but knew his injured leg would not withstand the demands of the rocky path.

Marcus turned back, reaching Pokey and pulling himself into the saddle. "It's a start," he whispered to the chestnut, then returned to the woods from which he'd come.

7

"Sarah, wake up."

Sarah wrapped her arms around her feather pillow and burrowed farther into its downy softness.

"Sarah, now. Please."

She reluctantly opened her eyes. The dim light filtering through the edges of the heavy damask bed curtains told her it was barely morning.

The grave look on Nigel's face told her it was not going to be a good day.

"Nigel, what is it?" she asked, sitting up hastily.

Her brother swiped the hair from his eyes, revealing anguish and fear. "It's Jasper. I can't find him."

"He's most likely in bed," Sarah answered, swinging her legs off the four-poster bed and standing.

"I've been to his house, and Clive's. No one's seen him since we left last night."

Sarah put her arm around Nigel's shoulders, her worry growing as the boy accepted the support with uncharacteristic ease. "Tell me exactly what happened."

"Well," he began, sagging against Sarah, "when we arrived, Charles was in a nasty temper—going on about a lord's demands or some such nonsense. He asked Jasper to stay behind while he sent Clive and me off to the Boot. By the time we returned Jasper was gone and Charles told us to go home."

Sarah squeezed Nigel's shoulder. "And?"

"The two of us did as we were told, but I . . ." Nigel paused, his cheeks growing red.

"You were worried about Jasper, as any true friend would be," Sarah finished for him. "So you went looking for him."

Nigel nodded. "As I said, he's not with Clive or at his home."

"And the cove?" Sarah asked.

"I didn't want to go alone," Nigel whispered, tears welling up in his eyes.

Sarah released her brother and rushed behind a dressing screen, quickly removing her night rail then slipping into the breeches and shirt she kept on hand. Quickly returning, she cradled Nigel's face in her palms, tilting his head to search his eyes. "You did the right thing, Nigel. There's nothing to be ashamed of.

"Come." She reached for her boots and took his hand, padding across the blue and rose carpet. Silently easing the door open, she peered up and down the hall, sighing with relief when she found it empty.

The two crept silently down the hallway to the stairs, avoiding the third step from the bottom, which always squeaked on contact. Reaching the landing, Sarah checked the longcase clock in the hall, reading half past four.

Nigel had spent nearly the entire night searching for his friend.

Despite her brother's obvious distress, however, Sarah was certain Jasper would be found. *Most likely asleep in his father's barn,* she thought. This was not the first time one of the boys had gone missing, only to be found the next morning snoring peacefully in a farmer's hay field. Nevertheless, the sooner Jasper was found, the better for all concerned.

She grasped the front door's brass handle and noiselessly eased the heavy oaken door open enough to slip through, waiting until Nigel was standing outside before carefully pulling it shut.

Nigel took off at a trot. Sarah hastily donned her boots then followed closely behind. The woods were dark, the faint morning light barely strong enough to seep between the thickly growing trees.

At last, they broke through the tree line and into the clearing, the sound of the waves reaching their ears.

"Come along, then," Sarah said coaxingly to Nigel as she carefully began to pick her way down the narrow rocky path.

The two reached the cove and looked about, but saw only the charred remains of a doused fire to tell them the smugglers had been there.

"Check the caves," Sarah instructed, gesturing down the beach toward the favorite haunt of Lulworth's youth, "and I'll go this way."

Nigel nodded solemnly and turned north.

Sarah watched him go, his shoulders slumped as he walked away. There was every chance that Jasper had fallen asleep in the cave. She expected to hear a rousing "Oy!" from Nigel once he reached his destination and found the boy.

Still, she turned to her task, making her way across the rocks and onto the soft sand. The tide was just beginning to turn. With every step she took, the incoming waves wiped the small indentation left by her boot clean away. Normally she was entranced by the sea life here on the shore, but this morning she barely noticed the small crabs scuttling sideways in an attempt to avoid being swept away with the next lapping wave.

Sarah picked her way carefully around an outcropping of rocks. She'd played on the rocks as a child and gazed upon them perhaps a million times since. They were as familiar to her as Lulworth itself, and something in the small tide pool just near the junction of the two main outcroppings did not seem right.

She stepped closer, squinting to bring the scene into focus.

The sight that met her made no sense at all. Sarah closed her eyes tightly and gritted her teeth, willing the truth before her to reshape itself.

And when she opened her eyes, Sarah found it had altered, though not in the way she'd wanted. The truth of it was still the same: Sarah had found Jasper Wilmington's lifeless body. Only now, he appeared to her in deeper, more disturbing tones, as if the longer she looked, the more of the tragedy would be revealed.

Sarah staggered back, her hand pressed to her mouth to hold back the scream of protest welling within her. She heard the suck and squish of someone running along the wet sand. Twisting about, she saw Nigel racing toward her.

"Go and get Father," she shouted, pointing toward the cliff path.

But Nigel continued to race straight toward her. "Is it Jasper?" he yelled, panic thick in his voice.

"Go, now!" Sarah replied, dashing toward him. She restrained him from going any farther, her hands gripping his arms tightly. "Do as I tell you."

Nigel struggled against her hold, desperately trying to peer past her.

"Nigel." Sarah instilled as much command into her voice as she could, willing it to remain firm as she forced her brother to meet her gaze. "Go. Now."

He stilled, the hurt on his face nearly undoing Sarah.

And then he broke her hold and ran for the path, throwing himself up the narrow cliff trail as if the Devil himself followed.

Sarah turned and walked back to the tide pool. Jasper's bloated body moved softly with the ebb and flow of the water, his arm awkwardly crooked over the edge. She crossed the sharp rocks; she could no longer feel their sting through her soles.

Sarah knelt near Jasper's head where it rested against the rocks. The brash young boy with the cheerful smile that she'd known so well was nowhere to be found here. His body was battered and broken, black bruises and dried blood all that remained.

Sarah instinctively reached out and touched his brow, tracing the length of it with her fingers.

Days before she'd threatened to kiss Jasper and he'd run for his life, his young, fit body allowing him to flee what was the most clear and present danger any young boy could encounter.

Sarah bent her head to Jasper's and placed a light, sorrowful kiss on his cheek.

And then she began to cry, wondering if she'd have the strength to stop.

That moment in Miss Sarah Tisdale's barn had ruined any hopes Marcus had harbored for sleep. After tossing and turning for what felt like hours, he'd gone and saddled Pokey at dawn and rode aimlessly along the cliff tops. Miss Tisdale dominated his thoughts. The last thing on his mind was Nigel's late-night wanderings with his friends.

Until the youth nearly unseated him when he appeared from the mouth of the cove path and launched himself toward Marcus.

"My father. I need to find my father," the boy said, a troubling quaver to his cadence.

Marcus reassuringly patted his horse then swung his leg over Pokey and dismounted. "Nigel, what are you doing out of your bed at this hour?" he asked firmly.

The boy grabbed Marcus's arm and pulled, urging him toward the cliff path. "It's Sarah. She's on the beach. I don't know what happened—she wouldn't let me near. You've got to help."

Marcus's gut clenched at Nigel's words. He swiftly handed the reins to Nigel and backed the boy and horse up to a safer distance from the cliff. "Take Pokey. And ask that your father fetch the constable as well."

Marcus waited long enough for the boy to nod before he took off for the path, navigating the drop with as much speed and precision as his leg would allow.

He reached the beach and looked about the cove, catching sight of Miss Tisdale near a rocky outcrop. Ignoring the pain in his damaged leg, he ran across the pebbled verge and onto the wet sand, cutting a direct line to where she sat.

He slowed as he drew near, relief flooding him when a closer view told him the woman was not injured. She appeared to be wearing men's clothing, the cotton fabric of her white linen shirt soaked and streaked with muddy sand. She stared at a tide pool just beyond her.

"Sarah—Miss Tisdale," he corrected himself, calling softly to her.

Her hands lowered slowly from her face as she turned to look at him. The movement allowed Marcus a better view of the tide pool beyond.

A body lay twisted and still, half in, half out of the water.

Marcus closed the space between them and pulled Sarah into his arms. He turned her to shield her body with his own. "Are ye all right?" he demanded roughly, his Scottish burr becoming more pronounced.

She buried her face against his coat, nodding wordlessly.

Sarah's head tucked beneath his chin, Marcus looked over the crown of her head at the body in the pool. The dawn light was brighter, clearer, and it allowed him to see the color of the boy's skin. The ashen pallor told him the lad had died a few hours ago—perhaps a day at the most.

"Sarah," he repeated gently, his arms tightening about her protectively. "Do you know this boy?"

Her sobs lessened, the weight of her body against his easing as she composed herself and attempted to step back.

She flattened both palms on his chest and pushed, her thick lashes lowered to conceal her gaze.

Marcus reluctantly loosened his hold, every inch of his body fighting the necessity of releasing her.

"I apologize, Lord Weston," she said barely above a whisper. "I needed a moment to compose myself."

"Do not apologize for having compassion and a soft heart, Sarah," Marcus insisted, her statement piercing his heart. "Not to me—not to anyone."

She looked up, her green eyes dark with shock and pain—and relief. "Thank you," she replied, fresh tears trailing their way down her cheeks.

She wiped them away quickly and swallowed hard. "It's Jasper Wilmington. He is a dear friend of Nigel's."

She turned to look at the cliff path and above, as if waiting for her brother's appearance.

Marcus gently caught her arm. "I sent him on Pokey. I'm sure they'll be here soon," Marcus told her reassuringly.

They slowly began to walk toward the cliff, Marcus deliberately moving Sarah away from the site. "Was Jasper one of the boys involved with the smugglers?"

"Yes," she answered, affection vying with grief on her expressive face. "Nigel, Clive, and Jasper are a fearsome bunch to be sure—or were, rather," she amended in a whisper.

She stopped suddenly, her brow furrowing. "Nigel mentioned that Charles was in a foul temper last night," she said, her voice filled with dread and foreboding.

"But I cannot think this was anything other than a horrible accident, can you?"

Marcus didn't have the heart to tell her he'd seen black and blue bruising encircling the boy's neck—indicative of strangulation.

He paused, dropping his gaze to the rocky shore while contemplating an appropriate response.

As he did so, he caught sight of Sarah's boots, one tinged with blood just near the toe.

She followed his gaze and looked down, sweeping the length of her rumpled, stained clothing before settling on her boots. "You've truly seen me at my worst, Lord Weston," she said quietly, her gaze returning to him. "And you're still here."

The pull of the emotions racing through his body and mind threatened to break loose. He didn't want to respond to what was surely more than just a simple statement.

He couldn't.

And so he gave in to his Scottish drive for action and firmly lifted her into his arms, and made haste for the cliff wall.

Not fully realizing that he'd answered her all the same.

He'd carried her the entire length of the cliff path until they'd reached the top and discovered Nigel, her father, and the constable about to descend the path themselves.

Marcus had carefully placed her on Pokey's back and instructed Nigel to walk her home, where he would meet them after assisting Sir Arthur and the constable.

She'd not wanted him to let her go.

Now Sarah stared unseeingly at the ceiling above her bed, knowing that she should prepare for the daunting day ahead.

But she could not quite pull herself from the comfort

and warmth of the familiar linens, especially in light of such a revelation.

She'd not wanted Lord Weston to put her down, even though she knew full well the man's leg must have ached from the effort of carrying her.

Even though he'd failed to acknowledge the weight of what she'd said.

Even though she was covered from head to toe in mud and sand, sea air and salt water.

She'd wanted to stay in his arms.

Forever.

Sarah rolled to her side, allowing the coverlet to dip below her shoulders.

She sensed that there was a side to Lord Weston that he hid from the world.

An untamed one that he feared polite society would never countenance from a man such as he.

It completely enthralled Sarah.

And in truth, his brusque treatment—such as she never would have accepted from any other man—was the only reason she'd left the beach with some semblance of her sanity intact.

She'd needed him to take control, and he had.

Sarah blew out a breath and willed herself not to cry.

She'd feared that she would perish on the beach alongside Jasper, the task of continuing on in the face of such a horrifying loss seeming too much to bear.

Strength and fortitude had never been attributes Sarah found lacking in herself; on the contrary, they were what she relied upon most.

But the sight of Jasper's lifeless body had forced her to doubt.

And then Lord Weston was there, asking little but doing so much.

Suddenly her vulnerability felt more an asset than a weakness.

"Sarah?"

She turned to find Nigel standing in the doorway, the purple-hued smudges beneath his eyes stark against the unnatural paleness of his skin.

He slowly walked toward her, the once-confident, carefree twelve-year-old slipping away to reveal a shocked and weary young boy.

Sarah pushed herself to a seated position and held out her arms in wordless comfort, as if the past years of his fearless independence had never existed.

He swiftly closed the distance, dropping to his knees and laying his head in her lap. "We did it for a lark—that's all. We never thought . . ."

Nigel's voice trailed off as he pressed his face into the bed linens.

Sarah wanted to cry. Or scream. She wanted to tell Nigel that everything would be all right, because it always had been.

Before today.

Before today, she'd marched her way through life with the knowledge that if she did not do for herself, no one else would. She'd found comfort in that fact and always taken for granted her ability to accomplish every task without aid from another.

Before today.

She softly stroked Nigel's fine hair with one hand while the other rested reassuringly on his shoulder. The growing boy shuddered as he began to cry, sobs shaking his small frame.

The memory of Lord Weston's sudden appearance at the cove flashed in Sarah's mind, compelling her to admit what she'd been struggling with since returning from the beach: Lord Weston's help had not only been welcome, but wanted. Wanted.

And freely given.

Despite the sadness that filled her heart for Jasper and

his family, Sarah felt an odd sense of hopefulness, as if all, within reason, could be put back together. "Shhhh, Nigel. I'm here," she murmured soothingly.

Marcus joined Sir Arthur in the drawing room. The older man's color had improved considerably in the hours since Marcus had left him on the beach, but he still seemed haggard. Marcus took a seat in an armchair near the window, noting the brandy bottle balancing precariously on the mahogany table just to the baronet's left.

"Someone provide Lord Weston with a glass," Sir Arthur commanded, gesturing toward the bottle. "We all need a little fortification right now."

Sarah rose from the upholstered settee and crossed to her father. "Of course," she said simply, taking the bottle from the table.

Marcus ran a weary hand over his stubbled chin, wincing as he realized how mortified Sully would be over his appearance. In fact, he was surprised Sarah's mother had allowed him into her drawing room.

Sarah. He'd used her Christian name for the first time that day.

He supposed there was a perfectly good explanation for using such familiarity. Death was never easy, especially for those inexperienced with such things. And the death of a child? Marcus counted himself lucky to have never borne witness to such a crime.

Until today.

Given more time, he would have taken better care with Sarah after discovering her on the sand. Perhaps he should have been gentler, less forceful, but his instinct to protect had demanded he remove her from the scene immediately. Her tears and grief had stirred a possessiveness that, even now, he refused to regret. She was safe here in her father's home, and that was all that mattered.

His brooding gaze followed her as she walked the

length of the room to a rosewood serving table. Wordlessly she poured him a glass, and then crossed to where he sat.

Marcus looked up into her face as she handed him the drink, her freshly scrubbed skin and pale blue gown fading for a moment, replaced by a swift mental image of her kneeling on the beach. The sight was seared into his memory—her tangled auburn curls teased by the morning breeze, her breeches wet from the driving tide. The mixture of terror and disbelief on her face.

"Lord Weston?"

Marcus blinked and realized he was now staring at the glass of brandy. The hand holding the glass belonged to Sarah.

He looked for a second time at her, relieved that it was not the Sarah from the beach who met his gaze. "Miss Tisdale," he responded belatedly, taking the glass. "Thank you."

She nodded as though she understood. Marcus assumed she believed he was rattled by the boy's death. And he was, to be sure. But even more, he was concerned for Sarah.

Marcus had half expected her to have retreated within herself, her emotions tamped down and all vulnerability safely encased in her usual confidence and self-possession.

But he was troubled to see the fragility still in her anxious gaze.

He suspected their relationship would never be the same after today, but as he looked about at those gathered in the drawing room, he realized that such a line of thought would have to wait.

He sipped the brandy slowly, savoring the liquor's burn as it slid smoothly down his throat, thankful for the distraction. "Sir Arthur, this has been a most disturbing day for your family," he began.

As the highest-ranking man in the county, he had

every right to involve himself in the necessary inquiry into the boy's death, despite Lady Tisdale's polite if frosty insistence that a man such as he surely had more important things to concern himself with. Even she could not deny the Errant Earl.

Parish constable Thaddeus Pringle, a small, wiry man with graying sideburns, had been summoned and now sat next to Sir Arthur. He pushed absentmindedly at the thick spectacles propped precariously on the end of his narrow nose.

The constable had proven himself useful on the beach, being the first to mention the bruising about the boy's neck. He'd aided admirably in removing the boy from the rocks, his strength belying his small stature.

"Mr. Pringle, has the boy's family been made aware of the situation?" Marcus asked, grimacing as his leg began to throb.

The question caught Pringle stifling a yawn with his closed fist. "They have, my lord. They're anxious to have the boy's body." Pringle paused, looking apologetically at Lady Tisdale and Sarah for mentioning such a thing. "For burial purposes, you see."

Marcus stretched his leg out, the throbbing growing immediately worse before abating to a dull, insistent ache. "Yes, of course. I'll see that my valet makes the arrangements."

Jasper's body had been carried to Lulworth Castle for safekeeping. Sully was, at that very moment, performing a thorough examination of the boy's corpse in the hopes that something might appear that would help with the case.

And so it begins, Marcus thought, realizing it would be necessary to take control by *any* means necessary if he was to gain ground.

Manipulation was not a game Marcus enjoyed, though the Corinthians were trained to be deadly precise. Judging from the day's events, Nigel knew more about the smugglers than he'd revealed in the past.

And while Marcus doubted that Sir Arthur had anything to do with the emeralds, he suspected the man would, if necessary, tell any falsehood to keep his son safe. As would, most assuredly, Sarah.

His gaze skimmed lightly over the family, knowing that he would ultimately expose and potentially destroy them if Nigel was tied to the jewels. The dull throb in his leg suddenly traveled directly to his heart.

Marcus took another sip of the brandy and closed his eyes, every emotion rebelling against this course of action.

"Mr. Pringle," Marcus began, "I believe you questioned the nature of Jasper's death, did you not?"

The constable hesitated, clearly uncomfortable with Marcus's question. "Are you referring to the bruising, my lord?"

"Yes, about the boy's neck," Marcus confirmed, watching Sarah from beneath half-lowered eyelids. "What do you make of it?"

Sarah's eyes widened and she turned in her seat to look directly at Pringle.

The constable pushed his spectacles up his long nose and cleared his throat. "If I had to say . . ." He paused, pressing the wire nosepiece though there was nowhere farther for it to go. "Well, I suspect the boy was strangled."

Lady Tisdale let out a dramatic gasp and all the attention in the room suddenly concentrated on her—except for Marcus's. He watched as Sarah remained silent, though her gaze next darted to her brother.

"Indeed," Marcus said in a low, shocked tone. "Nigel," he said, setting his glass down with an audible thud. "Clearly the men you've been dealing with are far more dangerous than we were led to believe."

It was the constable's turn to be shocked, his small body nearly vibrating at Marcus's words. "What's this?" he asked gruffly, discernibly upset over the revelation.

"I don't know," Nigel began, his tone anxious as he stood up from his chair, his movements jerky. "It was all in good fun—"

"Jasper Wilmington is dead, boy!" Pringle interrupted, raising his voice.

"This wasn't the plan. We were—"

"Plan?" Pringle sputtered, his anger growing. "What plan?"

Nigel began to shift back and forth from one foot to the other, his face anguished. "That's not what I meant," he pleaded, cringing when Pringle rose as well.

Marcus waited as the frenzy grew. Lady Tisdale shrieked as Pringle advanced on Nigel, which sent her husband flying from his seat.

Marcus knew timing was everything in such a situation. He watched as Sarah maintained her composure though the whole of her family looked to be tottering on the edge of hysteria.

Now, he thought, as Sarah rose from her chair, a desperate look in her eyes.

"If everyone would please sit down," he said in a commanding tone, rising to his feet.

All obeyed, save for Sarah, who crossed the room and joined her brother.

Marcus eyed her with compassion, making his concern for her—and, more important, Nigel—apparent.

Her tense posture eased ever so slightly at his silent support.

Then Marcus turned to the constable, adopting a stern bearing. "Pringle, the boy can hardly be expected to endure questioning at this time. Please go to Lulworth Castle and offer your help to my valet."

It was as if Marcus was a puppetmaster. All four of the Tisdales turned in unison to angrily stare at the man.

Pringle repositioned his spectacles once more before clearing his throat. "Yes, my lord," he replied in a thin voice, rising from his chair. "But the boy will have to be—"

"Of course," Marcus interrupted, gesturing toward the door. "We will speak this afternoon."

Pringle nodded quickly and left.

Nigel slumped into his chair, the lack of sleep and the weight of his friend's death clearly catching up with him.

Marcus eyed the boy with concern. "I suggest that Nigel retire to bed. I'll return to question him further this afternoon, and in the meantime I'll join Mr. Pringle to ensure Jasper is taken care of properly."

Tisdale nodded somberly while his wife stifled a cry. Sarah stood next to Nigel, her hand on his bowed shoulder.

As Marcus made his way toward the door she reached out and gently grasped his arm.

"Thank you," she said softly.

The sincerity in her eyes made Marcus want to hit something. Anything. As long as it was hard enough to break bone.

Better that than his heart.

8

A funeral for an aged fisherman or kindly grandmother was not an unusual occurrence in Lulworth. But
Jasper's was far from usual, the faces of those surrounding Sarah in the Church of the Holy Trinity filled with
shock and sorrow as they stared at the boy's casket near
the front of the sanctuary.

She inched along the hard pew until she was securely
pressed against Nigel, but her brother hardly seemed to
notice. His somber gaze was fastened on the vicar behind the pulpit.

He won't find what he needs there, Sarah thought to
herself regretfully.

No one would.

All of the reassurance in the world would not bring
back Jasper.

Nor would it provide any insight into why such a
heartbreaking death happened at all.

Sarah's gaze skimmed the gathering until she found
Lord Weston, his blond hair capturing a single shaft of
sunlight as it slanted through the simple stained-glass
window.

He'd insisted upon being present during Nigel's interview with the constable. Her brother had been terrified.
But Lord Weston's calm demeanor had set Nigel more at
ease. It was clear that Nigel had been much more forthcoming than he would have been if Mr. Pringle had been
allowed to pursue the interrogation on his own. The

constable meant well, but he lacked Lord Weston's natural compassion, and it was only when the earl had quietly assured Nigel that he believed him innocent of all
wrongdoing that the boy finally began to speak, spilling
forth a surprising amount of information.

First there had been a list of names. A lengthy list. Lord
Weston did not move a muscle as Nigel rattled them off,
but Mr. Pringle had literally jumped from his seat and
begun to pace, his wiry frame quivering with excitement.
His questions had grown more pointed, and his tone
harder. Nigel's eyes had widened with fear, but then Lord
Weston interceded again, this time with a reassuring hand
on Nigel's arm. Sarah, watching from the corner with her
parents, had seen her brother visibly relax.

"Page forty-six in your hymnals."

Sarah reached for the hymnbook at the vicar's direction and opened it to the proper page, holding the book
lower to share with Nigel.

The low, sad strains of the hymn began and the mourn-
ers' voices lifted in song. Sarah attempted to avert her eyes
from Jasper's mother, but it was impossible to look away
as Mrs. Wilmington stoically sang through her tears.

It was all so senseless. They weren't bad boys. They
had just been looking for adventure. And someone—

Sarah took a deep breath and tried to calm herself as
a burst of fury rolled through her.

Someone had killed Jasper. And that someone should
pay.

She glanced at Lord Weston once again.

Perhaps, she thought, swallowing past the tightness in
her throat, she was not helpless, after all.

Lord Weston's rank, his wealth and power—and the
very fact that he was a man—would allow him access to
people and places that a woman could never secure on
her own.

His interest in the boy's death was obvious enough.

And over the past few days, Sarah had sensed in him a desire for more from Lulworth, something she could help him with if only he'd agree.

If she could convince him that she was essential to his success, they might just be able to track down the individual responsible for Jasper's murder.

The hymn ended, signaling the close of the service. The casket was carried down the aisle, followed by the vicar, then Lord Weston, then Jasper's family.

Lord Weston nodded as he passed and Sarah inclined her head solemnly in acknowledgment.

Then it was the Tisdale family's turn. Sarah stepped out into the aisleway, standing aside to let Nigel join her.

She took his hand and they followed their parents, moving past pews filled with mourning villagers and out through the heavy oaken doors, leaving the dim church for the mid-morning sunlight and blue sky.

Sarah searched the stone steps and churchyard for Lord Weston, concerned that he may have already left.

Nigel's hand slipped from hers, drawing Sarah's attention.

"I'll just say hello to Clive," he said in explanation, nodding toward the boy, who stood near the vicar.

"Of course," she responded, watching with concern as Nigel slowly approached his friend.

"How is he today?" Lord Weston's deep voice, the merest hint of a Scottish burr shading the words, sent a shiver up Sarah's spine.

"As well as can be expected, I suppose," she answered, turning to meet his concerned gaze.

He glanced at Nigel once more, studying the two boys intently, and then returned his attention to her. "And you?"

"Truthfully?"

A small smile curved his lips. "I'd expect nothing less, Miss Tisdale."

"I'm so glad to hear it." She looked about as people began to make their way to the Boot. She gestured toward the tavern. "Shall we?"

At his curious expression, she explained, "Jasper's parents want to bury the boy, alone. We'll proceed to the Boot for the wake. A collection will be taken up on their behalf to pay for the funeral expenses. I'm sure Jasper's family would very much like for you to attend."

Lord Weston hesitated, turning his gaze to where Sarah's parents stood, her mother eyeing him critically. "The Wilmingtons may be the only ones to welcome my presence."

"You may be correct," Sarah answered succinctly, gesturing for Lord Weston to offer his arm.

She placed her slight arm in his substantial one, then paused, tipping her face into the light breeze off the water. The salt-scented wind teased the curls at her nape and temples, clearing the last of the funeral gloom from her senses. "Does it bother you?"

"Does what bother me, Miss Tisdale?" he asked in return.

Sarah squeezed his arm slightly. "Come now, Lord Weston, do we not know each other well enough to speak plainly?"

His face remained impassive. "Are you referring to the villagers' low opinion of me, then?"

"Yes," she answered succinctly. "I suspect that it does affect you."

"You do mean to speak plainly, don't you?" he replied, a low, reluctant chuckle escaping his lips.

"Lord Weston," she began, purposely slowing their pace further as they approached the Boot, "I've the desire to help you find your place in Lulworth and the means to do so."

"Why?" he asked quietly.

They reached the tavern's front door and Sarah tugged

him aside to allow the group behind them entry. "Because we are friends, Lord Weston. And I want you to be happy."

He nodded in understanding.

"And I want your help in finding Jasper's killer," she added.

"I see," he replied, moving toward the door.

Sarah stepped in front of him. "No, you don't," she argued, lowering her voice as two more made their way into the tavern. "I would not lie, Lord Weston. I do want you to be happy—"

"Miss Tisdale, there is no need to explain yourself."

Sarah balled her hands into fists at her sides. "Yes, actually there is. I'm not known for eloquence, that much you can attest to, I'm sure. But I am honest, would you not agree?"

"To a fault," he replied, looking up the high street.

"Then please believe me. I do care for your welfare. And I also care for the happiness of the townsfolk, which will not be secure until we find the man responsible for Jasper's death."

Lord Weston looked down into Sarah's face, his own unreadable. "If I agree, can we retire to the Boot? I find myself in need of a drink."

Sarah smiled widely. "Is that a yes—or should I wait on asking until you've had that drink?"

Lord Weston took her arm and turned her toward the door. "Perhaps until after the third."

Marcus loosened Pokey's girth strap, the big horse letting out a snort of pleasure as he did so.

Sully had been waiting for him in the stables. "Is she naïve, then, or too smart for her own good?"

Marcus lifted Pokey's saddle from the stallion's back and handed it to Sully. "I'm not entirely certain."

A stable hand hovered nearby, fussing with a pile of straw as he watched Marcus untack Pokey.

"Off with you," Sully told the man, adding, "The earl is perfectly capable of putting up his horse for the night."

The stable hand sketched a quick, awkward bow, and hastily headed for the stable door.

Sully walked the short distance to the tack room and dropped the leather saddle onto the wooden saddle stock, returning to stand next to Pokey's head.

"Well, my lord, stupid or smart?"

Marcus tossed a brush to Sully and leaned against the rough wood wall. Normally, he brushed Pokey himself but his aching leg warned him it needed rest if he was to rely on it.

As the valet began to gently tease the dirt from the Thoroughbred's hide, Marcus examined what he knew to be true of Sarah. Fearless, completely lacking in guile, intelligent, honest to a fault, passionate, utterly charming without trying one whit to be so, and a damned good kisser.

He shifted uncomfortably, lifting his aching leg, and settled the sole of his boot against the wood wall. He knew very well that the last attribute had nothing to do with whether or not Sarah knew more about the smuggling ring than she let on. So he tried again, this time focusing on what *would* make her suspect. He mentally rifled through the previous list and realized that, with only a few small adjustments in intent here and there, every reason for her to not be involved somehow was, in truth, every reason why she could be.

"Sully," Marcus began, standing up straight to stretch. "You called her a country bumpkin, did you not?"

"That I did," the valet confirmed, sweeping long sure strokes with the brush down Pokey's side. "But the more time I spend in Lulworth, the more I wonder who's *not* involved in running goods, rather than who *is*."

"And the Tisdales' financial situation?"

"Secure," Sully replied, reaching for Pokey's legs. "Modest, of course, but what a baronet's resources should be."

Marcus considered the valet's words. "And Nigel's list?"

Sully bent to brush firm strokes over the horse's girth. He came around Pokey's rump and started on the opposite side. "A nasty lot, those blokes. Charles is a doting grandmother compared to the rest. Marlowe's working on it. Should have some news within a day or two."

Marcus considered the information while watching Pokey's long, flaxen tail swish back and forth.

"Well then?" Sully pressed, capturing Marcus's attention once again. "What seems to be the problem?"

Marcus looked at the valet, puzzled. "I don't understand."

"Gah," the valet grunted, coming back around the horse to stand directly in front of Marcus. "You're not a laggard when it comes to judging people. So what seems to be the problem with yon bonnie lass?" Sully asked, borrowing Marcus's Scottish burr.

"I cannot see one," Marcus insisted, settling back against the wall. "The contrary, actually. She's offered to ease my way into Lulworth society if I help her ferret out the Wilmington boy's killer."

"If *you* help *her*?" Sully replied incredulously. "Well, that'll make it easy enough, then."

Marcus folded his arms across his chest. "Meaning?"

"Did you take a spill on your way home tonight?" Sully asked sardonically, slapping the horse on the rump. "It sounds as if she's nearly begging for you to use her to your advantage. And I've never known you to pass up such an opportunity."

Marcus felt a headache coming on. "You make me out to be—"

"Good at your job?" Sully interrupted, turning back to the horse. "Don't go growing a conscience now, my lord. It will do you no good."

He was right, and Marcus knew it.

Marcus pushed himself off the wall and strode over to a bucket full of carrots. He pulled out three and shuffled back to Pokey.

He snapped a carrot in two, laid it on the palm of his hand, and offered it to the Thoroughbred, watching the length of the carrot disappear quickly between Pokey's powerful teeth.

"So you like her, then?" Sully asked, nearly finished with the brushing.

Marcus snapped the next carrot in three chunks and fed them to his horse. "Does it matter?"

"I suppose not," Sully answered, his tone reflective. "Just that I've not known you to spend more than a few moments thinking on a woman—not when she's part of a case. Actually, even when she's not."

"Should I not be thinking about her, then?" Marcus questioned, keeping his gaze on Pokey's muzzle as he munched the carrot.

Sully dropped the brush into a grooming kit near the stall door. "Oh, I don't know that I'm the right one to ask about such things. But I had to ask—mustn't keep the gossipmongers waiting."

"Tell the wagging tongues that I'm merely a man anxious to make good on all that my title requires of me," Marcus replied, unhooking Pokey from the cross ties and leading him into the stall. "And do not delay. I've need to resolve this sooner rather than later."

"Missing London, are you?" Sully asked knowingly.

Marcus thought he could actually hear Sully wink.

"Yes, something like that."

"Hmph," Sully grunted with masculine disgust. "Cook's become demanding—insisting on flowers. Flowers!"

Marcus unbuckled and removed Pokey's halter. "Women, they're illogical." He stood back so the big chestnut could reach his hay.

"Exactly what I said—well, not to her, of course," Sully added sheepishly as he passed the iron bars of the stall window on his way to the tack room.

Marcus heard the grooming kit land with a thud as Sully dropped it onto the dusty floor of the tack room, just on the other side of Pokey's stall.

"Ready, sir?" Sully asked as he slid the stall door open.

Marcus toyed with the leather halter in his hands. "Not quite yet. Tell Cook I'll be in shortly."

"As if she's not already fit to be tied," Sully grumbled, closing the stall door behind him with force.

"I've faith in your ability to calm her—you are, by far, my most charming of valets."

"I'm your only valet and well you know it," Sully replied over his shoulder. He muttered a litany of verbal abuse that in all likelihood turned the dusky evening sky a deeper blue. The grumbling faded as he walked away from the stables toward the castle.

Marcus let out a long, low chuckle. "He doesna mean any of it," he assured Pokey. The Thoroughbred's ears pricked at the sound of his master's voice before he dropped his muzzle and resumed eating.

Marcus turned toward the western wall of the stall and flattened his palms against the rough, whitewashed wood, lowering the heel of his injured leg behind and stretching the aching muscles.

Sarah had shown an interest in his happiness.

Hell, she'd done more than that. The lass had all but pledged her love.

She could not hide what she felt for him—hadn't been able to for some time.

Other women had exhibited such feelings, though

their adoration had always been laced with pity for the poor half-blood earl.

Was it too much to hope that Sarah's love was the very thing Marcus's uncle had told him of so many years ago?

He couldn't know for sure.

And he hardly had the time to puzzle it out.

He slowly eased erect, straightening his injured leg and frowning unseeingly at the blank wall before him.

Frustrated, he slammed his fist against the rough wood wall. Pokey started, lifting his head with a worried whinny and shifting back, the straw bedding rustling beneath his hooves.

I cannot be in love with Sarah.

He'd thought often enough of the woman that his uncle had assured him existed. She loved him completely. Not out of pity or misguided helpfulness.

He slammed the wall again, frustration and self-loathing boiling up from his belly.

He'd once been fool enough to hope that he'd find a home in London. But the ton's thinly veiled curiosity about the half Scot had felt far from comforting.

He'd been wrong. He'd learned his lesson well. He had no plan to give Lulworth the opportunity to disappoint him again as well.

He flexed the aching fingers on his right hand, rubbing the trace of blood from scraped knuckles.

Besides, he thought, there was a chance that Sarah's brother was involved with the smuggling plot on a much deeper level than he was willing to tell.

And it was his job to find out. Nothing more. Nothing less.

"I willnae be growing a conscience now," he said aloud, the grim words earning barely a flick of sensitive ears from Pokey.

9

Sarah accompanied Lord Weston and her father as they walked side by side across the meadow, together carrying a bulky telescope. It was twilight, the sun having just set over the cove in front of her, the house and woods behind them now bathed in growing dusk.

"This will do," Sir Arthur instructed. The two men slowed to a stop and gently lowered the fragile device down to rest on the soft grass. Lord Weston supported the telescope itself while Sarah's father bent to assemble the wooden legs.

Sarah hugged a large wool rug to her chest. She was grateful Lord Weston had agreed to join them this evening to take in the stars.

She watched the men for a moment more before unfolding the rug. Firmly grasping two corners, she shook it aloft, the light breeze lifting and billowing the ashen gray wool before settling to allow her to spread the rug onto the grass in a perfect square.

She didn't know exactly why he'd agreed, but her request that Lord Weston help her find Jasper's killer had been met with some measure of enthusiasm.

Sarah knew that he was in no way obligated to say yes. Either the man truly did wish for acceptance in Lulworth or he wanted to spend more time with her.

Or both.

His behavior at Jasper's wake had done much to favorably influence the citizens of Lulworth. Jasper's father had told the entire town of Lord Weston's kindness. When he quietly paid the vicar for the funeral expenses and covered the cost of the wake, Weston rose measurably in the eyes of Lulworth.

Sarah knelt on the rug, a light worsted shawl about her shoulders.

In truth, she reflected, Lulworth's attitude toward Lord Weston had everything to do with his attitude toward Lulworth. His infrequent visits to the village since inheriting the title had done little to ingratiate him to the people who relied on the estate for income and advice.

Sarah's father bent down to peer through the telescope and Lord Weston stood for a moment, watching him adjust one knob and then another, an occasional "hmmph" escaping his lips.

"Lord Weston," Sarah called, motioning to him when he looked over his shoulder at her.

He walked slowly to join her, stopping at the edge of the rug before stiffly lowering himself.

"He'll be ages adjusting the mirrors just so," Sarah confided. "Better to rest until he's satisfied with the settings."

Lord Weston smiled. "I suppose if one is going to go to all of this trouble, one ought to be precise about it."

"Trouble?" Sarah asked, looking up. Stars were winking into view, sparkling like bright diamonds against the black velvet of the sky. "Hardly any trouble here. Now, in London . . ."

"Yes?" Lord Weston pressed.

Sarah looked at him, fascinated by the shadows highlighting his face beneath the moon's cool light. "Well, let me put it this way: When did you last see the stars in the sky over London, Lord Weston?"

"The night before I left for Lulworth," he drawled

with amusement. "There was Sophia Contadino, the Italian soprano onstage at the Theatre Royal—"

"Not *stage* stars, and well you know it," she admonished him with little heat. "Really, just look up."

He hesitated, as though to do as she asked would cost him.

"Up," Sarah insisted firmly.

He finally tipped his head back and raised his gaze to the sky, his hands propped on the rug behind him for support.

Sarah did the same, sighing with pleasure at the sheer quantity of twinkling heavenly bodies. "Now, would you not agree that an opera singer can hardly hold a candle to such as this?"

"I suppose not," he agreed without enthusiasm.

"Lord Weston," Sarah exclaimed with surprise, turning her head to fix him with an assessing stare. "You've need of me far more than I first believed."

He met her gaze, an appreciative male smile curving his lips. "And why is that, Miss Tisdale?"

"Well, you've clearly lost your mind if you cannot muster a suitable amount of excitement for all of this," she declared, gesturing to the setting. "Really, your mother must have instilled in you some love for the country and its pleasures, did she not?"

His smile disappeared, his features taking on a somber cast.

"I'm sorry," Sarah said quickly. Clearly, her spontaneous comment had struck a nerve. "It's just that—well, I cannot imagine a lovelier place than Lulworth."

"Do you remember what I told you, Miss Tisdale?" A brief smile eased the stern set of his jaw as quickly as it had appeared. "Never apologize. My mother acted with her heart when she married my father and she paid the price. The whole of Lulworth never forgave her—which made it that much harder for me to appreciate the district."

Sarah wanted desperately to reach out to him. To stroke his golden hair until the tension apparent at his temples eased. To set right what so many before her had clearly made wrong.

"Was it easier for your parents in Scotland?" she asked, folding her hands in her lap to keep from reaching for him.

"Have you ever been to the Highlands, Miss Tisdale?" Marcus asked, continuing to stare at the stars.

"No, though I wish I could say differently," Sarah answered honestly.

He shifted, wincing as he stretched his injured leg. "It's wild—beautiful, to be sure, but as rough and wild a land as you'll find. I'm afraid being half a Highlander is hardly being a Highlander at all."

The intimacy of their conversation made her ache for a physical connection, and Sarah's fingers itched to touch him. "And so to London you went," she confirmed, sympathy infusing her voice. "Has it become your home?"

"As much as anyplace else," he replied, though his words lacked conviction.

She could not fight it anymore. She unclasped her hands and reached for one of his. Her fingers felt small and slim entwined with his warm, large ones. She gripped his hand tightly in an unconscious bid of support.

"Lord Weston, you must come and see!" her father called enthusiastically.

Marcus released her hand gently and rose. "Have we found a star?" he asked dryly, his usual demeanor returned.

"Not just any star." Sarah's father clapped Marcus on

the back with infectious good cheer. "Here," he offered, gesturing for Marcus to look through the telescope.

Sarah sat very still, letting the light breeze cool her heated cheeks.

The armor of affable charm and witty humor had lowered for a moment, and she felt she'd glimpsed the real Marcus. But then, the shield had instantly risen once again and he'd retreated behind it with such speed that Sarah was momentarily disoriented. She found it necessary to breathe deeply, as though she'd run across the meadow and back without stopping.

What might he have said to her if her father had not interrupted? His eyes—oh, his eyes. Her body ached from the raw emotion she'd glimpsed for one brief moment burning in his green eyes.

And right then she knew it: He could break her heart.

A loud snuffle sounded much too close to her ear, followed by a damp swipe from an altogether too enthusiastic tongue.

"Titus," she chided, her arms automatically encircling the big dog in an affectionate hug.

"Is Nigel with him?" asked her father, still intent on peering up at the night sky.

Sarah looked back toward the house but saw no sign of a lantern bobbing toward them along the darkened path. "I'm afraid not."

She gave Titus a loving squeeze then used his broad back to steady herself as she stood.

"Was the boy to join us?" Marcus asked as he continued to look through the lens.

"Oh, yes," Sir Arthur confirmed, fussing with the telescope and making minute adjustments to the supports. "Normally Nigel would not miss a night such as this— the moonlight is perfect."

"I think he just needs a bit of time, is all," Sarah explained reassuringly.

She could have added that Nigel had, as of yet, not left the house after dark since Jasper died but decided against revealing the fact. She didn't want to worry her father further.

"Has he resumed his visits to the cove after dark?" Marcus asked as he relinquished the telescope.

"No—nor will he. I'll not allow such activities again," Sarah's father said firmly, a thread of worry shading his voice as he bent to the eyepiece.

"I think that's a wise choice on your part."

"Yes, well . . ." Sarah's father paused, and then cleared his throat. "Give me a moment, won't you? I think a small adjustment will bring both Ursa Major and Minor into view."

"Is there news?" Sarah murmured anxiously when Marcus pulled her arm through his and they strolled across the grass.

Titus let out a low bark, hefting himself up and lumbering after them.

"Interesting choice in chaperones, Miss Tisdale." Marcus lifted a brow, his mouth quirked with amusement.

Sarah tugged him to a halt and faced him. "Please, my lord."

"This is not a game," he admonished, all amusement gone.

"Do you think I don't know that?" Sarah ground out in an angry whisper. "With my father nearly reduced to tears—and not for the first time today. Every villager in Lulworth is terrified. If there's something that can be done I'll not wait a second longer."

"Dinna fash, woman." The words were a low, rumbled command, his Scottish burr revealing itself once more. "I asked a few questions at the wake," he began again, the fine English lilt returning. "It seems that a number of the men that Nigel mentioned are not known in Lulworth."

"Who told you this?"

"A few of the locals."

Sarah nodded. "I'm glad they were helpful."

"And I've you to thank for that," Marcus acknowledged.

The breathless sensation returned and Sarah bit at the inside of her cheek. "I think your generosity made quite an impression all on its own."

"I would not have been welcome at Jasper's wake if not for your open support and friendship."

Sarah considered Marcus's reasoning. "Perhaps you're right."

"There, now was that so hard?" he pressed, leaning in until his breath caressed the shell of Sarah's ear.

"You've no idea," she said, pleased she could still remain honest, even when the man was so disturbingly near.

"I think I've finally solved the problem," Sir Arthur called, his timing as impeccable as ever.

Marcus turned Sarah to walk back toward her father, Titus trotting behind.

"We make a good team, do we not?" Sarah asked, a sudden sense of exhilaration filling her.

Marcus looked down at her, his small smile returning. "We do, indeed, Miss Tisdale."

Marcus rode as close to the edge of the cliffs as he could, slowing to peer down the rough path that led to the cove below.

No light gleamed from a bonfire on the sandy shore, though that hardly meant the smuggling activities had ceased. More than likely, casks of wine, bolts of silk, and the Lord only knew what else were making their way either across the water from Calais or by land to London itself, where the items would be sold for a handsome profit.

Marcus surveyed the sea, stretching dark and unending toward the hidden shoreline of France.

Sir Arthur's firm refusal to allow Nigel any further participation in the local smuggling game had made Marcus wonder.

He could swear Sir Arthur had expressed guilt.

The question was, what, exactly, did the man have to feel guilty over?

Pokey's ears pricked up and he swung his head to the left just as a rider emerged from the woods.

"Marlowe." Marcus reined the Thoroughbred around to meet his fellow agent.

Marlowe slowed his bay and pulled him to a halt. "Weston," he replied good-naturedly. "You grow grimmer each time I see you. Isn't the sea air good for your constitution?"

"You forget, I'm attending house parties and country dances while you're gadding about the county," Marcus said in a mockingly bitter tone.

"Jealous?" Marlowe asked, his grin big enough for Marcus to readily see in the moonlight.

"Of course—though I do enjoy the occasional jig."

Marlowe laughed. "I'd pay good coin to see you dance a jig."

"Give me the information I need to close this case and I'll happily oblige," Marcus assured the Corinthian.

Marlowe fumbled in his saddlebag. "Turns out the boy's list includes some interesting frogs."

"Meaning?" Marcus pressed, leaning forward in his saddle.

"You start with Smith," he began. "A likely enough character—fisherman by trade, smuggler by necessity. There's a few more of his ilk. Then the list takes a turn."

Marcus recalled the contents of the boy's neatly written note. "What of the Frenchmen—Chenard, Boutin, and DuBois? Nigel made it clear he wasn't allowed near them—he didn't even know their first names."

"Hardly surprising if they're the men I believe them to be," Marlowe replied.

"Napoleon's men?"

"Not just any of Napoleon's men, no. These three, according to our sources, report directly to de Caulaincourt."

"Impossible." If Napoleon's valued minister of foreign affairs was involved, the situation was far more serious indeed.

"Not according to our contact," Marlowe countered, "and I'd trust him with my life."

Marcus considered Marlowe's assessment, one not made lightly by any Corinthian. "But why would men at that level chance crossing the English Channel?"

"The Orlov emeralds," Marlowe said succinctly.

"So you think it's true, then? That they're here?"

Marlowe nodded grimly. "Rumors are floating that Napoleon's patience has run out. Once he secures Russia's cooperation, he plans to take the rest of Western Europe in one fell swoop. The emeralds are all that he needs to move forward."

The wind picked up off the water, ruffling Pokey's mane as Marcus mulled this over. It would take a fortune the likes of which no monarchy had ever spent to secure such an army and the munitions necessary to win such a victory.

A fortune one would hardly entrust in the hands of just anyone.

"I don't suppose Nigel's list included those responsible for collecting the emeralds?"

Marlowe chuckled. "Now, that would take all of the fun out of it, wouldn't you agree?"

"Spoken like a true Corinthian," Marcus said, his mind already turning to likely suspects. "Any news of Dixon?"

"Other than that he's a smug, annoying bastard?"

Marcus acknowledged this with a dry tilt of his head.

"Hardly," Marlowe admitted, "though I'll continue to keep an eye on him."

"Do that."

Marlowe shifted in his saddle as his mount stirred restlessly. "Of course."

"Good," Marcus replied, patting Pokey on the neck. "Keep me apprised." He turned the big Thoroughbred back toward Lulworth Castle, kneeing him into a fast walk.

"I'll hold you to that jig," Marlowe said.

"I'd expect nothing less," Marcus called over his shoulder, his lips curling into a grin as the sound of Marlowe's laughter was carried away on the wind.

~❧ 10 ❧~

The Wilmingtons were not the poorest of Lulworth's residents. Their snug cottage, located just at the end of a rutted lane, was small, to be sure, the family of a fisherman simply glad to have a roof without leaks and fresh fish for the table.

But as Sarah reined in Buckingham, she could not help but think of the happiness that had once inhabited the house. A small impromptu Twelfth Night celebration last year when she'd brought a goose had truly been one of the most enjoyable times she'd spent in the company of her fellow villagers.

She couldn't have known the sadness that would befall the family, nor imagine the emptiness that now filled the once-cozy home.

"Are you all right?"

Lord Weston had somehow passed Sarah, though she hadn't been aware of it.

She quietly clucked at the gelding and he picked up his pace. "Tell me . . ." Sarah reined Buckingham next to Marcus's Thoroughbred. "Is this always so hard?"

He looked into her eyes, confusion in his. "Excuse me?"

"Comforting those who've lost so much."

Lord Weston turned to look at the cottage down the lane. "Well, I'm afraid I can't answer you. This is the first time I've done such a thing."

"Really?" Sarah asked quietly. "You've proven to be

quite a comfort to the Wilmingtons. I assumed you had some experience with such things. Perhaps while in Scotland?"

"Dealings with the clansmen were left to my father. They hardly wanted my or my mother's pity," he replied, the simplicity of his delivery belying the blow of his words.

Sarah reached across and placed a hand on his arm. "Their loss is Lulworth's gain, my lord."

"I'm not certain of that," he answered in a low tone, his eyes shuttering once more.

"I am," Sarah offered as his hand reached to cover hers. She couldn't be sure, but she thought that perhaps the man had taken her words to heart.

Small steps, she assured herself. *Small steps.*

"Well, from your lips to God's ears, Miss Tisdale," he drawled, taking her hand from his arm and setting it lightly on her horse's reins. "Though with you on my side, I don't know that I'll be in need of divine intervention."

Sarah gave a small smile in response, and they walked their horses on, soon reaching the cottage, where a small gig and horse stood. The dappled gray horse took in their arrival with mild interest, and then returned to munching on the long blades of grass that jutted out between the rocks in a well-worn path.

"Why, that is Hercules, Mrs. Rathbone's horse, I believe."

Lord Weston swung out of the saddle, knotted his reins through the iron ring set into a rough post, and walked to Sarah's mount. "You do not sound surprised to find him—or Mrs. Rathbone—here."

Sarah raised a brow and gave him a pert look. "What, precisely, might you be suggesting?"

He caught her waist and lifted her from the saddle,

lowering her slowly down the length of him. "You are determined, Miss Sarah Tisdale."

Sarah began to perspire. "You've no idea, my lord."

The cottage door opened and Mrs. Rathbone appeared, an empty wicker basket in her hands. "Sarah, so good of you to come," she said in greeting, turning her attention to Lord Weston.

He released Sarah's waist and bowed. "Mrs. Rathbone."

The woman smiled hesitantly and adjusted her poke bonnet, clearly pleased that the earl remembered her. "Lord Weston."

Sarah unclasped the silver buckles on her worn leather saddlebag. "Yes, well, Lord Weston insisted that we pay our respects and offer our assistance. Quite thoughtful of him, would you not agree?"

Though Mrs. Rathbone was a confidante of Lenora's, her amiable nature always prompted her to have a good opinion of everyone until proven otherwise.

Besides, she was, by far, the busiest gossip to be found in the county.

Yesterday, when Sarah had overheard Mrs. Rathbone speaking of her plans to visit the Wilmingtons, she'd hooted with delight—then been obliged to blame her outburst on Titus having learned to roll over. Which he could not actually do, but the women had returned to their talk, all the same.

"Yes indeed. Very good of you, Lord Weston," the woman agreed genuinely as she untied Hercules.

Sarah retrieved the food for the Wilmingtons, stifling a smile of success.

"Please, allow me," Lord Weston offered, taking the reins from Mrs. Rathbone and assisting her onto the bench seat.

She settled her skirts about her and took the reins

back. "Lord Weston, will we see you at the Bennington Ball?"

"I wouldn't think of missing it, Mrs. Rathbone," he answered, reaching for her hand and landing a chaste kiss on her kid glove.

"Excellent," she murmured, then gently nudged Hercules forward down the rutted road.

Lord Weston offered Sarah his arm and led her up the path to the rough-hewn door. "I suppose you're rather proud of yourself?"

"Obviously," she replied simply, and then rapped firmly on the thick panel.

The door opened slowly, its weight scraping against the worn stone floor within. Emily Wilmington's solemn face appeared, her tight-set mouth loosening into a welcoming, though sad, smile when she saw Sarah. "Miss Tisdale."

"Mrs. Wilmington, may we come in?" Lord Weston asked politely.

The woman looked confused for a moment, then craned her neck to peer behind Sarah, giving a start of surprise at the sight of him. "My lord, I didn't see you there," she apologized, bobbing an inelegant curtsy in her serviceable brown dress. "Please, won't you both come in?"

She opened the door as wide as it would go, revealing almost the entire interior of the cottage.

Sarah stepped over the threshold, noting the disarray in the usually neat home. Clothing in need of mending overflowed a wicker basket near a washstand. Dishes from the morning meal still lay piled atop the wooden table. A few logs sat on the unswept hearth.

Sarah nearly gaped at the scene, so unlike what she'd witnessed on every other visit to the cottage. She caught herself barely in time and managed a smile instead.

"I beg your pardon for the untidiness," Emily said,

closing the door behind them and shutting out what little light there was to be had. "I'm afraid everything has got away from me of late."

"It is we who must beg your pardon for arriving unannounced, Mrs. Wilmington," Sarah said. She held up the hamper. "We brought you some food."

Mrs. Wilmington blinked, her eyes glistening. She'd been crying when they'd arrived. Sarah suddenly felt like an interloper, trespassing on someone else's pain. It didn't seem to matter that she was there to pay her respects.

Mrs. Wilmington just stared at them for a moment, and then, as if a tiny piece of her awoke, she gave a little jolt and hurried to the table to make room for Sarah's hamper. "Thank you," she said, only allowing her voice to break when her back was turned. "I greatly appreciate the kindness."

It took Sarah a moment to realize she was referring to the food. An awful silence hung over the room, and Sarah instinctively began to fill it with idle chatter. "Of course," she said. "it is the least we could do, under the circumstances . . ."

She swallowed. That had not been the right thing to say. "I do hope you enjoy the chicken," she began again, setting the hamper down, "and two pies."

Mrs. Wilmington began to scurry about the room, trying to tidy up, filling her arms with shirts and utensils, crockery and the like, until the pile mounted as high as her chin.

"Allow me," Lord Weston said gently, reaching for every last item in her arms and stacking each efficiently in his own. He walked to the corner near the stove, where a large basket sat empty, and slowly lowered the things in, covering the lot of it with a wool blanket that had been slung over a rocking chair. "I may not be the most skilled when it comes to housework, but I am very creative." He smiled, his twinkling eyes inviting Mrs. Wilmington to join him.

Her shoulders relaxed a bit, her mouth faintly turning up at the corners. "I wish someone would have showed me that trick years ago, my lord."

"Ah, there you see—we men do come in handy on occasion," he declared, dusting his hands together as though he'd just finished a hard day's labor.

Mrs. Wilmington gestured for him to take a worn but respectable upholstered chair near the hearth. "May I offer you a cup of tea?"

"Mrs. Wilmington, allow me to put the kettle on," Sarah urged, gently placing her hands on the woman's shoulders and steering her toward the chair opposite Lord Weston.

He stood politely, taking his seat once Mrs. Wilmington was comfortably settled in her chair. "And where is Mr. Wilmington today?"

Sarah had wondered the very same, surprised that the man had not returned from the day's fishing.

"At the Boot, I suppose," Mrs. Wilmington said cheerlessly. "It's been hard for him here—without Jasper."

Sarah set the water to boil, and then opened the calico curtains wider to allow more light from the small windows to spill into the cottage. "And hard for you as well," she offered consolingly.

"Yes," Mrs. Wilmington agreed, her jaw tensing as she strained to control her emotions. "But it's different for Jacob. He feels . . . Well, he thinks he could have prevented it, you see."

The kettle let out a low whistle, demanding Sarah's attention.

"It must be very difficult—for both of you, of course. But it is unlikely that your husband could have prevented Jasper's death," Lord Weston said gently.

Sarah willed herself to remain silent, deftly preparing the cups as she waited for Mrs. Wilmington's response.

"No," Mrs. Wilmington said, shaking her head with exhausted sorrow. "Something had changed. Jasper told his father nearly a month past about this new crew of smugglers—all fancy and French."

When she didn't say anything more right away, Sarah stepped forward to hand her a cup of tea. Mrs. Wilmington nodded as she took it, then looked down at the steam rising from the surface. "Jasper said they were making people nervous," she continued, still not drinking. "Making demands."

Sarah handed a cup to Lord Weston, then pulled up a chair and sat next to Mrs. Wilmington, her own cup left neglected on the table. "Demands?" she murmured, prompting the woman to continue.

"Smugglers in these parts, as you know, Miss Tisdale, don't usually care who knows what they're hauling. But this lot . . ." Mrs. Wilmington sighed, her somber face troubled.

Sarah leaned forward, ready to press further, but Lord Weston quietly cleared his throat, giving her a look of warning when Sarah glanced his way.

"They were different?" Lord Weston asked, sipping his tea and appearing only politely interested.

Mrs. Wilmington began to stir her tea. "They were. Very particular about who opened the goods." Her spoon began to move more quickly, and by the time she spoke again, the tea was splashing from her cup. "Young Michael Higgins's curiosity got the best of him one night and he busted open one of the boxes when he thought no one was looking. Got a sound beating that night, he did."

Sarah finally picked up her cup from the table. "Did Michael tell anyone what was in the box?"

"He told Jasper," she answered, her tone changing. "Jewels and coin enough to 'fill the sea' is what he said."

"Do you believe Jasper may have tried to see the treasure for himself?" Lord Weston asked, a mixture of authority and acceptance in his voice.

Mrs. Wilmington finally took a drink of her tea, her eyes squeezing shut as she did so. "I think he did more than just look—if I know my boy, he tried to take a bit of it for himself.

"Jacob told him to leave well enough alone. But Jasper was never one for listening. And now he's dead."

She stood abruptly and carried her cup to the crude dresser.

"Mrs. Wilmington," Lord Weston began, rising to join her. "Did Jasper ever mention any names? Someone you and Jacob may not have recognized, outside of the Frenchmen?"

She set her cup and saucer into a washtub then took Lord Weston's from his outstretched hand and added it to the water as well. "Only one—a nobleman from the next county over. Fordham was the name. Jacob asked around about the man but no one knew anything."

"I see."

"Lord Weston, I didn't tell the constable any of this. It was clear he'd decided that Jasper was guilty of something—as if his death was—"

She stopped, her earlier anxiety and fear visibly returning as her shoulders sagged.

"We'll find your son's killer, I assure you, Mrs. Wilmington," Marcus promised with quiet authority. "You have my word."

"He's of no use to us now," Marcus said bitterly, staring down at Fordham's corpse.

The innkeeper let out a loud belch. "Oh, Christ, not another one. I'll send for the constable."

Marlowe pushed the man out into the dimly lit corridor, dropping several coins into the unshaved brute's hand. "Give us fifteen minutes, won't you?"

"Fifteen minutes and not a minute more—I've got paying customers in need of rooms."

Marlowe slammed the door in the man's face and turned back to Marcus.

"No need to be rude," the innkeeper bellowed as he trudged off down the hall.

"Sod off," Marlowe replied.

Marcus shot his fellow Corinthian a sardonic glance. "Are you always this subtle?" he asked, using his booted foot to prod the corpse and roll him onto his front.

"Always," Marlowe assured him, just as the body stilled.

Congealed blood circled a wound in the upper left side of Fordham's back.

"Pistol?" Marlowe asked, dipping to his knees for a closer view.

"Too noisy," Marcus answered, looking around the body. "A knife wound, though the killer must have taken the weapon with him."

Marlowe turned his attention to the room. "What was a man of Fordham's position doing in the Cock's Crow?"

Tucked out of the way directly off the quay in Bournemouth, the Cock's Crow was hardly a likely haunt for the nobility. No more than a warren of filthy rooms located over the equally dirty tavern below, the establishment's typical patronage looked to include whores, their customers, and those eager for a place to hide.

"My best guess is that he was lured here," Marcus answered, rolling the body back with his toe. "How did you find him?"

"Superior investigative skill," Marlowe offered.

Marcus reached into Fordham's coat pocket. "Blonde or brunette?"

"Both."

"Naturally," Marcus answered.

Marlowe exhaled loudly. "Did you happen to see a gray and white dog out front when you arrived?"

"The looks of a greyhound, only smaller?" Marcus asked, lifting a folded piece of foolscap from Fordham's pocket and standing.

Marlowe nodded, standing. "A servant identified the dog as belonging to Fordham. The beast follows his master everywhere, apparently."

"And was it the blonde or the brunette?"

Marlowe snatched the foolscap from Marcus's hand. "Just so we're clear, I do indeed possess superior investigative skills—and it was the brunette."

Marcus feigned concern. "Carmichael never mentioned how—" he paused for effect "—sensitive you are, Marlowe."

"Bastard," Marlowe muttered, unfolding and reading the note. "Nothing more here than a request that Fordham come to this fine establishment—date, time, but no signature."

Marcus gave the deplorable room one last assessing look before stepping over the body and stalking toward the door. "It's a start. See if your source knows who delivered the letter. And search the room one last time. There may be something of use that we've missed."

"Aye, aye, Captain," Marlowe answered sarcastically.

Marcus opened the door and stepped out into the hall, pulling it shut behind him.

"Sensitive, my ass," he heard Marlowe mutter aloud, and he could not help but smile.

Marcus made his way quickly down the shadowed

corridor, taking the narrow stairs with minimal pain in his leg.

He paused in the tavern, searching for the innkeeper. The lumbering fool stood behind the counter, near the back, shoveling stew of some sort into his mouth as he carried on a colorful conversation with a patron.

Assured that Marlowe would have sufficient time to complete the task upstairs, Marcus bid farewell to the hellhole and made his way outside to where Pokey was tied.

The horse snorted the moment he caught sight of Marcus.

"Do not start with me," Marcus said sternly, untying and slipping the leather reins from the iron ring set into the rough wooden post. "Your reputation may have suffered from appearing outside the Cock's Crow, but you'd do well to remember that it is I who had to venture inside."

As Marcus set his boot in the metal stirrup and swung into the saddle, he spied the little dog curled up against the rough wall of the alehouse.

The dog appeared bereft, his thin tail beating dejectedly upon the worn dirt.

"You're an idiot," Marcus muttered to himself. Pokey shifted in agreement.

Marcus stepped down from the saddle.

He looped the reins over his arm and ducked under Pokey's neck, walking to the thin canine.

"Well," he addressed the dog, "would you like to come with me?" Marcus bent his knees, leaning over to hold his hand out for him to sniff.

The dog instantly rose, his slim pink tongue darting out to lick Marcus.

Marcus gently settled his free hand on the dog's head, rubbing the silken, short fur between his ears. The dog leaned into Marcus's touch, his eyes closing with de-light.

"I'll take that as a yes," Marcus said with a satisfied grin.

Reaching around the dog's midsection, he lifted the lean canine into his arms and turned back to his horse. "Pokey, meet . . ." He paused, eyeing the dog. "Bones."

The chestnut sniffed the dog from head to tail, then resumed looking bored.

Bones shook and buried his head in Marcus's armpit.

"Come now, if Pokey had wanted to eat you he would have done so already," Marcus assured the dog, prying him from his chest.

Marcus once again placed his foot in the iron stirrup and lifted himself into the saddle, the little dog balanced in his arms.

Once over his initial shock, the dog settled into his makeshift mode of transportation nicely, his lean head resting on Marcus's thigh.

"Pokey, Bones here will require a slower pace. Under-stood?"

Marcus could have sworn that the chestnut rolled his eyes.

It wasn't that Sarah was angry.

She stood impatiently in the middle of Cove Road, the sun just finishing what was surely a glorious setting, but she'd hardly had the patience to turn about and enjoy it.

Perhaps it *was* that she was angry, though she feared she really had no right to be.

She'd learned from Lord Weston's stable boy, whom she'd met on the road into town, who'd heard from Mary the cook when he'd ventured in to break his fast, who'd in turn been told directly by Lord Weston's valet, that the earl had left for Bournemouth at the break of dawn.

"This," Sarah insisted out loud, "is precisely why he needs me." If their roles had been reversed, he'd hardly have possessed the connections necessary to have discovered Sarah's whereabouts.

Sarah had a niggling suspicion that he'd have simply asked her father, who, in truth, had become quite attached to the man. Marcus's interest in both brandy and astronomy had made him irresistible to the baronet.

Sarah kicked at a stone in the dirt road. She was growing more irritated by the second.

A horse and rider appeared in the distance and Sarah squinted her eyes in an effort to see.

They drew nearer, the horse's hooves raising a small dust cloud close behind.

Sarah recognized the massive chestnut's build, and then the rider, his golden hair tousled from a long ride. She was delighted to see he wore a small smile.

Which only irritated her more.

"Miss Tisdale," Lord Weston said, as he drew the horse to a stop. "How lovely to see you. Here, in the middle of the road. At sunset. *In the middle of the road.*"

"How dare you," Sarah hissed.

His eyebrows arched in inquiry. "I beg your pardon?"

"You cantered off to Bournemouth without so much as one word to me."

Lord Weston dismounted. Sarah stood so close to Pokey that Marcus loomed over her when he turned to face her, the lapels of his riding coat nearly brushing the bodice of her gown.

"We had an agreement," Sarah ground out. "An understanding. You were to help me and I was to—"

"Miss Tisdale," he interrupted, so near that Sarah felt

his words stir the curls at her temple. "I was simply protecting you."

"Protecting me? I am the one meant to protect you, Lord Weston." Sarah bristled with offended pride. "I know who can be trusted in this county and who can—"

"Fordham's dead," Marcus said bluntly. "Stabbed in the back by, I can only assume, someone involved in the smuggling scheme."

Shocked, Sarah could only stare at his grim face. She was too stunned to speak.

"And, with all due respect, you were never meant to protect me," he added with finality.

Sarah shoved her fear down deep inside and instead gave vent to her anger at his dismissal of her participation in their partnership.

"I am just as capable as any man when it comes to such things, Lord Weston, and you'd do well to not forget that." And with that, she rolled up her fist and punched him in the center of his waistcoat, just above his watch chain.

"Awa, ye crabbit besom." He sucked in a breath, his burr thickening his deep voice.

And then she kissed him. Cupped his annoying, frustrating, much-too-dear face with both hands and pressed her lips to his.

It was not artful, as she'd hardly had enough practice to become an expert, but it was certainly enthusiastic.

She pressed herself against him, the curves of her breasts flattening against the planes of his hard chest, her nipples tightening with excitement.

Sliding her arms around his neck, she tugged him closer and twined her fingers in his soft, golden hair.

For a moment, he didn't react. As if shocked into immobility, his lips failed to mold to hers and his arms hung loosely at his sides.

But Sarah had dreamed of this for too long. There were so many things she'd wondered about, puzzled over, daydreamed of—and with anger and sheer excitement fueling her actions, it didn't occur to her to stop. His lips were warm and firm against hers. She inhaled his scent and instantly needed to know if he tasted as delicious as he smelled. She parted her lips, the tip of her tongue tracing the seam of his mouth.

With a muttered curse, Marcus wrapped her in his arms and pressed her even more tightly to him. His lips parted and he sucked the tip of her tongue with sensual greed, coaxing her deeper.

Sarah instinctively pressed nearer, the cove of her hips cradling the harder angles of his.

He groaned and swung her into his arms, carrying her away from the lane and into the woods until they were out of sight of any chance passerby. He set her on her feet under an oak and pressed her back against the thick trunk.

"You are playing with fire, woman," he whispered, his voice deeper, rasping with arousal. He trailed his lips down the arch of her throat and lower, until his mouth reached the upper swell of her breasts just above the low neckline of her lace-trimmed bodice.

She didn't protest when he tugged her gown lower, air cooling her hot flesh until his warm hand closed over her breast. For a brief moment, she panicked and her hands gripped his biceps. "Tell me you want me as much as I want you," she demanded, her voice husky with desire.

"More," he growled, meeting her gaze with his. The heat in his eyes scorched, aroused, and reassured her. His mouth closed over the tip of her breast and he sucked, drawing the sensitive nipple into the wet heat of his mouth.

Instinctively, Sarah wriggled, trying to fit more tightly

against his hips. In desperation, she rose to tiptoe, and then hitched one knee around his waist, nearly groaning in relief when the new position pressed him deeper between her thighs. He shifted and began to move rhythmically back and forth, applying pressure exactly where her body most needed it. Heat built, fire racing through her veins and centering low in her abdomen.

She wanted to touch him. Lost to all reason or propriety, she tugged at his cravat and pulled it loose. Marcus helped her, making swift work of the buttons on his shirt.

Too impatient to wait for him to finish, she slipped her hands between the loosened edges of linen and flattened her palms on warm bare skin. He was marvelously made, with tanned skin that was supple and satiny beneath her sensitive fingertips. Powerful muscles curved over his shoulders, padded his ribs, and tapered to a trim waist.

She pressed herself against him, the feel of his skin on hers magical.

She wanted more.

"Please," she murmured, not knowing what it was that she needed so desperately.

He leaned into her, his mouth reclaiming hers in a deep kiss. One hand closed over her calf and urged her leg a fraction higher around his waist. Then he smoothed his hand beneath her skirts, stroking up her outer thigh until he reached her bottom. His hand lingered, tested, savored, then he pressed her hips tighter against his.

His other hand pushed her skirt higher and he flattened his hand on the slight curve of her belly, his thumb testing the shallow indent of her navel. Then he stroked lower and she gasped, clutching at him.

One finger brushed lightly against her curls and Sarah started with surprise.

His hand stilled at her response.

But Sarah was desperate, poised on the knife's edge of desire, and she pulled him closer, pressing her mouth and body tighter against his.

His finger resumed the teasing torture, until it slipped in between the wet folds and continued with a slow flicking motion.

It was the most exquisite feeling of frustration and need that she'd ever experienced.

The delicious tension built until Sarah was sure she would die. The fire of sense and satisfaction finally exploded within her, and she cried out for what felt to be an exquisite eternity. Then she sagged against the tree, her body pulsing with hypersensation.

She opened her eyes, to find him looking down at her, his breath coming hard as he stared into her eyes.

And then, just as Sarah's senses were returning, a dog barked.

"Aye, now he barks," Marcus growled.

His hand smoothed down her thigh and reluctantly lowered Sarah's leg, gently rearranging her gown until the hem covered her ankles. He stood, tugged her bodice into place once more, and then bent his knees to look into her face. He brushed an errant curl from her brow, his hands gentle, fingers lingering to trace the curve of her ear.

"Marcus," she whispered. "I—"

"Hush." He silenced her with the tip of his forefinger laid gently over her lips. "Come meet your new dog," he urged, taking her hand in his and pulling her toward the road.

Sarah was confused. Having never before been so intimately engaged with a man, she knew not what would be considered normal behavior—though she was fairly sure that, under most circumstances, a dog was not involved.

"I'm sorry, but, what?"

"Your new dog," he repeated, stopping once they'd arrived at Pokey's side. He released Sarah's hand and reached into the saddlebag to pull out a smallish dog. The little canine looked as confused as Sarah felt.

Her mind was reeling. "Where did you find him?"

"He's Fordham's, I'm afraid. Which," Marcus paused, setting the slim dog into Sarah's arms, "explains his need for a new home."

The dog settled in against Sarah's chest, his muzzle coming to rest on her arm.

"Oh, poor little, little . . ."

"Bones."

"Poor little Bones," Sarah cooed, distracted for a moment by the soft dog and its pathetic state.

Marcus turned to Pokey, buckling the bag closed once again. The movement pulled her attention back to earlier events.

"I hate to belabor the point, but *what was that*?" Sarah demanded, her gaze flicking to the tree and back to Marcus.

"You don't know?" he asked, clearly either genuinely surprised or entertained, Sarah could not decide which.

She could see no advantage, at this point, in evasion. She'd offered her body to the man—or he'd taken it, though she was glad either way—and she'd little left to lose.

"Lord Weston." She set Bones on the ground, stepping around him to stand directly in front of Marcus. She squared her shoulders and lifted her chin, her gaze meeting his without evasion. "I like you—in fact, I may love you, though having never been in love, I can't say for sure. I've no idea what to expect, no clue as to what will come. I'm not even certain of what I ultimately want. But there's no point in lying to you—not after *that* anyway."

She reached out, placing the flat of her palm on his chest. "I know I'm not what men like you want . . . or necessarily need. But I want to help you, to love you, if you'll have me."

Sarah suddenly felt exhausted. "Think on it," she commanded, then turned on her heel. "Bones," she called, waiting until she heard the patter of the dog's paws. With the little canine at her side, she walked steadily away from Marcus, leaving him to stare after her as she entered the welcome darkness of the forest.

11

"That woman will be the death of me," Marcus muttered, thrashing about in an attempt to rid himself of his cursed coat. Tailored to fit perfectly across his shoulders, the damned thing refused to peel off and Marcus was too impatient to wait for Sully to remove it.

A footman and an upstairs maid who'd made the mistake of crossing the expansive foyer at that precise moment scurried quickly out of sight, their gazes averted and focused steadfastly on the marble tiles.

Sully waited patiently for Marcus to stop moving, then deftly pulled on one coat sleeve and tugged the offending garment from his master's back. "What has Miss Tisdale done now?"

Marcus strode toward the kitchen in search of wine.

He was not about to tell Sully that he'd damn near taken the woman against an oak tree.

It was barbaric.

Foolish.

And so unbelievably sensual that his balls ached with the memory.

He stalked down the length of the hall. "How did she find out I'd gone to find Fordham in the first place?" he demanded, his sudden presence as he turned into the kitchen startling Cook and the kitchen girls.

The woman looked ready to reprimand Marcus for his intrusion, but thought better of it when Sully rushed into the room and placed himself between the two of them.

"Everyone out," Sully instructed, giving Cook a reassuring look before shooing her away.

Marcus made a circuit of the kitchen, gathering two bottles of wine, a loaf of crusty bread, a plate of butter, half a roasted chicken, and a wedge of cheddar. He set the food down on the scarred wooden table, pulled out a chair, and sat.

Sully reached for a knife and began to slice the bread. Marcus impatiently snagged the loaf from him and tore it in two.

"I may have mentioned to Cook that you'd be in Bournemouth for the day," Sully said, pushing the dish with the slab of butter toward Marcus. "I'm sure I never said anything about Fordham, though."

Marcus spread a thick layer of freshly churned butter on the bread and bit into it.

"If I may, my lord," Sully said mildly. "Whatever it is that the girl's done, I can't say that I mind the effect it's having on you."

Marcus frowned blackly, ripped another bite of bread from the buttered chunk and chewed vigorously. Sully had never been shy about sharing his opinions. As far as the valet was concerned, the cool, charming, reserved Lord Weston who moved efficiently through London's ton with debonair elegance was a complete sham.

And Marcus had to agree. Unfortunately, the fashionable, elegant version was what the ton wanted—and what the ton wanted was a gentleman.

He swallowed, gesturing toward a bottle of wine.

Sully reached for it. "She brings out the best in you," he said with a wink, pulling the cork from the bottle before handing it over.

Marcus washed down the fresh, crusty bread with a

long, cleansing drink. "You mean the beast, I believe," he growled.

"Fair enough—perhaps not the 'best.' But certainly something authentic."

Marcus chose not to admit the truth of his comment. "Marlowe's attempting to identify and track down whoever drew Fordham to the Cock's Crow," he said. "What about you? What are you doing?"

Sully gestured for the bottle. Marcus handed it to him.

"Preparing for the arrival of our guest," the valet answered simply, downing nearly half the remaining wine.

Marcus sliced off a chunk of cheese. "And who might that be?"

"Put down the knife and I'll tell you."

Marcus's fingers tightened their grip on the knife handle. "Who?"

Sully finished off the bottle. "Carmichael."

Marcus sent the knife flying through the air. "Goddammit all to hell!"

The knife cut through the air, narrowly missing Sully's head and coming to land in the larder door.

Marcus looked at the knife.

Sully looked at the knife.

The wooden handle quivered.

"I told you to put the knife down," Sully said with a long-suffering look. "You nearly took my ear off that time."

Marcus ripped into a chicken leg with his teeth. "Do you know why he's coming?" he said around the mouthful of poultry.

"I think the man misses you," Sully answered, completely straight-faced. "Look, you're in the wilds of Lulworth, Clairemont's on his honeymoon—Carmichael's lonely. He'd do well to get himself a bit of muslin, that one," he added with conviction.

Marcus set the half-gnawed chicken leg on a plate and

grabbed the second bottle of wine. "You're testing my patience, Sully," he ground out, yanking out the cork and tipping up the bottle to take a long swig.

"Well, of course I know why the man's coming, just thought I'd dress it up a bit," he replied, looking longingly at the bottle in Marcus's hand. "He doesn't leave London unless he suspects that something's wrong."

"And he'd be right this time," Marcus added grimly.

"Oh, I wouldn't go that far," Sully protested.

Marcus slammed his fist on the table, rattling the wine bottle and making the chicken leg jump. "I would. We've got a dead boy and a treasure that for all we know is making its way to France at this very moment."

"And Miss Sarah Tisdale, do not forget her," Sully added, looking as though he instantly wished he had.

As if I could, Marcus thought, drumming his fingers on the tabletop.

Sarah Tisdale had wormed her way into his heart. Actually, she'd done nothing of the sort. "Worming" implied stealth and skill—two attributes that the wee lass did not possess.

No, she'd tripped and fumbled her way beneath his defenses, the honesty with which she handled everything both shocking and irritatingly endearing.

But for all of her heart she gave to him, how much was out of pity? Was he just another stray animal for her to help?

That wasn't love.

"Any more news?" he asked, eyeing Sully.

"Well," Sully began, "the Tisdale boy swears that he knows nothing more. Dixon has been spending a fair amount of time at the manor, though that's likely to do with his designs on Miss Tisdale."

"Dixon?" Marcus asked incredulously.

Sully gave another longing look at the bottle and Marcus obliged, handing it to him wordlessly.

The valet took a long pull. "Not as pertains to the case, no. But the man's had his eye on the girl for quite some time. Seems she won't commit either way—nor will her father."

Marcus thought back to when he'd found Sarah hiding in the grass just to avoid speaking with Dixon. If he had to guess, her mercurial attitude toward the man had everything to do with his animals and nothing to do with any real feelings on her part.

Of course, his guess may have had *everything* to do with the fact that he'd kissed her breasts less than two hours before.

And felt her hot, wet release on his fingers.

Marcus shifted uncomfortably in his chair. "Reliable source?"

"I couldn't get much closer to the source if I tried," Sully answered, wriggling his eyebrows for effect.

Marcus rose from his chair, the day's physical activity beginning to catch up with him as the ache in his leg returned. "Keep an eye on Nigel and be sure that Marlowe continues to watch Dixon closely," he said curtly, limping slowly to the doorway. "But Sully, no more conversations with Cook, ye ken?"

The valet lowered the bottle, wiping his damp lips with the back of his hand. "Yes."

"Then he took his finger and—"

"Stop. Right there. Now," Claire begged, her eyes growing to twice their size.

"Are you quite all right?" Sarah asked dramatically, laying her hand on Claire's brow.

Her friend yanked Sarah's hand away and placed it in her own, shepherding her toward a patch of wildflowers. "Am I all right?" she hissed, incredulous. "You . . . you . . . And to speak of it here, in the middle of the Colbys' annual picnic. You . . . you . . ."

"Claire, you seem incapable of finishing a sentence," Sarah pointed out. "And besides—"

"*Whisper!*" she insisted, urgently straightening the skirt of her primrose-colored gown about her growing stomach in a desperate attempt to secure at least a modicum of propriety.

"And besides," Sarah murmured, her voice low and dramatically theatrical, "I thought you would be happy for me."

Claire's eyes somehow widened even more. "Happy for you? Happy for you?"

Sarah patted her on the back.

"What was that for?" Claire demanded, forgetting herself for a moment and speaking in an audible tone.

"You appeared stuck, my dear."

The two smiled politely as the vicar and his wife walked past, nodding and murmuring polite agreement when the man commented on the spectacular nature of the day.

"Did Weston make an offer of marriage?" Claire questioned once the two were out of hearing.

"Well, no," Sarah answered, the bubble of happy anticipation she'd felt at the thought of sharing her news with Claire quickly vanishing.

"Did he declare his feelings for you?" Claire pressed, smiling at her husband, who stood with Marcus across the meadow.

It occurred to Sarah that she could lie, but doing so would give credence to Claire's obvious concern. "No, he did not. But I declared mine. Does that count?"

"I vow," Claire said in a strangled voice, "I'm going to scream."

Sarah rolled her eyes. "Oh no, you are not. Here, take my arm," she replied, slipping her friend's hand through the crook of her elbow. "Did you really believe I would ever do things as they're meant to be done?"

Claire's eyebrows knit together as she considered the question. "I suppose not," she said with obvious reluctance.

"There," Sarah said reassuringly, patting her dear friend's hand.

"But did he give you any indication of his feelings?"

"Well . . ." Sarah hemmed, hesitant to answer.

"One word? A look? An impression?" Claire suggested, hope in her voice.

Sarah again thought to lie to her anxious friend, but decided against it. "A dog. Marcus gave me a dog."

Claire blinked rapidly. "I beg your pardon?"

"A dog," Sarah repeated, "named Bones. He looks to be a greyhound, though he's terribly small—"

"You called him Marcus," Claire squeaked.

Sarah blinked once, then twice. "I did?"

Claire squeaked a second time, making Sarah wonder whether she was truly going to scream. "You did."

"Well," Sarah began, "I suppose it's only natural after we . . . Well, what would one call it exactly?"

"Oh, heavens," Claire said, and then promptly let out a shrill scream.

"Bugger," Sarah muttered.

Gregory ran toward them, Marcus following closely behind.

"Claire!" Bennington said urgently, coming to stand next to his wife.

Marcus looked to Sarah, concern in his eyes. "What happened?"

"I shocked her, 'tis all," Sarah answered, vigorously fanning her friend with a lace-trimmed linen handkerchief. "It has happened before—and, I daresay, it will happen again."

Marcus's amused, faintly indulgent smile appeared. "Is there anything I can do?"

"Yes, actually," Sarah answered, pointing across the

lush grass to where the Colbys' servants had set out the picnic. "Go and fetch a pickled herring for me."

Brows lifting in surprise, Marcus appeared ready to question her, then thought better of it and set out across the meadow.

Claire squeaked, a scream clearly building in her throat. Gregory swore under his breath and fixed Sarah with a stern, irritated glare.

"What did you tell her this time, Sarah?" he asked as the picnic guests began to gather.

"I can hardly tell you here, now can I?" Sarah answered, looking about her at the curious faces.

Marcus returned with a small dish of the herring in hand. "Is this what you requested?"

Sarah gestured for him to hand her the serving dish, then offered it to Claire.

The woman licked her lips as though she were desperate to devour every last morsel.

"Get the gel something to drink!" Lady Colby barked, poking her husband in the arm with her parasol.

The round little man moved as quickly as his sixty-plus-year-old legs would allow, waddling toward a servant and waving his arms.

"My dear girl," Lady Colby continued, "a woman in your condition is prone to all sorts of odd behavior. Please, come and sit with me in the shade."

"You too, young man," Lady Colby yapped, snapping her fingers. "A husband's arm is most useful in these situations."

"I agree with Lady Colby; you should rest, Claire," Sarah chimed in, standing back so that Gregory and Claire might pass. "And eat. A lot."

Her friend paused to fix Sarah with a set smile, her eyes narrowing with threat. "This is not the end of our conversation."

"Refreshment! The woman needs refreshment!" Sarah said loudly, her voice infused with concern.

Lord Colby, who'd just arrived with a glass, jumped, spilling the contents down the front of his brown coat.

"Colby! Do be careful," Lady Colby scolded before turning her attention back to Claire and her husband. "Come, come. Don't dawdle."

"Let's not keep the woman waiting," Gregory urged, gently helping Claire follow in Lady Colby's wake.

Sarah watched the crowd disperse, Marcus remaining at her side.

"What did you do?" he murmured as he took hold of her elbow.

His warm hand on her bare skin had Sarah involuntarily licking her lips.

"You must understand, it takes very little to upset Claire."

He nodded solemnly, though a brilliant grin appeared upon his mouth.

"You practiced that smile as a boy, didn't you?" Sarah asked, leaning into his side though she knew she should not. "You used it at school too, I would imagine."

"Yes," he confirmed, a low chuckle rumbling in his throat. "Shocked?"

Sarah rolled her eyes. "Hardly. You men are as resourceful as any woman on earth. Shocked?" she countered.

"By you? Never."

"Really?" She eyed the crowd as it buzzed about Claire and Lady Colby. "Claire screamed because I told her of my deflowering. Is that the correct term? My virginity is still int—"

"I stand corrected," Lord Weston interrupted, steering her toward the edge of the meadow.

Sarah allowed him to do so, the feel of him at her side so . . . well, right.

"Sarah," he began, scrubbing his palm over his chin. "You should not have done such a thing."

"Told Claire, or allowed you to deflower me?" Sarah asked, truly confused.

"Both," he answered with frustration, then visibly checked himself. He let out an exasperated sigh. "And I did not 'deflower' you. Such a crime requires a bit more involvement on the part of my . . ."

"Do continue!" Sarah whispered, her mind greedily eating up the information.

Marcus turned his head toward the wilderness just beyond. "How do you do it?"

"Do what?" Sarah asked, beginning to worry.

He rubbed his jaw again. "Bring out the worst in me."

Butterflies gathered, fluttering wings of apprehension low in Sarah's abdomen. "I bring out what's real in you—the good and the bad."

Marcus looked back at Sarah, his eyes bleak.

"Do you not worry for your reputation?" he asked, the moment of vulnerability passing as quickly as it had arrived.

Sarah barely controlled the sudden urge to reach out and cup his face in her hands. "Claire would no more betray my confidence than I hers," she said. The butterfly wings fluttering in her abdomen soared upward beneath her ribs and made her heart pound with an anxious beat. "What troubles you?"

"God, woman, how can you ask such a question?" he insisted, his voice straining with the effort. "I took advantage of you—in the road, for Christ's sake," he added, his burr broadening the words.

"It was against a tree—and I wanted it. I wanted you," Sarah said simply.

His chest rose and fell hard as he drew a deep breath. "You do not know what you want."

"Do not underestimate me."

"My lord," a voice echoed across the meadow. Sarah and Marcus turned to see Thaddeus Pringle hurrying toward them through the thick grass.

"Stay here," Marcus commanded. He walked to meet Pringle, his long strides eating up the distance between them.

Sarah obeyed Marcus without question, apprehension and foreboding chilling her.

The constable reached Marcus, his wiry frame fairly quivering, alive with agitation. Marcus bent his head to the shorter man, both speaking in hushed tones. Try as she might, Sarah couldn't hear their words.

Their conversation was over as quickly as it began, the constable turning to hurry away, disappearing across the meadow while Marcus returned to Sarah's side.

"What is it?" she murmured, searching his grim face. Although none of the other guests stood close enough to hear, she was vividly aware the gossips were avidly watching for any hint of scandal.

Marcus's gaze flicked over the assemblage before returning to Sarah. "Clive Burroughs has been found strangled in the woods above the cove."

Sarah saw Marcus's lips move and heard the words he spoke, but she simply could not put them together in a way that made sense. Another child killed. *Another child.*

First Jasper, now Clive. She struggled to understand the reality of Marcus's statement but her mind recoiled in horror.

"Sarah," Marcus said softly, his warm hand closing around her elbow. "I need your help. Can you do that?"

She nodded, his touch steadying her, although she had the strangest sensation her body was slowly going numb.

"I must assist Pringle—"

"Do not leave me," Sarah whispered, sure of nothing else than that she could not endure the coming hours without him.

He drew her arm through his and urged her into motion, walking across the meadow toward the tree where Claire and Lady Colby continued to hold court. "I won't be far away," he said, "but I need you to organize assistance for Clive's family, then I need you to go to his parents and do what you can."

"But I cannot." Sarah's gloved hand gripped his sleeve tightly.

"You can, and you will," Marcus assured her. "Do not underestimate yourself."

Her words, repeated by him with such confidence and firm belief, suddenly meant everything.

Sarah drew in a deep breath, preparing her mind and heart for the hours ahead.

"Ladies," Marcus said grimly to those gathered beneath the tree, releasing Sarah's arm and bowing. "Duty calls me away and I'm afraid I must beg your leave."

And then he was gone.

"And the second boy?"

Marcus looked at Carmichael. The head of the Young Corinthians had arrived late in the afternoon to the news of Clive Burroughs's death. "Strangled and left dead in the forest."

"Interesting location, wouldn't you agree?" Carmichael looked out over the castle's expansive gardens from his seat on the terrace, his face unreadable.

Marcus nodded, watching the sun sink beneath the trees. "The killer wanted the boy found. He's sending a message."

"This is superb brandy," Carmichael commented, raising his crystal glass to his lips for another sip. "Though not worth dying for, I'd venture."

Marcus pushed his chair back violently, rising and stalking toward the stone railing. "It's hardly about the brandy, and well you know it."

"So you believe the rumors concerning the Orlov emeralds are true?" Carmichael replied, skepticism lacing his tone.

Marcus scrubbed his hand across his face and looked over his shoulder, anger at the death of another boy simmering beneath the surface. "Don't you? Wasn't that the reason for sending me to this cursed backwater?"

"To be completely honest, I thought the theory lacked merit—to put such riches in the hands of common smugglers, and some of them boys, no less. Such a simple plan as to appear ludicrous at best. Which—" Carmichael paused to taste the brandy once again, "—is exactly what makes it so brilliant."

"You admit you purposely sent me off on a wild-goose chase?" Marcus countered, gripping the stone balustrade with punishing force.

Carmichael leaned back in his chair, crossing his legs and fixing Marcus with a direct, unswerving stare. "I sent you here to recuperate, knowing full well that without a case of some sort you'd go mad."

"Madness is rather subjective, wouldn't you agree?" Marcus bit out, regretting his words instantly. He thrust his fingers through his hair and grimaced. "I apologize, Carmichael. It's been a long, trying day."

"Are you positive?"

"That it's been a trying day?" Marcus frowned at Carmichael.

"Trying" did not begin to describe the last twelve hours.

The child's death was unthinkable, to be sure. But there was something about Clive's murder that scared Marcus.

He'd grieved for the loss of Jasper as any compassionate individual would. But Clive's loss cut closer to his heart.

He was forming an attachment to the town.

And as for Sarah, he hardly knew where to begin.

Her honesty terrified him. She was the strongest woman he'd ever met—and the most vulnerable at the same time.

He'd very nearly shouted when he learned she'd confided their intimacy to Claire.

Despite Sarah's assurances that her friend would keep their secret, Marcus had his doubts that she would keep such news from Bennington.

Based on what his married friends told him, wives seemed to delight in telling their husbands everything.

Sarah was naïve beyond comprehension.

She was wantonness wrapped in innocence.

She was everything Marcus did not want or need in his life.

And he could not stop thinking about her.

Even now, he realized, as he stood before his superior with the responsibility for a badly botched case resting on his shoulders and the evidence mounting to suspect her brother's involvement in what amounted to treason.

She was there.

In every crack and crevice of his brain, until there was nowhere to hide.

Marcus closed his eyes and rubbed at his temples.

"Weston," Carmichael said in a firm, yet considerate tone. "I was not asking after your day—rather, your mental state."

Marcus let out a bark of laughter. He couldn't help himself. "Do you have to ask?" he countered.

"Sully believes that your days here have altered you in some way—that the carefree Weston is no longer."

"Does he, now?" Marcus asked, dropping his hands to the rough stone of the cool balustrade. "And you? What do you think?"

Carmichael smoothly pushed back his chair and rose to join Marcus. "I think you were never comfortable in the role to begin with."

"The society matrons wouldn't have allowed me into their homes were it not for this 'role.' I would have served no purpose—"

"No purpose?" Carmichael interrupted, a somber cast to his intelligent features as he looked out over the gardens. "Are you absolutely sure on that point?"

"That I'd not have been accepted in the ton were it not for my acting abilities?" Marcus asked incredulously. "Yes."

Carmichael turned his back on the view and settled against the waist-high balustrade. "Weston, not that I've ever doubted your loyalty, but your work as a Corinthian never seemed wholly satisfying to you."

"For a statement not meant to question my devotion," Marcus replied, "you've come close to doing just that."

Carmichael folded his arms across his chest. "Weston, your work is impeccable, but there's a difference between living to work and working to live."

Marcus was silent.

"My friend, did it ever occur to you that the Corinthians were but the beginning for you?"

"Are you cutting me loose?" Marcus asked grimly.

Carmichael raised his hand, signaling for him to stop. But he could hardly remain silent. "Because the case is not lost—not yet. Clearly the Tisdale boy knows more than he's admitting. I've hardly exhausted all—"

"Weston," Carmichael began firmly. "I'm merely suggesting that you view your time in Lulworth as an opportunity rather than an impediment."

He patted Marcus on the back. "Growth is never easy—and quite often, it's exhausting work."

"I've enough exhausting work," Marcus growled.

Carmichael pushed off from the railing and walked toward the doors. "You miss the ease of playing a well-rehearsed role—nothing more, nothing less."

"And," Marcus pressed.

"And the old Weston or—well, the 'new,' for lack of a better term—will crack this case. You mark my words."

It was late, that much Marcus knew. Countless servants had traversed the length of Lulworth Castle in an effort to draw him from the terrace.

But he would not—could not—move.

Not until he had a firm plan.

And not as long as he held any doubt concerning precisely what had to be done from the moment he rose from his chair.

Then, or when the second bottle of brandy he'd demanded was empty.

He reached for it, teetered, and fell out of the chair. He hit the cold, stone floor of the terrace with a thud, landing on his back, the legs of the chair scraping loudly as it skidded away from him across the floor.

He squinted up at the stars, calculating the spaces between constellations.

The smugglers responsible for the murders of Jasper Wilmington and Clive Burroughs were likely looking up at the same night sky.

Aye, the bastards could probably tell time by the stars and planets.

"Your bloody burr is coming out, Weston," he said aloud, the sound grating to his ears.

Sarah seemed to like his accent, though Marcus could not think why.

"Goddammit all to hell, Weston," he yelled, "get yer head on straight."

From smugglers to Sarah in no time at all.

To Sarah, who shivered at the sound of his burr and would probably worship him if he wore a kilt.

She was a wonderful woman, with nothing better to do than fancy herself in love with him.

She'd groom him and train him, just like Titus, though Marcus felt sure he'd take to the commands with a touch more skill than the mastiff.

"Leave the lass to her dogs, Weston."

He leaned up on one elbow, stretching to reach the table, grunting with the effort until he felt the weight of his brandy glass in his fingers.

"And pigs and horses. And a peacock. For the love of God," he added, spilling a minimal amount of the drink as he carefully lowered it.

"A sodding peacock!" he yelled, tipping the glass to empty it of brandy.

Oh, Carmichael had done an admirable job of meddling. So admirable that Marcus had spent his first hour alone on the terrace attacking his sobriety, while returning to his superior's advice again and again.

But Marcus had seen Carmichael in action before. Mighty men—the mightiest, to Marcus's way of thinking—had been reduced to happily married fools.

He'd never suffer the same fate, if he had anything to say in the matter.

And then the brandy had swiftly kicked in.

Or Marcus had come to his senses.

One or the other, it wasn't important.

He knew himself well enough to realize that he'd have difficulty solving the smuggling case when his mind was occupied elsewhere.

Namely with Sarah, whose very nature made him

question himself—down to the smallest of details. It was painful and, in all honesty, unnecessary.

And the hours between sundown and sunrise, when Marcus tended toward introspection, could be endured.

Would be endured.

Happily, if it meant this would stop.

That life would return to normal—or, at least, as normal as he'd ever known.

Resolution was at hand. He'd give up the bonny lass.

Now, if Marcus could only stand.

12

In the past, Claire had often commented on the lack of current fashion to be found in Madame Estella's in Lulworth. But as Sarah looked about the cozy spot, she realized *that* was precisely why she found it so dear.

The tiny establishment sat cramped between the butcher on one side and the baker on the other, a fact that irritated many of Lulworth's ladies to no end.

Sarah never quite understood why they were so annoyed with the placement of Madame Estella's. The convenience of purchasing bones for her dogs and a bun with plump currants for herself, all within a few steps, delighted her.

Sarah could not imagine a more pleasing shop than Estella's. True, the furnishings were slightly shabby. The damask settee probably should have been reupholstered the previous year, and Sarah suspected that the chintz curtains would not pass a close inspection. But the rows of fabric that lined the shop added an endearing touch. In London, the bolts of silk, satin, and velvet were mysteriously tucked away, to be brought out for each individual lady's attention.

And then there was Estella. Sarah watched the seamstress as she deftly completed the final fitting of Claire's periwinkle gown, pins between her teeth and more pins neatly stuck in the edge of one sleeve.

"A touch more here," she mumbled around the pins, not waiting for Claire, Sarah, or Lady Tisdale's approval before she expertly folded a tuck in the silk just below Claire's arm, the half inch of fabric making all the difference in the fit of the gown.

Lady Tisdale nodded in approval. "You do have a way with silk, Estella."

The woman looped a graying curl behind her ear and humphed in appreciation.

Sarah smiled. Even her mother had to admit that Estella was as talented a needlewoman as one would find for miles around—not an easy thing considering the fact that Estella had gotten her start stitching fishing nets and sailors' sturdy breeches.

Her business had been born from necessity when her fisherman husband was washed overboard in a storm at sea, leaving Estella with a rundown cottage and three babies to feed.

Now the talented woman expertly produced everything from rough woolen box coats for seamen to finely beaded ball gowns for the local gentry. Only in Lulworth could a woman do such a thing, Sarah thought to herself with pride.

"Sarah?" Claire asked, looking down at her friend. "What do you think?"

Sarah lifted Bones onto her lap, much to her mother's clear consternation, and adjusted her skirts. "Estella was right. The bodice needed to be taken in just a touch."

"Of course." Claire raised her arms so Estella could continue pinning. "But my question is about the ball. I don't know that we should go forward with it in light of all that has happened."

"You're being foolish, Claire," Lady Tisdale declared stoutly. "The Bennington ball is a Lulworth tradition. The entire county looks forward to it with great anticipation—and most especially will this year, I've no doubt."

Estella slipped the pins from her mouth and set them down on a worn worktable. "A ball might be just the thing to take everyone's mind off those poor boys."

She gestured for Claire to turn around, viewing the back of the bodice through narrowed eyes.

"Exactly," Lady Tisdale said briskly. "You would be doing Lulworth a disservice if you canceled the event. Besides, it is tomorrow. You could hardly cancel with so little notice. I do think—" She cut herself off when Bones sneezed. "Really, Sarah, must you bring that creature in here?"

Sarah ignored the question in favor of what she considered a far more important issue. "But Mother, aren't you the least bit concerned for Nigel's safety?"

"Why on earth should I be?" Lady Tisdale asked confusedly, scooting as far from Bones as the length of the settee would allow.

Estella threaded a pin through the silk just at the apex of Claire's shoulder. "Something to do with his dearest friends being murdered in cold blood would be my guess," she muttered.

"Estella!" Lady Tisdale cried, shock and dismay written across her features. "Did you not just a moment ago agree with my judicious reasoning as to why the Bennington Ball should proceed as planned?"

Estella stepped back, ran a searching gaze over Claire from head to toe, and with a nod of satisfaction gestured for her to remove the gown. "That I did. But your boy's safety is an entirely different kettle of fish."

"Exactly, Mother," Sarah agreed, calming a quivering Bones, who'd jumped in fright when Lady Tisdale had responded to Estella's statement. "Nigel's dearest friends—and smuggling cohorts, I might add—are dead. And not by accident. They've the bruised necks to prove it."

The women fell silent for a moment, all four struggling to absorb the unthinkable truth, for perhaps the hundredth time.

"Be that as it may," Lady Tisdale said with a resolute sigh, "Nigel is hardly in danger. It's rumored that Jasper and Clive *absconded* with a treasure of some sort."

"Is that a fancy word for stealing?" Estella asked, carefully taking the gown from Claire and draping it over her sturdy arm. "I'll help you dress, my lady."

Lady Tisdale nodded grimly. "Exactly. So you see, Nigel has nothing to fear."

Sarah looked at her mother, then Claire, and finally Estella, who was gazing at Lady Tisdale with disbelief. "Am I to understand you believe Nigel played no part in the theft?"

"Of course. Nigel is not like those other boys. He has no need to do such a thing."

For the first time in her life Sarah wanted to slap her mother senseless.

Actually, that wasn't quite true. She'd wished so before, but never had she come so close to following through.

Sarah had initiated numerous conversations with Nigel in the hopes of discovering some forgotten fact that would lead to the killer. But he'd only assured her that he knew nothing more—a statement that Sarah found hard to believe.

"Mother, I realize your daily activities do not often bring you into close contact with Nigel and his friends," Sarah began, wrapping her hands about Bones's midsection to assure they were otherwise engaged. "But allow me to enlighten you: Twelve-year-old boys need no reason to steal. Twelve-year-old boys need no reason to consume Cook's strawberry tarts until they gag, nor a reason to swim naked in the ocean in the middle of November."

Lady Tisdale began to fidget with her shawl.

"Mother," Sarah demanded.

"He claims to know nothing of the trouble—"

"He's hardly going to admit to such a thing at this point. His two dearest friends have been murdered!"

Lady Tisdale swallowed hard, her nervous fingers plucking at the shawl until Sarah thought she might tear a hole in the soft cashmere.

"We've given him no reason to steal—Sir Arthur and I have set the most moral of examples—"

"You're not listening," Sarah interrupted, gently setting Bones on the floor and shifting across the settee to her mother's side. "He's a *boy*. Boys do rash and reckless things every single day of their lives."

Estella disappeared for a moment, returning with a teacup and saucer. "Here, my lady, drink this. It will do you good."

Lady Tisdale reluctantly released her shawl and took the cup and saucer, avoiding Sarah's gaze as she sipped. She gasped, her eyes opening wide as she let out a heavy breath. "This is not tea!"

"Good Lord, no," Estella answered. "A time such as this calls for juniper cordial."

Lady Tisdale rested the cup and saucer on her lap, her earlier forcefulness subdued. "What are we to do?"

"Lady Bennington holds the ball, because that's what the county needs. And you make sure that the boy is locked up safe and sound," Estella answered resolutely, as though it was the simplest thing in the world.

Lady Tisdale looked ready to say something, but apparently decided against speech in favor of a second fortifying nip of Estella's cordial. "I should not have denied Lord Weston's request," she moaned after swallowing.

"What request?" Sarah sat upright, foreboding filling her. Claire immediately crossed the room and sat in the dainty chair next to the settee.

"Lord Weston came to the house yesterday and asked

to speak to Nigel. I believe you were visiting the Burroughses, Sarah. I refused, of course. And when he offered to send one of his own servants to protect Nigel—"

"You refused?" Sarah interrupted. "Mother, how could you?"

Lady Tisdale drained the cup. "I hardly realized the danger—and who is Lord Weston to barge into my house and make demands of my family?" she added truculently.

Claire placed her arm about Sarah's shoulders—whether to comfort or restrain, Sarah could not be sure.

"*Who* is Lord Weston?" she repeated. Anger at her mother's determined refusal to see reason after the events of the last two days had Sarah clenching her fists.

"He's surprising the lot of Lulworth, I can tell you that," Estella interrupted, collecting the cup and saucer from Lady Tisdale. "My nephew told me Lord Weston has given his entire staff leave to attend the Michaelmas Fair."

Lady Tisdale's eyes widened until they were round as saucers. "That's all well and good. But it hardly makes up for years of—"

"And I heard Mrs. Rathbone telling Mrs. Wyatt, in this very room, mind you, of the kindness Lord Weston has shown the Wilmingtons," Estella continued with purpose. "It appears that *everyone* has noticed Lord Weston's efforts."

Lady Tisdale cleared her throat uneasily. "Well, I can hardly be expected to think on the man while my poor little boy is in danger."

Claire squeezed Sarah gently, a subtle reminder to hold on to her temper. "Lady Tisdale, who is with Nigel at the moment?"

"Cook. The boy simply will not stand for being on his own these days," she answered, a flicker of alarm in her eyes. "Sarah, you must talk some sense into your brother. You're the only one he will listen to."

"Of course she will," Claire answered for Sarah, gesturing for Estella to refill Lady Tisdale's cup.

The dressmaker produced a small flask from within the folds of her corduroy skirt and poured. "For your health," she urged encouragingly, handing it to Lady Tisdale.

She did not hesitate this time, taking a drink immediately. "We'll get this all sorted out, won't we, Sarah?"

Sarah nodded, though she felt anything but sure.

Nigel had lied to Cook.

It wasn't the first time, nor, he suspected, would it be the last.

But the woman had been so awfully kind to him, allowing him anything in the larder, that Nigel felt guilty.

He'd told her not to worry, that he just needed a bit of rest in his room.

And then he'd run as quickly as he could toward the abandoned well on the northern end of Lord Weston's property.

He tripped over a tree root and fell full length on the ground, scraping his palms on rocks in the grass.

He could feel tears welling in his eyes—just as they had again and again since Jasper and then Clive had been killed.

"Bloody baby," Nigel whispered, sucking in a deep breath and screwing up his mouth as tightly as he could in an effort to stop himself from crying. A hard, tight knot lay heavy in his chest and it was difficult to swallow.

He dug into the deep, brown dirt with both hands, the feel of the cool earth beneath his nails comforting.

But he couldn't lie there forever—though he wanted nothing more than that.

He pushed himself up on his knees, looking about quickly to ensure that no one had followed him.

Standing, he took a moment to swipe his palms over his hot, wet cheeks, and then he was off again.

Nigel had been as horrified as anyone when he'd heard of Jasper's death—just as confused as well.

It wasn't until Clive told him what he and Jasper had done that Nigel realized what kind of trouble the two were in.

After spying the emerald and coin, Jasper had gone to Clive and suggested they take a bit off the top—not too much, so that no one would notice—but enough that their families could live a better life than the one the sea provided.

Only they'd stolen something that was far more valuable to the French than either boy could have imagined.

Clive had seen one of the Frenchmen question Jasper and then strangle him, right then and there on the beach.

He'd known there was nothing he could do and so he'd waited. Pissed his pants with fright, and waited for the men to leave. And then waited some more.

Finally, he'd run all the way home, dug the emerald from under the straw pallet on his cot, and taken it to the well.

He figured they couldn't kill him if they didn't know where the jewel was. Some protection, Clive had said. He'd make a deal, gain a bit of blunt, and hopefully keep his head attached to his neck.

He and Jasper hadn't involved Nigel because, being the son of a baronet, he wanted for nothing.

Nigel had felt oddly sad, as if risking death would have been worth it to have been included in his friends' adventure.

But now his heart pounded as he raced toward the well.

He thought about the conversation with Clive over and over.

His friend had been so sure that he could handle the French. That he'd come out on top despite what had happened to Jasper.

Nigel turned off the path and fought his way through the bracken and fern, fronds slapping at his arms, his chest, his face.

He pictured Clive as he'd last seen him, at Jasper's funeral.

Nigel slowed as the well came into view, dropping his pace to a jog as he crossed the grass.

Clive had begged him not to tell anyone.

He shouldn't have listened.

Nigel reached the stone well and placed both hands on its worn surface, catching his breath.

He'd gagged at the news of Jasper's death.

And wanted to die himself when he'd heard about Clive.

He gritted his teeth, blinked moisture from his eyes, and pulled at the worn length of rope, hand over hand.

The bucket scraped against the mossy stone as it pitched precariously from side to side, coming into view just as it threatened to upend.

Afraid it would tip over and lose its contents, Nigel yanked, and the bucket flew past him, landing with a soft thud on the ground.

He sank to his knees and reached for the small package, no larger than the palm of his hand, wrapped in filthy muslin.

Nigel didn't bother to unwrap the treasure. He had no desire to see what had caused the deaths of his two friends.

Jasper and Clive were gone—all because of this stupid emerald.

"I'll get the bloody bastards responsible," he said out

loud, looking up into the canopy of trees. "I'll make them pay with their lives."

He shoved the small, dirty parcel into his pocket and took off running again, needing to be home.

He'd no idea what to do next.

He was afraid to do anything at all.

But as he ran breakneck back through the forest toward Tisdale Manor, he knew that he had to do something to make them pay.

Marlowe followed Nigel silently through the woods, making sure the boy returned to Tisdale Manor safely.

Then he doubled back and sought out the path through the woods that would take him to the cliffs. From there he planned to cross to Lulworth Castle, where Carmichael and Weston awaited him.

He'd been twelve himself once. And as such, Marlowe knew the boy's pledge to seek revenge ought to be taken seriously.

Never mind the fact that the scrawny youth was hardly a match for Napoleon's cohorts.

No, the boy would not give up on his goal easily.

Something needed to be done. And quickly.

Marlowe reached the stately front door of Lulworth Castle and rapped loudly. The door opened wide and Weston and Carmichael appeared before him, both with fowling pieces lying casually over their forearms.

"Up for a bit of hunting, Marlowe?" Weston asked, stepping out onto the stone steps and heading for the drive.

Carmichael followed and Marlowe fell into step. The men walked in silence for some time, one occasionally firing off a round at the sudden, desperate flight of a bird.

"Marlowe, do you have news?" Carmichael asked, squinting at a copse of trees.

He reached for Weston's gun, readied it, and fired at nothing in particular. "The boy is in possession of the emerald—and a healthy appetite for revenge."

"Meaning?" Weston asked, taking his gun back.

Marlowe smiled. "Come now, you were twelve once, were you not? My guess is that he'll use the jewel to arrange a meeting. And then he'll do his damnedest to take revenge."

"He could not possibly think he would be able to carry out such a task," Carmichael said.

Marlowe reached for a long blade of grass and began to split it into two. "Well, I'd wager that he doesn't know who he's dealing with. Either way, he'll get himself killed."

"The boy is no good to us dead," Carmichael replied sternly.

Weston took hold of the barrel with both hands. "Good God, Carmichael, he's more than a means of information."

"Of course. But his safety is a priority, would you not agree?"

Weston twisted his palms about the gun ruthlessly, nodding in agreement.

"We'll move the boy to Lulworth Castle as soon as possible. Marlowe, your success with the Mercier interrogation was quite impressive. I'll leave the boy to you."

Weston swung the gun to the ready and fired into the trees. "If I remember correctly, Mercier nearly died."

Marlowe sent the bits of grass in his hand flying on the breeze. "We got what we needed from him, didn't we?"

"This is a twelve-year-old boy we are speaking of," Weston pressed, his voice laced with anger.

Carmichael looked at Marlowe, then at Weston, his brow furrowed. "Do you wish to interrogate the boy yourself, Weston?"

"Do I have any other choice?"

*   *   *

The house was silent. Blissfully, forgivingly silent as Sarah sat at her rosewood table, writing.

She'd suffered through Claire's final fitting and accompanied her mother home, struggling to maintain her composure. Not until she'd seen Nigel with her own eyes had she felt the easing of the iron fist of fear around her heart.

After a brief hello, she'd quietly closed the door to Nigel's room and fled the confines of the house for the open air. She'd run. And just for good measure, run some more.

The air and space had restored her equanimity sufficiently to sustain her through dinner—even when her mother insisted that Sarah speak immediately, if not sooner, to Nigel.

Her brother had refused to attend the meal, choosing instead to dine in his room.

Sarah suspected Nigel needed time.

She fiddled with the quill pen, rolling it between her fingers. Though writing in her journal was hardly a habit for Sarah, she picked up the pen now and again at Claire's insistence. Good for the soul, her dear friend had assured her.

"Bugger."

Nigel needed time, that much was clear. But for what, exactly?

She simply could not believe he would knowingly involve himself in something so sinister. But unknowingly? Of course such a thing was possible. Nigel was twelve. And he was, well, a boy, as she'd had to point out to her mother that very afternoon.

And he was surely terrified by now, no matter the depth of his involvement. Sarah wanted to take him in her arms and assure him that everything would be all right. But she could not. She would be lying if she did so.

She looked down at the foolscap, the name "Marcus" scrawled in her hasty script.

She needed so much to see him.

She needed him. Wanted him. Felt sure that he would put right everything that plagued her heart and soul at present.

Not that she believed he was a miracle worker—hardly. He was far from perfect, but it didn't matter. In some way, his imperfections made him perfect—for her. All that Sarah wanted was *all* of him. The good, the bad, and otherwise.

Before meeting Marcus, she'd never thought to rely on a single person for aid—it simply had not occurred to her.

But Marcus had her considering the unthinkable. Believing in the unbelievable. Wanting what she'd always assumed she could never have.

She closed her eyes and ran the smooth quill feather over her lips. In the midst of chaos, her mind turned to him.

She was neither embarrassed nor apologetic. He'd witnessed her for who she was, with her clumsiness, spontaneity, boldness, and candor. And still, he was there.

She loved him.

And though she would have wished for such a realization to occur in the midst of a time of joy, Sarah suspected that peace and happy times would never have brought to the surface her true feelings for Marcus. She gently set the quill down.

Nothing had ever been so simple in her life.

Nor would anything ever be again.

13

"It's charming, this little town of yours," Carmichael commented with interest. He stood just inside the terrace doorway with Marcus, observing Lulworth society as the ladies and gentlemen arrived at the Benningtons' for the much anticipated ball.

Marcus's laugh was a low sound of amusement. "It's hardly mine," he responded, smiling as two men he'd met at the Bennington house party passed by and nodded in friendly recognition.

"Well, perhaps not," Carmichael conceded. "Though it appears you've made up for your lack of attention to the county in the past."

"Yes, well—" Marcus gestured for Carmichael to accompany him out onto the terrace, "—it's amazing what taking a bit of initiative will do, especially when it involves a crime."

The two left the stately room, Marcus allowing Carmichael to pass through the opened doors first.

The swell of attendees spilled out into the warm night. Decorative lanterns swung gently in the light breeze off the sea. Their golden glow cast circles of soft light, revealing and then concealing the guests as they strolled.

"That, and the help of a good woman," Carmichael added, smiling at the sight of two guests who'd wandered off the path and into an alcove half-concealed in the tall laurel hedge. He clasped his hands behind him and glanced sideways at Marcus. "Sully mentioned a Miss Tisdale."

The muscles in Marcus's jaw tightened. "Miss Tisdale has been quite helpful. She offered to ease my way into Lulworth society, if you can believe such a thing."

"It appears she's been successful," Carmichael replied, noting with some interest yet another party who strolled by and smiled in greeting.

Marcus nodded briefly, returning the gesture of goodwill with a charming wink. "Yes, I suppose. Her connections with the townspeople certainly made the investigation easier in the beginning."

"Is that all?"

"What else would there be?" Marcus asked abruptly. "I won't be spending any more time here than is completely necessary—and may I remind you, Miss Tisdale's brother is wrapped up so tightly in this case that he can barely draw breath. No, the woman fancies herself in love with me—a notion I'll be putting a stop to immediately."

"Why?" Carmichael asked quietly.

Marcus's hands curled into fists. "I've my reasons. Besides, I told you, I've no desire to stay here."

This was not going well.

And then there she was. She stood in the doorway like some enchanted creature, the candlelight from inside the ballroom highlighting her curves in a blue silk gown.

Marcus ignored the swift stab of pain in his chest, just over his heart. Without taking his gaze from Sarah, he cleared his throat. "And there she is now."

"Oh," Carmichael replied, his voice devoid of emotion.

Sarah's searching gaze found Marcus and a smile lit her face. She quickly stepped onto the terrace and began to thread her way toward him through the throng of strolling, laughing guests.

A trio of men hurrying toward a cluster of young ladies passed too closely behind Sarah and one of them knocked into her while attempting to avoid another lady. He bumped her hard enough that she faltered in mid-step and tripped on the hem of her gown. In an instinctive attempt to catch her balance, she raised her arms as counterweights.

Unfortunately, a servant chose that precise moment to dart past her with a tray of fluted glasses.

The servant managed to remain upright.

The tray did not. The crystal fell with a crash to the stone floor of the terrace.

Carmichael turned to take in the chaotic scene, along with seemingly everyone else on the terrace. "She certainly knows how to make an entrance."

Sarah's cheeks were flushed with embarrassment as she looked past the apologetic servant to Marcus.

He wanted to stalk across the intervening space and toss the clumsy youth over the balustrade, then sweep Sarah away from the raised eyebrows and judgmental glances, but he had a charade to play tonight. The game didn't include defending Sarah—quite the opposite, in fact.

With effort, he schooled his features into a frown of disapproval and turned back to Carmichael. "Yes, she does." His voice held no inflection whatsoever.

Carmichael's shrewd gaze met Marcus's and he lifted an expressive brow.

Head held high, Sarah made her way through the onlookers and joined the two men at last. "Lord Weston," she began, dropping into a graceful curtsy. "I do hope you're not excessively thirsty. I've reason to believe the supply of spirits has been somewhat depleted."

"So we've heard as well," Marcus answered coolly, turning to Carmichael. "Miss Sarah Tisdale. May I present Lord Carmichael, a friend just down from London."

Marcus watched as Sarah curtsied, careful to execute it perfectly.

Carmichael took Sarah's hand and brushed a light kiss against her knuckles. "Miss Tisdale, a pleasure."

"It's an honor to make your acquaintance," she replied with just the right tone of politeness, clearly determined to erase the impression created by the scene just enacted behind her.

"A lovely evening for a ball, would you not agree?" Her gaze moved over the guests as they chatted, sipped punch, and made use of the gardens beyond.

"Yes, quite," Carmichael answered. "This is my first trip to Lulworth, and I must say, the sea air and breathtaking scenery does much to recommend the town. I'm quite pleased that Weston encouraged me to stop on my way to Cornwall."

Sarah beamed with delight, clearly pleased by Carmichael's praise of her village. "I'm so happy to hear of it."

"Yes, acceptable weather indeed," Marcus drawled in a bored tone. "Though I do have to wonder at the delays."

"I beg your pardon?" Sarah asked, confusion furrowing her brow.

Marcus feigned forgetfulness. "My apologies, Miss Tisdale—I'd forgotten that you've spent little time in society," he said. "In London, the dancing would have begun long ago and this—" he gestured to the crowd milling about on the terrace and garden below, "—would never do. It's as if the Benningtons are eager to invite scandal. Would you not agree, Carmichael?"

"We are not in London, Weston," Carmichael said repressively.

"Precisely," Sarah said, her voice quivering ever so slightly.

He'd wounded her—just as he'd planned to. And it hurt like hell. There were times when Marcus hated being the bastard he knew he was.

Her face had fallen, the impact of his condescending criticism written across her expressive features for the entire world to see.

"I'm sorry, Lord Weston," she said with quiet dignity. "I was under the impression you'd become quite fond of Lulworth—even with its quaint ways."

She wasn't putting up a fight, at least not to the extent that he knew she could.

Which meant the words he was about to utter would be unimaginably painful.

He shrugged. "Lulworth's charms were tempting. For a time. But I could not be happy in such a simple place. Never."

Sarah took a deep breath. Her hands fisted at her sides, her grip on the sticks of her fan punishing. "Are you quite sure?"

"Quite."

"Well, in that case . . ." She squared her shoulders, her chin lifting. "Since your time in Lulworth is drawing to a close, I suggest that we not waste a minute longer. I'll speak to Claire about informing the musicians."

With admirable dignity, she nodded briefly at the two men and turned, lifting her skirts to quickly disappear into the throng.

"What was that?" Carmichael demanded, his disapproval clear.

"*That* was necessary," Marcus answered. "Come, I've need of a drink."

*   *   *

"Why would he say such a thing?"

Claire inspected the poached salmon with a critical eye before nodding at the servant, who lifted the platter and disappeared among the seemingly hundreds of cooks and servants currently engaged in serving the expansive buffet.

"Come with me," Claire ordered, taking Sarah by the hand and towing her toward the larder.

No fewer than five anxious individuals attempted to impede their progress, a pheasant in need of tasting, a pudding that lacked the desired consistency, and three dishes that Sarah could hardly identify.

Though Claire was well known throughout the county for the iron fist she wielded over such an affair, she refused all requests, opened the larder door, and shoved Sarah inside.

She followed, closing the door tight. "Are you sure he was speaking of you?" Claire asked pointedly.

"Yes, of course," Sarah answered. "I might be naïve, but I'm hardly stupid."

"I was not suggesting that you're stupid, Sarah," Claire said reassuringly. "I simply needed to know."

She paused, as though she was considering her response—or as if she truly did not want to continue.

"Claire," Sarah begged, "why would he say such a thing?"

She took Sarah's hands in her own. "Because it's true."

That was hardly what Sarah had expected to hear. "Well, I could have reasoned that out. Come now, Claire, you're usually so insightful—"

"Sarah," Claire interrupted, squeezing her dear friend's hands. "It's not fair, but I fear that he speaks the truth."

Sarah slipped her hands from Claire's and sat down

on an upended bucket, her legs suddenly losing the ability to hold her.

"Men are hardly known for their steadfastness, Sarah," Claire began in a calm tone. "And when they've, well . . ."

"Yes," Sarah prompted her friend.

Claire frowned. "Oh, Sarah, I fear Lord Weston got what he wanted from you on Cove Road."

Sarah propped her elbows on her knees and dropped her head into her hands. "No, it can't be."

"I'm sorry," Claire said with regret, the sound of a bucket scraping across the floor followed by the swish of skirts as Claire sat accompanying her apology.

"I know he has feelings for me," Sarah protested. "I saw it in his eyes."

Claire's delicate silk dancing slippers came into Sarah's view as she stared at the floor.

"I'm sorry, Sarah. More sorry than I've ever been."

"What can be done?"

"To Weston? Well, I've a few ideas of my own—all involving a very sharp knife."

Sarah dropped her hands into her lap and looked up into her friend's face. "What can be done to win him back?"

"Sarah, dear," Claire replied, brushing aside a stray curl that clung to Sarah's tear-damp cheek. "I don't think he was won to begin with."

And then Sarah cried, not the few tears that had begun when she'd first entered the kitchen, but large, hot drops of moisture that threatened to carry her away.

"Bollocks."

The sound of such a vulgar term spilling from Claire's lips shocked Sarah.

"This is what we are going to do," she said firmly. Her voice was militant, resolute, as she stood and pulled Sarah up beside her.

She fussed with Sarah's hair, looping a few errant strands about her finger, removing and replacing pins to repair the damage.

"You are going to march upstairs and thoroughly enjoy the evening." She paused, reaching for a length of linen and dabbing the evidence of tears from Sarah's face. "No, you are going to march upstairs and enjoy this year's Bennington ball as you've never enjoyed a ball before."

"But Claire, I've never liked balls," Sarah replied flatly. The storm of crying had been replaced with an emptiness that seemed to multiply by the moment, spreading throughout her body, numbing her.

Claire continued to do her best with the linen. "Well, *he* hardly knows that, now does he?"

Sarah took the damp cloth from Claire's hands and blew her nose loudly. "And how will this help me?"

"Your mother really did fail you when it came to explaining these things, didn't she?" Claire teased, and then pulled Sarah into a warm embrace, hugging her fiercely before holding her at arm's length and fixing her with a ferocious gaze. "You've tried honesty and look where it got you. Now you'll employ what God gave you—and make that man pay."

Being honest did have its advantages.

Sarah knew exactly which of her attributes could be relied upon to capture the attention of the male sex.

Not her legs, for they were, though well turned, somewhat on the short side. Her hips and posterior were all well and good, but she'd never learned to walk in a way that showed them to the best advantage.

But her breasts? *She'd* never seen anything out of the ordinary about the pair, but she had witnessed men ogling them time and time again.

It always made her angry—though in the back of her

mind, she pitied the fools for being controlled by two ar-
bitrary mounds of flesh.

"Present them," Claire hissed, smiling as Gregory and
Mr. Dixon walked toward them.

As they'd exited the larder, Sarah had not been entirely convinced that she could proceed with the plan.

Now she was sure she could not. "You said nothing of
Mr. Dixon," Sarah whispered back, opening her fan and
holding it in front of her bodice.

Claire's gaze darted toward the corner of the room
where lords Weston and Carmichael were engaged in a
lively conversation with several of Lulworth's most no-
table eligible females. "We must take the opportunity
when it arrives."

" 'It' is precisely the problem," Sarah muttered, lowering her fan reluctantly as the vile man approached
with Claire's husband.

She glanced in Weston's direction but was unable to
discover whether he was looking at her.

She wanted to slap Marcus, then dissolve into a puddle of tears.

He'd reduced her to this—worse, she'd allowed him
to do so.

And for what? Sarah could not fathom why Marcus
had behaved so cruelly.

"Lady Bennington, Miss Tisdale," Mr. Dixon said in
greeting, bowing low.

Claire nudged Sarah with a circumspect poke of her
folded fan. Sarah responded by slightly arching her back
and thrusting her breasts out in what she hoped was a
subtle fashion.

Judging from Mr. Dixon's expression, she'd been successful in gaining his attention.

"May I have this dance, Miss Tisdale?" he asked, trying very hard to focus on her eyes.

He failed miserably.

Bugger, Sarah thought resignedly, allowing him to take her arm. "I would be delighted."

And so it begins.

Courtship had always been a nasty business, but for Sarah, the absolute worst part of it all was the lying.

One lied about a preference in food or drink in order to appear more amiable. One lied about a particular talent or skill so that a man would think you more deserving of bearing his children. One lied about lying.

"Quite a fine evening, wouldn't you agree?" Mr. Dixon asked as he steered her toward the dance floor.

"Yes, quite," Sarah agreed, mentally rolling her eyes at the sound of her own voice.

Two lies within the space of thirty seconds, and for what?

To make Marcus regret having tossed her over?

At times, it felt to Sarah as if she were the only sane person in the whole of England.

She didn't want to make him regret anything—not yet anyway. She wanted the truth. What was so difficult about the truth?

"Oh, good, a quadrille. 'Tis a favorite of mine," Mr. Dixon said with satisfaction, positioning Sarah as though she were a little girl and taking his place across from her.

Sarah sighed, pasting a flat smile on her face. The music started, and she waited, watching as the head couple began to dance. When it was her turn, she nodded politely at Mr. Dixon and concentrated on making her feet move to the music. But she could not make her mind think of anything but Marcus.

She'd thought to never feel this way.

She had promised herself that Lulworth and the little world she'd built for herself would be enough.

What had Marcus done to tempt her away from the comfort of that idyllic, if limited existence?

Claire's encouraging face appeared in Sarah's view as she spun to the right, Mr. Dixon's superior sneer when she returned to the left.

And as she clapped three times, then turned to take the man's hand, she saw Marcus.

Sarah failed to read his face, though the dance continued at such a clip she doubted that she would have been able to even if she was not spinning in Dixon's arms.

Marcus.

The memory of his name scrawled across her journal flashed through her mind.

And she felt . . . She felt embarrassed? No, Sarah thought, turning once again. Not embarrassment.

Shame.

Though she knew deep in her heart that she'd done nothing wrong, there was no denying the emotion as it swept over her.

"Are you feeling well, Miss Tisdale?" Mr. Dixon inquired as they completed yet another turn.

"Perfectly well, thank you," she lied amiably, smiling at him.

He released her hand and they parted, each returning to their places.

She convinced herself to send the man a coy look as they stood across from each other, punctuating the glance with a slight shift of her shoulders. She was no fool. She knew exactly what the motion would do to her breasts.

Mr. Dixon looked as if he was about to lick his lips in anticipation.

Sarah noticed her mother near the edge of the dance floor, observing with keen interest her progress with the man.

And the flicker of anger bloomed stronger.

This was what had been expected of her all along.

This was what she got for her trouble.

The music ended and Mr. Dixon moved to her side, placing her gloved hand on his coat sleeve and covering it with his, the move possessive. "You've always claimed to abhor dancing, but I must say, Miss Tisdale," he paused, his gaze lowering to rake her breasts once more, "your passion for the art is truly inspiring."

Sarah needed to be free of him. Free of the house and all the people in it. Free of the fear that she'd betrayed herself and her emotions tonight.

She pulled her hand from beneath Mr. Dixon's and walked away without any explanation. She didn't look back, her pace increasing until she was nearly running, moving swiftly toward the terrace doors.

She slipped through them and picked up the blue skirt of her gown as she raced down the steps to the gardens. She didn't stop running until her legs refused to go on, far from the lights of the ballroom, far from the gathering of polite society.

And there, in the middle of the Bennington gardens, where the most charming of gazebos stood flanked by roses and hydrangeas, Sarah stopped.

She pulled at the pins in her hair.

Kicked off her slippers.

Ripped the long, white gloves from her arms and flung them to the wind.

She reached beneath the skirt of her blue gown and ripped the silk stockings from her legs, leaving them to lie where they fell.

Then, and only then, did Sarah let loose with a string of profanities so coarse that a blue streak could surely be seen from as far as the next county over.

The woman could run.

Even if Marcus's leg was completely healed—or, better yet, never injured at all—he'd have been hard-pressed to keep up with her.

She'd left the ballroom so abruptly that there was little time to react.

Dixon had simply stood there, looking annoyed until skulking off toward the dining room.

Claire had been intercepted by Lady Colby, with no hope of following after her friend.

Lady Tisdale was frozen in place on the edge of the dance floor, obviously torn between concern for her daughter and fear that any further action would bring unwanted attention.

"Either you go after her, or I will," Carmichael told Marcus.

And so he had, using a circuitous route so that no one would connect his exit with hers.

He'd run full bore for a time then dropped to a jog when he heard a woman's voice.

It was Sarah, all right, the tone elevated, but still recognizable.

She was swearing up a storm. Literally.

Marcus stopped dead in his tracks and listened, noting with some interest the clouds that threatened in the east.

The moment reminded Marcus of when he'd first met her that day at the pond.

She'd shocked him, wild and unabashed. Her appetite for life had terrified him.

It terrified him still.

But he should have known then what was so clear now: One could not avoid falling in love with Sarah Tisdale.

It was impossible—*she* was impossible.

And Marcus could no longer deny what was right in front of his eyes.

He continued toward the gazebo, circling around to where Sarah stood.

She stopped abruptly as he approached, a look of disbelief forming on her face. "What do you want?"

Her tone, so raw yet so sharp, cut him like a knife.

He'd hardly thought on what he would say, words usually rolling off his tongue like autumn leaves falling off a tree.

But this was different. This was not a lie.

This meant something—everything.

"You."

"Really," she countered, her arms akimbo as she moved to stand near him on the platform, her eyes level with his. "I understood you had grown weary of Lulworth's charms—"

"Please," Marcus interrupted. Hearing his words repeated by her twisted the knife in his gut.

Lightning flashed, brightening the dark sky, and a soft breeze stirred the warm night air, followed almost immediately by the loud roll and crack of thunder.

And then Sarah slapped Marcus so hard across his cheek that his ears rang as though a second roll of thunder had arrived.

"Why did you hurt me?" she demanded, her voice thick with pain and anger.

The rain began, fat drops landing on Marcus's shoulders and quickly dampening his coat.

He thrust a hand through his hair, roughly raking it back from his brow. "You cannot know what a risk it is for me—to be with you." Even as he spoke the words, he could hardly believe he was exposing a truth he'd never uttered aloud before. Not to anyone. "No one has ever wanted me just for me."

Sarah raised her hand again, but she brought her palm to his heart instead.

"I want you for this," she said, pressing firmly, as though marking him with a permanent imprint on his flesh. "And this," she continued, moving her soft palm to his forehead. "You bloody stupid, ridiculous, arrogant ass. I want all of you—and nothing less."

The rain continued to fall, soaking his hair above her small hand, running in rivulets down his face, yet Marcus couldn't move.

"Can you say the same for me?" Sarah's fingers trembled as she gently brushed back a lock of his wet hair.

She gazed into his eyes with heartbreaking honesty and hope—such forgiveness in her deep green eyes. Marcus knew beyond a shadow of a doubt that she spoke the truth.

He stepped up onto the platform. "Sarah." He wrapped his arms about her waist to lift and carry her to a bench tucked toward the back of the gazebo. "I don't have the words," he said as he set her on her feet.

"Then show me."

She half twisted away from him, turning her back. Tucking her chin, she pulled her mass of curls to one side and forward over her breast, the move exposing the row of tiny buttons that ran down her spine.

"Aye." His fingers fumbled with the tiny pearls as one after the other popped free.

Sarah tugged the bodice down over her breasts, slipping her arms free from the sleeves until the gown pooled in a circle of blue silk about her feet, leaving her clad only in her chemise and corset.

She turned to face him and he slid his hands into the silky mass of her auburn hair. He bent to kiss her shoulder and the soft spot where arm met torso and the side of her breast. The taste and scent of her skin sent impatience roaring through him and he unlaced her corset to peel it free and toss it aside.

With matching haste, Sarah reached for the buttons at his waist, her nimble fingers eagerly attacking each one, his cock throbbing under the brush of her fingers.

She pushed his breeches and smalls down his thighs, taking the length of him in one hand while the other closed over the heavy crown.

"Christ Almighty, woman!" Marcus ground out, tearing his coat and waistcoat off.

"Oh!" She looked up at him through her lashes, but her curious hands didn't still. "Is this wrong?"

Marcus groaned as he licked her right breast through the soft, thin chemise. "On the contrary. It's very right."

"Lovely," she breathed.

She released him and pressed hard on his chest, forcefully pushing him back until his shoulders were against a supporting beam.

Then she sank to her knees, her warm breath stroking him as she descended. Marcus's muscles clenched, shivering under the erotic brush of her quick breathing as it skimmed over his skin.

Kneeling at his feet, she pulled off his slippers, tugging first one, then the other free to toss aside. She caught the edges of his breeches and smalls and shoved them the rest of the way to the floor, easing them off over his feet.

She placed her palms on his thighs, careful to avoid his healing wound. She sank back on her heels, her gaze moving slowly upward. Marcus felt the brush of her stare like a brand moving over his skin and when those emerald eyes finally looked into his, he caught his breath.

His lust roared out of control and he reached for her, but she shook her head, stopping him. Her gaze left his, following her stroking hands, totally absorbed in his body. She explored him slowly, her fingers petting, stopping to touch here, caress there, until both settled on his testicles, cupping and squeezing until Marcus groaned aloud, his muscles bunching as he clenched his fists to keep from reaching for her.

She looked up and smiled.

"Are you enjoying yourself?" Marcus ground out, determined to let her have this moment, though his cock throbbed almost painfully with anticipation.

She arched an eyebrow. "Oh, very much so."

Her hands encircled his thick shaft, stroking the sensitive skin until Marcus groaned again and muttered a guttural curse.

His head rolled back and hit the beam, though he failed to notice anything except the feel of her fingers on him.

But when her mouth came down on him, hot and wet, every inch of his body felt the force of it, her lips lightly clasping as her tongue swirled and her teeth ever so slightly tugged.

Marcus sank his hands deep into her hair and held on, gently urging her into a rhythm that made him grit his teeth.

She grabbed his buttocks, her fingernails raking the skin. He had barely enough presence of mind to grab her shoulders.

"For the love of God," he growled. Her mouth left the head of his cock as he pulled her up and into his arms. "Where did you learn such ways to bedevil a man?"

"Claire." She looped her arms around his neck, her fingers threading into his hair as her mouth sought his in a kiss desperate with need.

"Remind me to thank her," Marcus said a moment later, lifting his head before his mouth took hers once again and his tongue ravaged the slick inner surfaces of her sweet mouth.

He walked her backward to the bench and she wrapped her legs around his waist as he laid her down, the cove of her hips rocking against the hard angles of his.

Marcus looked at her, lying beneath him, beautiful in all her unfettered glory. Her skin glowed with arousal, her eyes filled with passion and promise.

"Are you certain? Is this what you truly want?" he asked her, his body clenching against the possibility that she would deny him.

Her hips lifted, pushed, and rocked against him again and she smiled as only Sarah Tisdale could. "I've never been more certain of anything in my life."

"I love you." The words had come of their own accord, but Marcus did not regret for one moment having said them.

Her green eyes flared with fierce emotion, her hands tightening about his arms.

Before she could answer, he shifted, nudging the blunt head of his arousal against her soft core. She gasped, shuddering as he entered her with a slow, steady thrust.

Sarah's breath caught in her throat and Marcus stopped, fearful that he'd caused her pain.

"I know," she whispered.

Mine, he thought for one fierce moment before his lust raged out of control. He partially withdrew before rocking his hips forward, burying himself in her farther with each slow, powerful stroke.

She bucked against him, demanding more.

Marcus breathed in the scent of her skin and hair and the smell of sweat and female arousal. He quickened the pace. She breathed faster, her body arching like a bow beneath his. She strained, desperately reaching for the summit.

And then she cried out, her legs wrapping more tightly about him as she shuddered beneath him.

His hand closed over her thigh and he drove into her with several quick, deep thrusts before he stiffened, the intensity of his climax tearing a deep groan from his throat.

He rolled to the side, taking her with him while still so deeply embedded in her body he couldn't tell where his ended and hers began.

"Trust me—no matter what happens," he whispered into her hair. "Promise me."

Her hands came to rest on his face. "I promise. With all of my heart."

And he believed her.

14

There did not seem to be enough sausage nor coddled eggs in the world to satisfy Sarah's hunger.

"Did you run the length of Lulworth?" her mother queried, referring to the previous night's disappearance—and this morning's appetite. "And truly, all for a case of the vapors? Surely remaining indoors would have been much more prudent."

Marcus had created an alibi, insisting that Sarah memorize the story.

"I simply needed the fresh air—and it was hardly the length, Mother." Sarah buttered her toast and hid a smile. "Lord Weston sent his valet to fetch me from the garden. It was not my fault that the man could not keep up."

"Nor mine that your best dress was ruined, thanks to the rain," Lady Tisdale complained, gesturing for Sarah to pass the strawberry jam. "Really, if only Lord Weston's man would have shown some concern, you would have been fetched straightaway."

Sarah set her toast down and reached for the jam pot. "I'm sure the Almighty is, at this very moment, re-thinking the storm, Mother." She passed the pot then retrieved her toast.

She could not deny that the lovely dress had been ruined, though the rain had little to do with its demise.

Sarah shivered as she remembered just how the creases had been pressed into the blue silk. The soft material wasn't meant to be so carelessly tossed into a heap in the damp night air.

Marcus had cursed under his breath when he buttoned her back into the ruined gown, his deep burr making the vulgarity sound like a delicious invitation.

She'd suggested that next time perhaps her dress should stay on, in the interest of tidiness.

Sarah took a second bite from the toast point and chewed with enthusiasm.

"Well, no matter the storm or the dress, it was kind of Lord Weston to offer you use of his coach," Sarah's father joined in, eyeing his wife before neatly folding the ironed newspaper in half and burying his nose in the stories of the day.

Lady Tisdale reluctantly nodded in agreement.

"Indeed," Sarah chimed in, making a heroic attempt to keep a smile from her face.

How could love find one in the deepest pit of despair one moment, then soaring among the clouds the next?

Nellie, a trusted servant, entered the room and bobbed a quick curtsy in front of Sarah's father. "Beg your pardon, sir, but Lord Weston awaits you in your study. He says he must speak with you at once."

Sarah choked on her toast and half rose from her seat in a rush.

"Gracious, Sarah, do sit down," her mother insisted. "Lord Weston asked for your father, not you. Though I've no idea why the man would be so presumptuous as to call quite so early."

Sarah swallowed the last bite of bread, which had temporarily stuck in her throat. "Really, Mother," she began as she sank back into her seat. "Lord Weston has shown our family nothing but kindness and consideration since returning to Lulworth. Even your dearest friend, Mrs. Rathbone, has examined her heart as regards the man. Can you not do the same?"

Lady Tisdale began to furiously apply jam to her toast. "Really, Sarah, I've no idea what you're referring to. I've not harbored any ill will toward the earl—though, in truth, I suppose we all—"

"Ladies," Sarah's father interrupted. "No need to quarrel. Let us put this behind us, shall we? The man is sitting in my study as we speak."

"Yes, quite," Lady Tisdale agreed, the layer of jam now an inch thick on her toast.

Her father's words caused Sarah's stomach to roll. Was Marcus going to ask her father for her hand? They'd hardly had time to talk of such things last night. She couldn't decide if she was excited or terrified.

Sir Arthur set the folded paper down next to his half-empty plate and rose. "Very well. Don't want to keep Lord Weston waiting," he said cheerfully, giving Sarah a merry wink before walking from the room.

Did her father suspect the same? And for that matter, Sarah continued to speculate, was it possible that her mother did as well?

She turned and narrowed her eyes at her mother, who sat contemplating her shirred eggs.

"Sarah?"

Sarah ignored her mother's query and leaned forward, searching for some small sign—a twitch, perhaps—that would indicate what her mother was thinking.

"Is there something on my face?" Lady Tisdale touched the linen napkin to her lips, the gaze she fixed on Sarah questioning.

"No, Mother." Failing to discern anything useful from her mother's behavior, Sarah turned to stare at the doorway. She picked up her teacup, lifting it to sip, but was suddenly too nervous to do so. She set the cup back into its saucer with a click. Absentmindedly, she turned it this way and that, this way and that, until the sweet brown liquid spilled over the lip and onto her hand.

She hardly noticed.

"Sarah?" her mother said for the second time, though in a far more irritated tone.

Sarah's father appeared in the doorway, worry clearly written on his face. "Where is Nigel?"

Sarah pushed up from her seat, confused. "What does Nigel have to do with—?"

"Your brother, where is he?" Sir Arthur demanded.

"In his room, Father. Why?"

Lady Tisdale dropped her linen napkin next to her place setting on the table. "Really, what is going on here? First Sarah, and now you. Has the whole world gone mad?"

"Lenora, see to it that Nellie packs a bag for Nigel."

Lady Tisdale huffed indignantly and drew herself up, clearly annoyed. "I'll hardly do such a thing without knowing why."

"You will do as I say, Lenora. Now!" Sir Arthur snapped.

His temper was so unlike his usual placid self that Lady Tisdale was speechless. Heart filled with foreboding, Sarah dashed around the dining table to run from the room, desperate to speak with Marcus.

But her father's study was empty. She peered out the window and caught sight of him just outside, as he untied Pokey's reins and lifted himself into the saddle.

Sarah turned to run for the foyer, catching her hip on the edge of her father's desk and falling hard.

She picked herself up, ignoring the pain as she threw the entry door open wide and raced down the steps.

"Stop!" Sarah called, startling the big chestnut as she darted around him to catch the stirrup.

Marcus looked down at her, his face grim.

"Please, tell me," she pleaded, searching his face for answers. "Why is my father sending Nigel away?"

Marcus captured her hand with his and held tight. "Do you remember what I asked of you—that you would trust me, no matter what?"

"I do."

"Remember your promise." Marcus released her hand then took up the reins and urged the Thorough-bred into a gallop.

And he was gone.

It had gone well enough, considering all that could have transpired.

Marcus's conversation with Carmichael, precisely two hours past the most extraordinary sexual experience of his life, had not set well.

Not at all.

Carmichael had judiciously avoided any probing into the nature of Marcus's time in the gazebo.

Marcus slowed Pokey to a trot, hardly anxious to return to the castle. He wanted whatever happened between them to be about only the two of them. Not the Young Corinthians. Not the smugglers. Not his family nor Sarah's. Whatever the outcome, Marcus needed to know that he'd been true to his heart and hers.

He looked out over the cove, the throaty bark of a gray seal carrying on the wind.

She'd made it so simple for him. There'd been no blame, no conditions—just one surprisingly powerful slap and all was forgiven.

Marcus fingered his cheek where her hand had been, heat spreading as he thought about other parts of his body those hands had touched with sensual abandon.

Sarah hid nothing—apologized for nothing—demanding that he match her willingness and give himself over completely. And for the first time in his life, Marcus felt he could do so. She gave him courage in a way he'd hardly known he was lacking.

He'd executed his work with the Young Corinthians with ease and skill, never questioning his ability to face dangerous situations. But what Sarah offered required that he give of himself—not his skill nor his valor, but his heart and his soul.

Nothing less.

She made him believe he could do anything.

Ahead of him, Lulworth Castle came into view. Pokey nickered and trotted a bit faster.

Marcus hoped that he had inspired in Sarah the ability to do the same.

She'd kept her composure earlier, though he'd given her very little opportunity to do otherwise, he reflected. He suspected that, at this very moment, she was none too happy with him. But he'd known that a quick retreat would be wise. Sir Arthur would explain the situation and, though fabricated, the story would hopefully satisfy Sarah—at least for the time being.

Carmichael had insisted that the boy be brought to Lulworth Castle, as much for his own safety as for questioning. The constable would be blamed for requiring his confinement, thereby preserving the anonymity of the Corinthians and Marcus's involvement with them, including Carmichael's cover.

They'd wasted enough time as it was, Carmichael had stated in his famously taciturn way. He hadn't blamed Marcus directly for the investigation's lack of progress, but he hadn't needed to. Marcus knew the truth of it already. His feelings for Sarah were getting in the way. Which would only put Nigel in more danger. Marcus would sort out his involvement in the Corinthians once the boy was safe and the smugglers captured, but not before.

Sarah would have to be patient, he realized. Hardly an easy task for the woman, but she'd promised. And Marcus felt sure—more sure than ever before in his life—that she'd not let him down.

He pushed Pokey into a fast canter. It would hardly do to have Sully and the boy reach Lulworth before he did.

"Outrageous!"

Sarah very nearly rolled her eyes at Mr. Dixon's outburst, but she discovered she had neither the interest nor the energy to do so.

The man stood near the mantel, drinking her father's brandy and acting as though he owned Tisdale Manor—and everyone within its walls.

Sarah's mother moaned with dramatic flair. "That is precisely what I said." She fidgeted with a tassel on the needlepoint pillow in her lap. "My poor boy," she wailed. "Taken from the bosom of his family—"

"It is for his own safety," Sarah's father interrupted.

Mr. Dixon set his glass on the stone mantel and clasped his hands behind his back, rocking on his heels with self-importance. "That may be, but has anything been proven?"

"There's speculation that the boys stole from the smugglers," Sir Arthur answered, taking a slow sip from his glass. "Surely you've heard it. The entire village can speak of nothing else."

Lady Tisdale moaned again and covered her eyes with her lace handkerchief.

"Mother, we've already discussed the likelihood of Nigel's involvement in such a crime, whether knowingly or not."

"Yes, but is it really necessary for them to take him away?"

Sarah had wondered the same thing, though she was hardly going to feed her mother's melodramatic tendencies at this point by appearing to be in agreement. Marcus had asked her to keep her promise. And she would.

"I will go to Lulworth Castle at once and confirm the boy's comfort," Mr. Dixon decreed, giving Lady Tisdale a reassuring look before he turned to Sarah and rested a comforting hand on her shoulder.

Sarah recoiled, covering her instinctive revulsion by turning to her father, the move allowing her to slip out from beneath the man's touch. "Father, do you truly think this is wise?"

"I have Lord Weston's word that Nigel will be treated with the utmost kindness, which is enough for me," Sir Arthur replied with a firm nod.

Lady Tisdale burst into tears.

"That being said," Sir Arthur continued, "if you wish to call upon Lord Weston for your own assurance, Dixon, I can hardly stop you."

Mr. Dixon nodded condescendingly. "I would consider it an honor to look after the interests of your family."

He walked at once to the doorway, bowed low, and was off.

"I must admit," Lady Tisdale began, wiping delicately at her eyes, "Mr. Dixon's eagerness to aid us at such a time is of great comfort." She dropped the pillow on the settee and moved slowly toward the door, her body drooping disconsolately. "I believe I will lie down."

"Rest well, my dear," her husband offered. When his wife disappeared through the doorway, he slumped back into his chair.

"Father." Sarah rose and crossed to Sir Arthur, kneeling on the floor next to his chair, her skirts a pool of sprigged yellow muslin against the blue wool carpet. "Mr. Dixon can hardly be trusted to look after anyone's interests but his own. He'll only get in the way."

Sir Arthur sighed, his gaze troubled as he laid a hand on Sarah's cheek. "As I said before, I cannot control

Dixon. But if I know Lord Weston, he won't let the man interfere."

"But Father—"

"Sarah," he interrupted, his tone weary, "this is far more serious than any of us would like to admit. Please, do not question me further. When I have news of Nigel I will tell you. Until then, we wait."

Sarah nodded, covering his hand with hers.

The last thing she was about to do was wait.

15

Sarah watched Mr. Dixon's carriage trundle down the drive of Lulworth Castle before leaving her hiding place to approach the portico.

She rapped the carved knocker against the heavy oak panel and waited, Titus and Bones close behind.

A liveried servant opened the door and peered out at Sarah. "Yes?" he asked impatiently.

"Miss Sarah Tisdale to see Lord Weston," Sarah said succinctly, moving to step inside.

"I'm sorry," the man said in a clipped tone, barring her way. "Lord Weston is not available at the moment."

Sarah stepped back. "I'm certain if you tell him my name, he will make himself available."

"I have been told that Lord Weston is not available to see *anyone*, which it seems to me would include you, Miss Tisdale."

Titus growled low in his throat.

Sarah had half a mind to release the big dog on the obnoxious man.

If he wasn't lying, then Marcus meant to keep her from Nigel.

None of this made sense. "I'm sure we could clear this up if you would only let me in—"

"No," the servant said with finality, and shut the door in Sarah's face.

Sarah turned on her heels.

"Bugger!"

Both Titus and Bones barked loudly at the vulgarity.

"I promised to trust him."

Growling ensued.

She felt just as the dogs sounded.

If she could only speak with Marcus and make him understand. Sarah fully supported the constable's need to not only question Nigel further, but protect him from the very real danger. If Marcus heard these words from her lips, Sarah felt sure he'd allow her entry.

She could be useful, after all. It was true that her attempts to ferret out Nigel's involvement in the smuggling scheme up until this point had proven fruitless, but she'd hardly pressed the point, confident that in time her brother would reveal all. She'd made a mistake waiting, that was clear to her now.

Her father's words echoed in her ears: "This is far more serious than any of us would like to admit."

Sarah looked at the circular driveway, then down the long, straight, graveled path that would take her home. "Come along, boys," she said to the dogs. She lifted her skirts and picked her way down the steps, then took a sharp turn toward the back of the castle.

Marcus sat across from Nigel in the nearly bare room. All excess furnishings and adornments had been removed, leaving only two simple chairs and a small wooden table in the corner.

"Thirsty?" Marcus asked the boy, who looked ready to cry.

Nigel nodded, his eyes remaining fixed on the floor.

Marcus stood up and crossed the room to a porcelain pitcher on the table. He poured a cup of watered wine and returned to where the boy sat, slumped in the straight-backed wooden chair.

He handed the cup to Nigel and took his own seat once more.

Marcus knew the boy was near collapse.

The constable had gone after him like a dog with a bone. Tears had filled the boy's eyes when he was told his family was in danger.

Pringle had grimly related the grisly details of just how Jasper and Clive had left this cruel world, their necks wrenched until their heads nearly fell from their bodies.

The constable had even threatened to give Nigel over to the smugglers and be done with him if he didn't tell them all that he knew.

Marcus would never have guessed that Pringle had it in him, his wiry frame humming with angry energy as he relentlessly questioned the boy.

Just as surprising was Nigel's response. Though visibly shaken, he had endured Pringle's onslaught with a strength Marcus suspected few twelve-year-olds possessed.

He was, after all, Sarah's brother.

Sarah, Marcus thought as he watched Nigel take a drink.

He'd known she would come, though he hadn't guessed she'd arrive right on the heels of Dixon.

The man had protested loudly when he'd been refused entry to the castle. Everyone in the room had paused when the sound of Dixon's outraged, angry bellowing reached the small room on the third floor.

Pringle had even used Dixon's outburst to his advantage, telling Nigel that the smugglers had come for him. The boy had begun to shake with terror, but still, he'd remained silent.

Marcus glanced at Nigel, who'd drained his cup of weak wine and resumed staring at the floor.

Marcus gritted his teeth until it felt as though his jaw would break. Interrogation was, in essence, upending the balance of power through physical and mental manipulation.

Marcus had never thought twice about using such tactics on hardened criminals.

But Nigel was not a hardened criminal. He was a child—and even more, the brother of the woman Marcus loved.

The pain in his jaw spread to his temples, a gnawing headache threatening to take over.

Marcus was glad that Sarah would be nowhere near Lulworth Castle when he finally broke Nigel.

He wished to hell he was anywhere else but here himself, with anything else to do but this.

Pringle had prepared Nigel, and now it was up to Marcus to finish the job.

It could be done slowly—certainly easier on the suspect. Or quickly—which, depending on how one looked at it, could be considered a kindness in its own way.

Marcus was out of time, which, in his experience, had a way of making things clear.

He stood and stretched, preparing for what he must do.

A swift and well-executed break was considered a badge of honor within the Corinthians.

Marcus had to wonder whether any of his fellow agents had been asked to apply such skills to a twelve-year-old boy.

He scrubbed a hand roughly down his face, took a deep breath, and savagely knocked the cup from the boy's hands.

Nigel's head shot up, his eyes wild with fear.

"I'm done indulging you, Nigel." Marcus purposely injected a menacing note in his voice, raised his foot to the rung of Nigel's chair, and shoved.

Nigel gripped the sides of the chair as it skittered across the floor and crashed into the opposing wall.

Marcus had calculated the move in order to ensure that he'd not do any real harm to the boy.

But he'd clearly scared him; Nigel jumped up and raced to the table in the corner.

"The table will afford you no protection from me." Marcus stalked across the room to reach the boy cowering in the corner.

He paused, the sight of Nigel shivering with alarm making his gut clench.

Nigel needed for this to end.

As did Marcus.

In one swift move he grasped the table and threw it across the room, the wood fracturing into several pieces and sending the pitcher crashing to the floor.

"I didn't know what Jasper and Clive had stolen until it was too late—I swear. You have to believe me!" Nigel cried, sliding down the length of the wall and pulling his legs in to rest on his chest.

Marcus let out a rough breath and turned, freezing as he caught sight of the open door.

Sarah stood in the doorway, her face bone-white beneath the red of her hair.

"How did you get in here?" Marcus demanded.

"Sarah!" Nigel screamed, scrambling up from the floor and running to his sister.

Sarah met him halfway. She wound her arms tightly around the boy and pinned Marcus with eyes bright with tears and betrayal. "You said I could trust you."

Two Corinthians burst through the door. "Lord Weston—"

"Would someone please tell me how this woman gained entry to my home?"

"She bribed the scullery maid," one answered.

"I did not bribe Emily," Sarah ground out. "I simply asked after her sickly brother William and one thing led to another."

The two agents looked abashed.

And Marcus was ready to knock their heads together.

"Well, at least now I know why you refused me entry." Sarah gripped Nigel tighter. "You didn't want anyone to see you torture an innocent child."

"Now, wait just a bloody minute, woman," Marcus began grimly.

"Weston," Carmichael called from the doorway, his tone as calm as ever despite the tense situation.

"What?" Marcus snarled.

Carmichael leaned against the doorjamb, surveying the room. "I believe you need to speak with Miss Tisdale—alone."

He pushed away from the door and walked to where Sarah and Nigel stood. "Come now," he said gently to Nigel. "We'll see if Cook has something for you."

"No," Sarah protested, her arms tightening around Nigel.

"Miss Tisdale, you have my word that your brother is safe," Carmichael told her, his gaze meeting hers with direct honesty.

She stared at him, her expression reflecting her indecision until Nigel straightened, glancing up at Carmichael. Something about the older man's gaze must have reassured him, for Nigel released her, squaring his shoulders as he turned.

"It's all right, Sarah," he said with barely a tremor in his voice. "I'm hungry."

Sarah hesitated, clearly torn, but Nigel eased out of her grip and moved to stand by Carmichael.

"Pattinson, Stewart," Carmichael said over his shoulder to the two agents. "I've need of you below-stairs."

The agents snapped to attention and followed Carmichael and Nigel out into the hallway, shutting the door behind them.

"How could you?" Sarah's hands were curled into

fists at her side, her entire body stiff with anger. "If I had a gun, I'd shoot you."

"I've no doubt you would."

Her soft lips compressed into a thin line. "Explain this." One arm lifted in a jerky motion, indicating the room about them.

Marcus flexed his fingers. "Do we have to do this?"

"You assaulted my brother." Her voice rose, threaded with outrage. "So yes, I demand an explanation."

"God, woman," Marcus snarled, gripping the smooth wood of the chair next to him. "Why will you Tisdales not do what is best for you? If you'd just do as you're told—"

"Do as I'm told?" she ground out in disbelief.

"Yes, do as you're told." He shoved the chair, sending it skittering away across the floor, and thrust his fingers through his hair, raking the blond strands off his brow in frustration. "How am I to keep you safe otherwise?"

The chair slammed into the wall and broke.

Sarah stared at the splintered wood, and then at Marcus, who had moved to the window, his back to her. "What is going on?"

"The men that Nigel and his friends worked for . . ." He yanked at his knotted cravat, loosening the linen around his neck. "They're not your commonplace smugglers. They've direct ties to Napoleon. And the jewel those boys stole was meant for him."

Sarah's knees went weak and she backed up to the wall, leaning on it for support. So many questions filled her head that she hardly knew where to begin. "How do you know such things?" she whispered.

"I'm not your commonplace earl," he said grimly.

"A smuggler, then?" Sarah asked in disbelief, the very notion sounding ridiculous the moment the words left her mouth.

He leaned the point of one shoulder against the wall, crossing his arms over his chest. "Hardly, though there are times I wish it were that simple."

With sudden impatience, he pushed away from the wall, gesturing for her to come to him.

Sarah thought to deny him, but the agony in his eyes was too much for her to bear. She walked slowly nearer, slipping her hand into his outstretched palm.

"I am part of a group that works for Whitehall—a group that specializes in cases such as these."

"You're a spy?" Sarah asked, her pulse quickening.

"Of sorts, yes," he confirmed. "It's hardly what you're likely thinking, though—not the sort of thing you'd find in a Drury Lane melodrama."

Sarah's mind raced. "Were you sent to Lulworth expressly because of this treasure? Did you know of Nigel's involvement before you came? Is your wound real?" she asked, brushing her knee against his leg where she approximated the injury to be.

"Ow, dammit, woman." Marcus growled, wincing as he shifted his leg out of her reach. "Yes, the wound is real, and that's all I'm going to tell you. It's all I *can* tell you."

"Why?" she pressed.

"Have you heard nothing I've said?" he demanded. "The less you know, the safer you are."

Sarah squared her shoulders and frowned at him. "Have I not kept up with you thus far?"

"No, you have not," he replied sardonically. "Look at you, your dress is torn in three places and you've bits of greenery in your hair."

"But I made it into Lulworth Castle, all the same," she countered.

Marcus stalked back to the window. "You have to trust me. Just as I needed you to leave Nigel to me, I need you to let this lie."

"So you weren't intending to harm Nigel?"

"No. The boy was close to telling us everything after the constable's questions. He required a small push, that was all."

Sarah followed him, slipping her arms around his waist, her cheek against his coat just below his right shoulder blade. "But I can be of use."

"Not if you're dead," he said in a desperate tone, turning and crushing Sarah to his chest.

"Marcus," Sarah responded, going up on tiptoe to gently turn his face to hers so she could kiss him.

He needed no encouragement to deepen the kiss, his tongue pushing into her mouth to claim hers. "I love you, Sarah." He lifted his head to look down at her, searching her eyes with his own. "If I lost you . . ."

Sarah wanted to tell him that he didn't have to do this alone. That she'd learned to trust him and he could do the same with her.

But she sensed he simply could not hear such words from her now.

"I'll do as I'm told," she said quietly, burying her face against the warm comfort of his broad chest.

She would try.

"Where is Miss Tisdale?"

Marcus stalked into the billiards room and dropped into an armchair upholstered in deep brown leather. He propped his feet on the matching ottoman and crossed his ankles before answering. "Safely at home with two Corinthians to watch over her and her family."

Carmichael nodded his approval, and then took aim at a ball. "Not Pattinson and Stewart, I hope."

Marcus smiled. "I wouldn't be too hard on them. Sarah is a force to be reckoned with."

"That, Weston—" Carmichael paused, expertly wielding his billiard cue, "—is an understatement."

Marcus heard the cue tip crack against the ball before the sphere heavily rolled across the table. "Well done."

"Hmmph," Carmichael grunted in satisfaction, then returned the cue to its slot in the carved holder against the paneled wall. "How much did you tell her?"

"Enough to keep her safe," Marcus replied, resting his head against the back of the chair and closing his eyes.

Carmichael perched on the arm of the heavy, masculine leather chair opposite. "I was under the impression that there wasn't enough information in the world to guarantee such a thing."

Marcus purposely kept his eyes closed. "We've reached an understanding," he answered, making it clear that he had nothing more to say on the topic.

"I'm not one to pry—"

"Carmichael," Marcus interrupted. "Don't forget that I've seen you in action. Clairemont, Marlowe—"

"Marlowe did not follow my advice and look where that got him."

Marcus nodded. "All right, I'll give you Marlowe, but you can hardly deny your meddling handiwork with Clairemont."

"I simply advised the man, nothing more."

Marcus opened his lids far enough to give Carmichael a disbelieving, narrow-eyed stare. "Yes, well, be that as it may, they are now married."

"Happily married, mind you," Carmichael added. "And besides, who said anything about marriage? I'm hardly prepared to lose another agent to a marital union."

Marcus dropped his feet to the floor and sat up straighter. "You don't fool me for a minute, Carmichael. You're like the gander to all of us goslings—"

"I'm fairly certain that the gander, if given the chance, kills his young," Carmichael said mildly.

Marcus muttered a pithy oath. "Nor will you throw me off with wit." He pointed an accusing finger at his superior. "I'll not be led astray—or be shown the path. Whatever it is you do."

"Well, you clearly feel quite strongly about all of this," Carmichael replied affably, folding his arms over his dark blue waistcoat.

"I do." And he did, Marcus realized with surprise. "Tell me," he said with an abrupt change of subject, "did you make any progress with Nigel?"

Carmichael nodded. "The boy knew nothing of the theft until after Jasper's death. That's when Clive told him about their scheme, but by then it was too late. Nigel was in possession of the emerald—which we already knew, of course—and it's currently locked away in your study. He'd planned on using it to arrange a meeting with Charles and the others."

"What for?"

"The opportunity to avenge his friends."

Marcus scratched at the morning stubble on his cheek. "The arrogance of youth."

"To be sure," Carmichael answered. "They've killed two boys, what would one more be to them? Besides, they need to ensure that no one knows the truth behind the treasure—at least not until it's in Napoleon's hands."

"And the local tie to the French?"

Carmichael sighed. "Nothing. Nigel claims he never saw anyone outside of the regulars—and the three Frenchmen, of course." He stood and stretched, yawning. "I'm to return to London in the morning."

"Shorthanded, are we?"

Carmichael pulled on the gold chain of his pocket watch and peered at the time. "Yes, actually. But there's also been another burglary—or attempted burglary, I should say. We intercepted the emerald, though the thief killed himself before we could question him."

"I'll have Marlowe begin negotiations with Charles and see if I can't make a bit of progress on the local front," Marcus said.

"You'll have a time of it repairing things with the boy," Carmichael added, turning toward the door. "But it's important that you do so."

Marcus closed his eyes and leaned his head against the padded backing of the chair once more. "You're not one to pry, remember?"

"I remember everything, Weston."

16

"This, I could become accustomed to," Marlowe declared, eyeing the female residents of Lulworth as they danced, sang, and drank their way through the Michelmas Fair.

Marcus sighed wearily. "Yes, I imagine you could, but let's focus on the task at hand, shall we?"

"And I'd been told you were by far the merriest of the Corinthians," Marlowe answered with mock disappointment. "Rusticating in the country has had a most disagreeable effect on you."

Two colorfully dressed jesters stopped to juggle a series of plates next to them, drawing a burst of applause from the surrounding onlookers. Marlowe eyed them with a narrowed glare and they quickly disappeared into the boisterous crowd.

"Was Charles difficult to find?" Marcus asked.

"Not at all. Holed up in the Boot as if he'd been told to do so, which—" Marlowe paused, taking a pint from a serving wench "—I suppose he was." He pulled a coin from his pocket and tossed it, winking when she deftly caught it and slipped it into her bodice.

Marcus shook his head, refusing the woman's offer of ale. "And the fair—was that his idea?"

"He insisted. I'd hardly arrange an exchange in the middle of a crowd."

As a general rule, Marcus didn't mind crowds. Experience told him the throng often made it easier to shield oneself from detection. But he had much more than himself to be concerned with today. The emerald sat nestled in an inner pocket of his waistcoat.

And the Tisdales were in attendance as well.

His first inclination, upon hearing of Charles's demand to meet at the fair, was to lock the whole lot of them up in Lulworth Castle.

But he could not be in two places at once.

And so they'd accompanied him, Lady Tisdale flitting about, talking with one friend and then another. Sir Arthur sat at a table brought out for the festivities, slowly sipping at his pint while Dixon spoke to him. Sully stood close by, conversing with a handful of farmers, though he'd been instructed to keep a close watch on the family.

Sarah had heartily agreed when Marcus had insisted she not tell her parents of the Corinthians' involvement. She feared the knowledge would only upset her father further—and allow her mother yet more opportunities to sigh, moan, cry, and faint—something that Marcus readily agreed was a valid concern.

Counting himself and Marlowe, that meant only two agents plus Sully to complete the exchange and see to Nigel and Sarah's safety. Not the numbers Marcus would have preferred, but hopefully enough to ensure an uneventful exchange.

A battered fishing boat manned by agents Pattinson and Stewart, with two local ruffians along, lay in wait for the smugglers near the entry to the cove.

"The grimace does not become you, Weston."

Marcus elbowed Marlowe low in the ribs. "Go. I want to know exactly when Charles arrives and who's with him when he does."

Marlowe swept an exaggerated bow and sauntered off, twirling a woman in his arms as he passed, then heading for the pie-maker's stand.

Marcus couldn't quell the unease roiling in his gut. He would feel more comfortable when the exchange was complete and Sarah was out of danger. Still, he knew life wouldn't return to normal—at least, not the normal that he had known before he met her.

Leaning against the side of a booth, he watched Sarah attempt to coax her brother into dancing with her around the maypole. She'd succeeded in getting him to hold a length of red ribbon in his hand, but hadn't yet managed to actually convince the boy to move.

Marcus had no doubt she would succeed in winning him over, and no sooner had the thought crossed his mind than Nigel begrudgingly shuffled his feet. He slowly followed Sarah around the pole, a small smile of amusement lighting his features.

Apparently Sarah had the same power over her brother as she did Marcus. "A force to be reckoned with," Marcus had called her when speaking with Carmichael.

And she was.

He smiled as she bobbed and weaved with her purple ribbon in the fading sun.

He was so unbelievably grateful to have her on his side.

He was a lucky man indeed.

The dancers slowed as the fiddler finished, laughter filling the air about them, while the villagers who'd been unable to wrap the pole precisely struggled with their ribbons.

Sarah gave Nigel a loving pat on the head before untangling him.

Marcus was glad to see that the dancing seemed to have done some good for the boy. His demeanor was visibly more relaxed as Sarah took him by the hand and led him away from the pole.

Dixon, who'd left his position with Sir Arthur and

made his way toward Sarah and Nigel, approached from behind and lightly tapped Sarah on the shoulder.

Marcus stiffened and pushed away from the booth wall. He caught Sully's attention then looked to where the Tisdales sat, signaling for the valet to stay close to the two.

Dixon took Sarah by the arm and forced her to walk with him toward the edge of the clearing.

Dammit. Marcus hardly relished leaving Nigel, but hoped that his dealings with Dixon would be over quickly.

Marcus moved faster as he shoved his way through the crowd, breaking into a run. Ahead of him, Dixon and Sarah walked into the shade of the woods.

He ran after them, bounding into the underbrush.

"Stop right there," Marcus called out to the two.

Dixon's stride slowed as Sarah dug in her heels and refused to go any farther.

The man swung around, still holding tight to Sarah's arm. "Weston," he said with irritation, his words clipped. "What do you mean by this intrusion?"

"Surely, even in Lulworth, forcing a woman into the woods is not acceptable courting practice?" Marcus countered, flicking a quick glance at Sarah.

She appeared slightly alarmed, though mostly annoyed.

Marcus gave her a faint reassuring nod, then looked pointedly at Dixon. "Let Miss Tisdale go."

"I was merely anxious to discuss the situation concerning her brother." Dixon's eyes gleamed with impatience.

"I'm well aware of the situation." Marcus's mind raced, swiftly considering and discarding options for removing Sarah to safety. The man hadn't eased his grip on her arm; Marcus fought down the urge to attack and force Dixon to release her; Sarah's safety was paramount.

"Well, of course you are, Weston," Dixon continued in an irate tone. "After all, it is, in part, because of you that the poor boy was held captive for no apparent reason, leaving his family to wonder whether they would ever see him again."

"I'm afraid I have little patience to continue this conversation in Miss Tisdale's presence, Dixon. Release her."

"Not just yet," Marlowe's familiar voice called.

Marcus shifted slightly, enabling him to keep track of Dixon while looking toward the clearing.

He was surprised to see Marlowe walking toward them, with Nigel and a large, brutish man following closely behind.

"Hardly ideal timing, Marlowe, but it will have to do," Marcus replied, turning back to fully face Dixon.

"Sorry, my friend," Marlowe said sardonically, walking past Marcus to where Dixon stood. Nigel and the other man, presumably Charles, followed him.

Marcus turned back to Dixon.

"Nigel, take your sister—"

In an unexpected move, Marlowe attacked Dixon, landing a savage kick to his midsection. The man swayed and Marlowe lashed out again. Dixon hit the ground hard and was rendered senseless.

Marlowe stealthily snatched Sarah and spun her around so that her back was tight against his chest. One hand wrapped around her waist to hold her immobile.

With his other hand, he plucked a gun from the waistband of his breeches and held the weapon to her temple.

"Marlowe," Marcus said calmly, though his blood ran cold. "Oddly enough, I do not remember discussing this portion of the plan."

"No, you wouldn't." Marlowe tightened his grip and Sarah stiffened as the gun's barrel touched her skin. "Give the emerald to Charles, Weston."

The brute grabbed Nigel and shoved him, causing him to stumble and land against the trunk of a large oak tree.

"No!" Sarah screamed in protest, struggling to free herself from Marlowe's grip.

"That wasn't part of the plan, either," Marlowe said with a grimace.

"And if I agree to hand over the jewel?" Marcus asked, commanding Marlowe's attention.

"Oh, that's the fun part," Marlowe said, his faint smile sardonic. "You'll have to choose between the two. The boy or the woman—one goes with us, and the other stays."

Marcus wanted to kill the man with his bare hands.

Then kill himself for allowing such a situation to occur.

But blind rage would not prove helpful now.

"Come, Marlowe, that's hardly fair," Marcus said, somehow managing to keep his voice casual and light.

Marlowe squeezed Sarah's waist, forcing a cry from her throat. "You forget that I'm well aware of what sent Carmichael scurrying back to London. He's in possession of the seventh emerald." He gave a little shrug. "I somehow doubt you'll be inclined to hand it over without the proper inducement."

"I see. So, assuming that I choose one, how am I assured that the other will be returned safely?"

Marlowe smiled, his amusement palpable. "You're not. But come now, Weston, there's no reason this needs to turn ugly. It's simple enough. Choose."

"I'll go," Sarah got out, her voice quavering with emotion.

"No, Sarah!" Nigel protested. Charles planted a beefy

hand in Nigel's back and pressed him harder against the rough tree bark. The boy cried out in pain but continued to struggle.

Marcus weighed his options. From his training Marcus knew he could not save both Tisdales, and the emerald. One wrong move and Sarah would be dead, with Nigel's head bashed in for good measure.

If he'd not lost possession of at least one, then perhaps. If Marlowe had not surprised him with his traitorous act, maybe. But all of the ifs in the world would do no good now.

Carmichael had called him an exceptional agent. But even the most extraordinary of spies could do nothing against these odds.

He'd sacrifice now, and then wait for the opportunity to strike. The very thought sickened him, but he had no other choice. If he could manage to get close enough to Marlowe, there was some small chance that he could use the knife stowed away in his boot to wound the man— perhaps enough to slow him down.

But he'd still have to decide between the woman he loved and the boy who was inexorably tied to her happiness—and, in turn, his happiness.

He gave Nigel one last look, nodding at the boy with conviction.

"I've your word that the boy will not be harmed?" he asked in a collected tone.

Marlowe smiled, then squeezed Sarah tightly about the waist. "As much as it's worth, Weston, yes. You have my word."

"Give me Miss Tisdale." He reached into his coat pocket and pulled out the muslin pouch that contained the emerald. "And I'll give you the jewel," he told Marlowe, moving forward slowly.

"Stop right there," Marlowe demanded loudly, causing Sarah to flinch from the force of his words. "First, I'll ask you to rid yourself of the knife in your boot."

Marcus swore under his breath as he bent to retrieve the blade.

"Now toss it into the bushes, if you'd be so kind," Marlowe continued, his eyes expertly trained on Marcus's hand. "And, in case you've not taken note before, I've the reflexes of a cat. The woman would suffer a blade to the face at the very least—a bullet to the head at the most."

Marcus paused, weighing Marlowe's words with care. Though he'd not watched the man closely enough over the last weeks to know whether he spoke the truth, he would hardly think to question the statement with Sarah's life hanging in the balance.

He savagely threw the knife to his left without taking his eyes from Marlowe and Sarah, the sound of the blade piercing a tree trunk making Marlowe smile.

Dixon groaned and made to get up. Marlowe kicked him in the stomach twice and the man fell silent.

"Now toss the emerald to me."

Marcus obliged. The small pouch sailed through air, passing Sarah as Marlowe shoved her away then leveled the pistol at Marcus.

Sarah lost her balance and pitched forward. Marcus caught her and pulled her close.

"No!" she screamed, twisting in his hold as she tried desperately to reach Nigel.

But Charles had already dragged Sarah's brother with him deeper into the woods, the two disappearing beyond the thick of the trees.

"Wise choice," Marlowe commented, testing the weight of the emerald in his hand with a slight toss. He pointed the pistol directly at them. "And I wouldn't follow if I were you. Two boys have been killed—it would hardly be an inconvenience for my associate to take care of a third."

Sarah lashed out at the man, struggling to free herself from Marcus's arms in an attempt to launch herself at Marlowe.

Marcus tightened his grip around her waist and held on, murmuring in her ear as Marlowe backed away, then turned and vanished.

"Are you going to kill me?" Nigel asked as another swell of cold salt water washed over the side of the small wooden boat.

A seagull cried overhead, accompanying the boat as it bobbed along.

The man Weston had called Marlowe looked down at him, his face unconcerned. "Come now, boy, don't look so glum. There's always hope."

Charles rowed toward St. Aldhelm's Isle, his large, muscled arms flexing with each stroke.

Nigel and his friends had heard often enough of the island being used by smugglers. The ghost stories told for generations had successfully kept away any curious customs officials and the like.

The three friends had planned a trip to the island at the end of the summer. Nigel had wanted nothing more than to set foot on the beach and claim it for his own.

But now there was nothing he wanted less than to touch its rock-hewn beaches. The island's bulk loomed ahead of them, a blacker outline against the night, ominous and no longer fascinating.

"You'll kill me even if you get the last emerald, won't you?" he pressed, a sudden eerie calm settling over him.

"Shut up with ya," Charles spat, sweat dripping down his ruddy face. His huge muscles bulged, flexing and straining below his sleeveless leather jerkin.

Marlowe nudged the boy with his knee. "Remember, boy, there's always hope."

Charles began to sing in time to the swells:

In Scarlet town where I was born,
There was a fair maid dwellin' . . .

Nigel knew the song well. He'd sung it often enough with Jasper and Clive as they'd gone about their odd jobs for Charles and his men. It seemed almost perverse that Charles would choose the tune at such a time, but oddly enough it comforted Nigel.

He sent his man in to her then
To the town where she was dwellin' . . .

Marlowe nudged Nigel a second time. "Come now, boy, sing along." Nigel did as he was told, his voice low, near a whisper. Marlowe sang out as if every last creature in the ocean was listening, his voice strong and deep.

So slowly, slowly rose she up,
And slowly she came nigh him . . .

Nigel's voice grew louder, until the seagull squawked with disgust. But Nigel hardly cared. He feared if he stopped singing, he'd be unable to hold back the tears that clogged his throat.

When he was dead and laid in the grave,
She heard the death bell knelling.

The three ended with great gusto and Marlowe threw his arm about Nigel as the last line grew to a crescendo and then faded away.

" 'Tis a pity we'll have to kill him, the boy has a good enough voice," Charles said with a tinge of regret, starting in on "Old Maid in the Garrett."

Nigel willed himself not to cry, holding fast to the strange nothingness that had plagued him off and on since Jasper's and Clive's deaths.

Nothingness, it seemed, was preferable to fearing for one's life.

"Hope, boy. There's always hope," Marlowe repeated before joining Charles in song.

Sarah watched as Marcus closed her parents' carriage door then conferred with the driver. A short conversation ensued between the two and the driver climbed atop his perch.

Marcus made his way to where Sarah stood fidgeting with the ribbons on her straw bonnet.

"How did you explain Nigel's absence?" she asked, attempting to smile assuredly at her mother, who stared after the two.

Marcus looked to where they'd emerged from the forest minutes before. "I lied. They believe he's with Stewart and Pattinson."

Sarah nodded, trying desperately to control her emotions. "Why did you choose Nigel?"

Marcus scrubbed a hand over his face, his chin rough with beard stubble beneath his palm. "Sarah, there is no point in discussing this further."

Sully appeared just over the hill alone, walking at a brisk pace.

"Where is Dixon?" Marcus demanded, his voice eerily calm.

The valet cleared his throat. "Gone by the time I arrived—must have woken up and made a run for it."

"Accompany the Tisdales home. I'll go back and try to find him," Marcus said tersely.

"I'll just fetch my horse, then," Sully said plainly. "We'll need to be off—"

"I'm well aware of the time. Go now. I'll send Sarah over straightaway," Marcus interrupted brusquely.

"There is every point in discussing this," she said once Sully had gone, her voice growing frantic.

Marcus flexed his fingers then drew them into fists. "Because I could not bear for them to take you. There, is that what you wanted to hear?"

Sarah caught her breath, her lungs suddenly unable to draw air. "I'm sorry." She reached for him, then realized she could not touch him as she wanted to—not here. "I didn't think beyond the shock of the moment. Of course the choice must have been impossible for you."

He bowed. Readying to take his leave, he pressed a kiss to the soft skin on the inside of her wrist where her pulse beat with frantic haste. "Please, Sarah, don't apologize. I should have protected you both."

"You could not have known that Marlowe was a traitor," she replied softly.

"I should have sensed something was amiss," he said darkly, his face grim.

"I'll not let you blame yourself for this," she said simply.

Marcus pressed one last lingering kiss on the warm skin. "Well, that's hardly of concern at this point. My first priority is to retrieve Nigel."

"Will we go right away, then—rather than wait for the last stone? We should speak with Thomas at the Boot first, as he deals in smuggled—"

Marcus pinned Sarah with a deadly serious stare. "Let me make this perfectly clear: There is no 'we' as concerns Nigel now."

"You cannot possibly expect me to sit at home sewing while my brother is missing," Sarah protested.

His nostrils flared as though preparing to emit flames.

"You've advised me to begin with Thomas, which I will do. Your place is with your parents now."

"Bollocks!" she whispered vehemently. "You want me safe and sound, locked up tight where—"

"It's enough that Nigel's been taken," he asserted ferociously, his jaw clenching with the effort. "So yes, I want you where no harm will come to you. I cannot do what needs to be done unless I know you're safe."

The hard cast of his features brooked no argument, no appeal. "You will remain at Tisdale Manor while I go in search of Nigel—wherever the hell Marlowe may have taken him. On this I will not waver. Do you understand?"

Sarah's heart swelled with love for the man, even though she found herself supremely frustrated by the situation.

She understood it all perfectly well. And she'd done her best to abide by his terms up till now—something she'd never considered for anyone else.

But she could be useful—should be useful, especially at such a time.

"I want my brother back, Marcus, and I'll do whatever it takes to bring him home."

"He'll be home soon, Sarah. You have my word," Marcus swore, as he escorted her across the grass to where her parents waited with Sully.

One way or another, she'd hold him to his promise. Even if she had to take matters into her own hands.

17

"Do you take me for a fool, Miss Tisdale?" Sully asked with a deep frown. He stood in front of Sarah's doorway, blocking the threshold, his arms crossed.

Sarah considered telling him that he'd prove himself one if he didn't get out of her way, but she suspected that a sweeter tack was needed. "Mr. Sully, I've a bargain for you."

"It's just Sully," he told her, unmoving, "and I'm not interested in bargaining."

Sarah bit the inside of her cheek, considering her options. "Really? Then am I to understand you've no interest in Mary O'Riley?"

His stony expression didn't ease, though Sarah noted with pleasure that a slight tic seemed to be developing near his left eye.

"What's Cook have to do with this?" he asked suspiciously.

Sarah crooked her finger, beckoning him to come in.

He obliged, frowning when Sarah closed the door.

"Lord Weston warned me about you, so don't go getting any ideas—"

"Mary's had an offer of marriage from one of the local farmers," Sarah interrupted, nearing to stand directly in front of him, her gaze fixed on his. "He's a good man—and, quite honestly, Mary would be a fool to refuse him."

The tic increased in speed until Sully appeared to be

winking at her repeatedly. "She's said nothing of this to me."

"She would hardly want it to seem as though she's blackmailing you, now would she?" Sarah replied determinedly.

The tic intensified until Sarah wondered if it could do permanent damage. "Sully, if you'll help me, I'll make certain Mary refuses the farmer."

"You'd ruin Mary's chance at happiness?" Sully ground out the words through clenched teeth.

"Hardly. Mary admires the farmer, but she does not love him," Sarah continued, stepping closer to him, her voice lowering to a whisper. "She *loves* you."

The tic stopped. "Are you lying?"

"I would never lie about such a thing," Sarah assured him. She willed herself to remain still though she could feel the seconds slipping by.

"Dammit all, Miss Tisdale," he muttered, walking around her toward the fireplace. "Lord Weston will have my hide if I don't look after you."

Sarah took a deep breath, feeling victory within her grasp, and turned. "Sully, I think I know where they've taken Nigel—and the emerald—or at least I have the means of finding out. And I'd insist that you accompany me, of course," she added. "I'd hardly go traipsing about after dark on my own."

She held her breath. His expression told her he was considering her words, but she knew the battle was not yet won.

He paced, frowning. "You would do exactly as you're told?"

"Of course."

Turning, he paced back and forth, muttering to himself.

"And this information, how likely is it that Lord Weston will have any luck tracking it down on his own?"

Sarah clasped her hands behind her back in an effort to contain her surge of hope. "I'm not sure he could secure this information on his own. I don't know how much the townsfolk truly trust him yet, and he must talk to them for answers. Sully, I can help."

He walked toward her, his eyes hard. "You get yourself into any trouble and it's my head—and I've got a nasty side to me. You understand?"

Sarah swallowed hard. "Of course."

"I'll wait in the hall while you dress."

Sarah looked down at her linen shirt and pair of breeches and boots that she'd bought off a local boy. "I am dressed."

"You . . . you can't mean to go out in *that*?" Sully asked disbelievingly. "I thought you'd dressed to visit your animals."

Sarah glared at him. "Are we going to stand here and argue about my clothing?"

Sully grabbed her by the shoulders and turned her toward the door. "No. And saints preserve us," he muttered, guiding her through and closing the door behind them.

Marcus crashed through the aged door of the Boot with such force that every last occupant of the tavern looked up from their cups, owl-eyed and confused.

He hardly had time for explanations. He'd returned to the fair only to confirm that Dixon was truly gone, whether dragged off by who the hell knew or having left of his own accord, Marcus could not say.

It did not matter, as Marcus could do nothing about it. Carmichael had promised to send more men if he could, but the man didn't know the immediate urgency of the situation. Sully was watching the Tisdales, and Stewart and Pattinson were waiting in the harbor, leaving Marcus alone to find Nigel.

He stalked to the back of the tavern, not stopping until he was standing across the bar from Thomas.

"You'll not be getting any brandy tonight, Weston, so if that's what you've come alookin' for, you might as well leave," the tavernkeeper said pointedly.

"Nigel Tisdale has been kidnapped, and I have reason to believe you can be of some help," Marcus ground out, willing himself to remain somewhat collected.

The man could not hide his concern for the boy, but he hesitated just the same.

"Your cousin Henry, he's a footman in my home, is he not?"

"What's that to you?" Thomas countered, distrust coloring his countenance.

"I'll assume then that you've asked after me?"

Thomas looked to deny it, and then thought better of it. "And?"

Marcus stood so that his eyes met Thomas's. "I need your help. Now, you may not like me, but I'm inclined to believe you've made up your mind as to whether I'm a man who can be trusted."

Thomas stared back, his face set in a grim mask.

"Will you help me?" Marcus pressed, his tone deadly serious.

Just then, a young boy emerged from the kitchen and tugged on his sleeve. Thomas bent down and the boy stretched up to whisper in his father's ear.

Thomas frowned and shook his head at the boy, but the young one persisted, clutching a fistful of his shirt and whispering faster.

Thomas nodded at last, stood tall, and turned to Marcus. "Don't say I never did nothing for ya. Come with me."

"I'm in no mood for tomfoolery," Marcus said, hopeful the man heard the sincerity of his tone.

"Neither am I." Thomas's voice was gruff, his words just as terse.

Marcus followed Thomas through the door to the kitchen, where several cooks and servers stopped working to gape at the lord.

"Mind your business," Thomas yelled, gesturing for Marcus to follow him down a set of crude steps.

Marcus kept pace with the man despite the nagging soreness in his leg. They reached a low room where casks and barrels of flour and sugar, wine and brandy stood along all four walls.

"All right, then," Thomas called, his deep voice loud in the silent room.

Two figures emerged from one corner. Marcus slipped from his boot the knife he'd retrieved earlier, palming it with one swift smooth movement.

"I told you this was a bad idea."

Poised to throw, Marcus squinted into the dim light. "Sully?"

The valet stepped into the light. Behind him, dressed head to toe in boy's clothing, was Sarah, her hair concealed beneath a cap.

Fury, red and hot, burned through Marcus. "I do *not* have time for such antics," Marcus snarled. "Take her home, Sully." He slid the knife back into the sheath inside his Hessian and made to turn back to the stairs.

"Please," Sarah begged, stepping around Sully. "Listen to what we have to say."

"This is not the time, Sarah," Marcus ground out.

"My lord," Sully began, his voice slow but steady, "I realize that you're angry, but the woman knows how to find Marlowe."

"Well, I think I do," Sarah added, nodding at the giant tavernkeeper. "Thomas, you know the comings and goings of Charles and his men. Can you tell us where they'd be likely to hide?"

"Come now, miss, I've a business to run, after all."

Sarah stepped closer to Thomas and looked up at him with honesty in her eyes. "You can trust Lord Weston."

Thomas's gaze shifted to Marcus and narrowed with suspicion. "Well, my lord, *can* I trust you?"

"You have my word."

Thomas stared hard at him for a tension-charged moment. Then he muttered under his breath and threw the filthy towel he still carried in his hand onto the top of a cask. "Been talk of supplies being run out to St. Aldhelm's Isle. Good money to be had for those who keep their mouths shut. Frenchies with deep pockets out there, some say."

Marcus turned toward the stairs. "Sully, come with me. We'll need a boat. Sarah, you're to stay right here until I come for you."

"You're not thinking of going to the island now, are ye?" Thomas asked before Marcus reached the second step.

Marcus slammed his fist against the rough banister. "I've hardly time to explain myself—"

"Because you'll not get far," the man continued. "There's only one spot to put ashore and it's a hard one to find in the daylight, never mind the black of night."

Marcus realized the man was right. Marlowe had been the Corinthian agent assigned the task of discovering where Napoleon's men awaited the final gems, the coves and caves of the coast affording any number of possible hideouts. He hadn't shared that information with Marcus.

"I can help."

Marcus squeezed his eyes shut and took a deep breath. "Sarah."

"I've been to the island. I know the spot Thomas is speaking of," she pressed. "And you'll not find another man tonight sober enough to take my place. Those not upstairs right now are home sleeping off the fair. You know I speak the truth."

"Goddammit," Marcus swore under his breath.

"Besides, it will be far easier to see to my safety with me by your side, wouldn't you agree?" she added.

Thomas pulled a wool coat from its peg on the wall. "Take this," he ordered, "and mind the pocket."

Sarah reached for the coat and nodded in thanks.

Marcus had no other choice.

"We've no time to waste. Sully, go and ready the horses."

"Oh, there'll be no need for that," Thomas interrupted, walking to the long row of stacked casks along the north wall and pulling first one then the other from their place, to reveal a hidden doorway.

"I told you, I have a business to run."

Sarah huddled into Marcus's side, the wind light but cool as it glanced off the low side of the boat and ruffled her tangled tresses.

"Why did Nigel not tell me of the tunnel that led directly from the Boot to the cove?" Marcus asked angrily of no one in particular.

Sarah pressed against him. "He did not know, I'm sure of it. We spoke at some length after you questioned him. He was terrified—too terrified to have kept such a thing secret. It does not matter now."

Sully rowed through the blackness, his powerful strokes sending the boat slicing through the waves. The lamp of the Lulworth Cove lighthouse illuminated the surrounding area just enough to reveal the dark outline of Aldhelm's Isle.

"Of course it does," Marcus replied in a low tone. "You're in danger—danger that might have been avoided had I known all of the facts."

"I'll be all right," Sarah whispered to Marcus, placing a hand on his cheek. "I'm with you."

His jaw tensed, the muscles tightening and flexing under her sensitive fingertips. "You've no idea what these men are capable of, do you? And I've put you here."

Sully turned the boat toward the southwestern side of the island and the minuscule cove nearly hidden there.

"I do understand the danger—but you must know that I'm safest when I'm with you."

"Fire," Sully warned, pointing toward a small blaze on the shore.

" 'Ello!" a man's voice called out to the boat, the sound of the waves slapping against the vessel alerting him to their presence. "Reinforcements, then?"

Marcus shoved Sarah down and she crouched in the bottom of the boat, her head hidden below the oarlocks. "You are not to leave this boat," he ordered.

Sarah struggled to sit up, spying the man as he waved from the shore. She knew he could not make out their faces from this distance. Still, they'd have to convince him that they meant no harm. She did the only thing she could think of.

> *I had just come home and I took a room,*
> *I was all settled down to recline,*
> *When I saw a delectable maid go by . . .*

Sarah's voice, though high, to be sure, was passable as long as she kept her chin tucked low while singing. "Join in," she hissed, launching into the second chorus with appropriate gusto.

> *And when she stretched out on her bed,*
> *I couldn't stand no more . . .*

Marcus and Sully took up the bawdy shanty tune as though born to do so, and Sarah had never been so glad for her unique coastal education.

She didn't say a single word,
But she took me in her arms . . .

The man on the shore had joined in, his lusty singing carrying on the waves.

"Ready yourself," Marcus told Sully.

That night I rode in glorious style,
And other things besides . . .

"Glad to hear, I am, that you're not those Frenchies," the man shouted as he leapt into the water and waded toward the boat. "That smug lot hardly knew one tune among them."

The keyhole in the door, my boys,
The keyhole in the door . . .

The man leaned back at the last of the chorus and bayed at the moon, stopping midway when the length of rope Sully had thrown hit him square in the face. "Patience now, you can hardly 'xpect—"

He stopped, eyeing Marcus and the others warily.

"Hey, now, what's this all 'bout—"

Sully launched himself from the boat, his hands closing around the man's neck, choking off his voice before the two of them disappeared beneath the waves.

Sarah gasped and Marcus shoved her hard, flattening her against the bottom of the boat. "Stay down," he ordered, then went over the side himself.

Sarah peered into the dark water, surprised when Sully broke the surface of the water, gasping for breath.

"Are you—"

Sully made for the shore. "Stay down, woman."

His words echoed in her ears as she saw the smuggler's body rise to the top then gently float past.

Marcus waded through the cold salt water, the temperature numbing his leg wound. He reached the beach, pausing briefly to get his bearings. Scrubby bushes grew in thick tufts all the way to the edge of the pebbled beach, and a narrow path was visible between two of the larger bushes just in front of where Marcus stood.

He slipped his knife from his sodden boot and signaled Sully to follow him.

The sound of someone disturbing the foliage reached their ears just as they started across the beach. Marcus gestured, silently ordering Sully to flatten himself against the rocks.

Marlowe, Charles, and another man rounded the bend to the right and walked out onto the beach.

"Grimes?" Charles bellowed.

"Where'd ye get off to?" the other yelled into the night. He glowered and half turned to look behind him. "I don't see him, Marlowe."

Charles looked out on the water, squinting as he caught sight of the small boat. "Is that a boat?"

Marcus and Sully rose silently to their feet.

"Christ!" the other yelled, pulling a knife from the folds of his shirt as Sully lunged at him.

And then all hell broke loose.

Marcus threw himself into the fray, attacking with a ferocity born of duty and anger.

He dispatched the armed man quickly with a swift slice to the throat, and then went after Marlowe, who'd retreated up the path the smugglers had descended.

Marcus reached a clearing and stopped abruptly.

Marlowe stood in the middle of it. He held Nigel in

front of him, one arm trapping the boy. Nigel thrashed and struggled against his hold.

"Where the hell have you been, Weston?" Marlowe demanded in a low voice. He held a pistol in his free hand, his arm at his side. "We drowned Pattinson, Stewart, and the rest hours ago."

Marcus blinked, narrowing his gaze over Marlowe's features with deadly precision. "It took some time to find a guide to land us in the cove, but you knew it would."

"I'd always heard you were unstoppable, Weston," he continued. "I must say, I'm somewhat disappointed with your performance. As for mine? Well, I think that it speaks for itself."

"I've grown tired of your games, Marlowe. Give me the boy," Marcus replied, slowly walking toward the two, his knife at the ready.

Marlowe lifted his hand, holding the pistol to Nigel's temple—steady despite the boy's struggles. "Do you think I'd make things so easy for you?"

Nigel went still, his face whitening, his eyes ablaze with fear.

"You'd kill an innocent boy, turn traitor to your country—all for a bit of blunt?" Marcus's voice was lethal.

"A bit of blunt?" Marlowe's smile flashed, white in the moonlight. "You know *nothing*. And as for killing the boy—why wouldn't I? He's no longer necessary."

Before Marcus could move, Marlowe spun Nigel around then hit him squarely in the temple with the pistol. The boy staggered and collapsed. Marcus leapt but he was too late to catch the boy.

Marlowe disappeared into the underbrush and Marcus made a quick decision to attend to Nigel and let Marlowe go.

He knelt beside the fallen boy, checking for a pulse

and drawing a deep thankful breath when he felt the strong pound of blood at his throat.

"Nigel!" he said clearly, sharply tapping his cheek.

Nigel came around with a start, sucking in a deep breath and coughing as the air filled his lungs.

"Are you all right?" Marcus asked.

The boy nodded.

"Then come with me."

Sarah waited anxiously in the boat. From her vantage point, she'd watched as Marcus disappeared down the path away from the beach and into the interior of the island while Sully dispatched his foe.

The wind picked up, and the waves grew in size, making the boat bob up and down with increased roughness. The rolling and pitching did little to calm Sarah's nerves.

Suddenly, a figure appeared, silhouetted briefly on the cliff top before jumping over the edge and down onto the beach. Small pebbles flew as the large bulk of a man raced for the water.

Sarah squinted, narrowing her eyes in an effort to make out his identity. With sudden shock, she recognized Marlowe, just as the sea water reached his thighs and he dove forward to swim toward the boat.

"Bugger!"

Sarah stood up, only to quickly sit back down when the boat rocked alarmingly and she realized she had nowhere to run.

Frantic, she caught up the wool coat Thomas had given her before they left the Boot and began to run her hands over it. "Mind the pocket," he'd told her.

She muttered an oath when something heavy slipped from the pocket and fell with a distinct thud to the bottom of the boat.

Sarah looked up. Marlowe was cleaving through the

rough water, making impressive progress and drawing nearer with every stroke.

She grabbed the bag and upended it into her lap, sorting swiftly through the items that fell out.

"Do not come near this boat," she shouted at Marlowe, then noted that he continued his brisk clip as if she hadn't spoken.

"Bollocks!"

Sarah grasped Thomas's pistol and lifted it in both hands, half cocking the hammer. "I'm armed!" she yelled in warning, dread building in her belly.

She'd watched closely as her father had instructed Nigel in the proper way to load a gun. But that occasion had been in the daylight with nary a threatening individual in sight.

With grim determination, she picked up a smaller cloth bag and poured what she hoped was the proper amount of gunpowder down the barrel.

Then she rammed a lead ball down the barrel.

The sound of Marlowe's arms slapping the water as he swam closer reached her ears.

"Bloody, bloody hell," she muttered. With ruthless focus, she made herself concentrate, fingers nearly steady as she sloshed a measure of gunpowder into the flintlock's pan, snapped the frizzen into place, and fully cocked the hammer.

The boat suddenly dipped on the port side and Sarah screamed. Marlowe's hand was visible on the gunwale.

She pointed the gun at him shakily. "I'll shoot," she warned again.

"Find Dixon—use it on him," Marlowe said, tightening his grip to lift himself into the boat.

Sarah fired and the shot knocked her flat on her back. Shaken and bruised, she pushed herself upright and scrambled toward the bow.

She peered into the water where just a moment before Marlowe had been.

He was nowhere in sight.

Swallowed by the rough sea as if he'd never been.

"Sarah," Marcus yelled.

She looked toward the beach, where the men stood all in a row, Nigel the very last.

"Are you all right?" she demanded of her brother.

"Yes," the boy yelled back. "And you?"

"Better than Marlowe," she whispered, setting the gun down and returning her gaze to the deep, dark water.

18

"All of it—Jasper's death, Clive, even Marlowe—for an emerald?" Sarah asked. The moonlight seemed to strike sparks that flashed and glittered, distracting her as her thumb swiped back and forth across the egg-sized gem in her palm.

Marcus pulled her in close, sheltering her against his formidable body as the guinea made its way back to the Weymouth coast. "Well, for that one—plus seven more just like it," he answered quietly, rubbing her shoulder in comfort. "But all the same, it's an asinine reason for dying."

She dropped the emerald into his palm and closed his fingers around it. "Take it. I don't ever want to see it again."

Marcus dropped the emerald into the small pouch and pocketed it. "Are you all right?"

"No," Sarah answered simply, "but I will be."

She looked forward to where Nigel sat in the bow. He bent over, his shirtsleeve wet from wrist to elbow as he trailed his hand in the water. "Will he?"

"Eventually," Marcus assured her, though he had his doubts. At twelve, Marcus had thought of nothing but the big wide world, far away from his homes in Lulworth and Inverness. Life had been full of possibility—open as far as Marcus's imagination could carry him beyond the realities of his world.

But Nigel had seen the worst of humanity at a very

tender age. Whether his faith in humankind could be restored depended on too many variables to calculate.

"With the love of his family," Marcus added, leaning
in to press a kiss on her soft brow.

The boat rocked abruptly, sending the pistol Thomas
had given her sliding to bump Sarah's boot. She bent
down and retrieved it, eyeing it wearily before flinging it
into the sea. "I never want to see that again, either," she
explained. "Though I suppose Thomas will be none too
happy."

"The loss of his flintlock is the least of Thomas's wor-
ries." Marcus added gruffly, "You could have killed
yourself with that damn pistol."

She settled back into the crook of Marcus's arm and
laid her cheek against his chest. "I told you I was safest
with you," she chided him gently.

Marcus was beginning to agree. All the reasons he
loved Sarah were the very same ones that told him she
could not be trusted on her own.

And that, he realized with more than a touch of relief,
suited him just fine.

He couldn't go on living as though his future relied
upon his past. He'd only hurt himself by refusing so
much, taking so little—by hiding from it all until he'd
hardly known who he was.

He kissed Sarah's hair, closing his eyes as he did so.
Marcus had thought himself brave, when all along he'd
only taken the coward's way out.

"Almost home now," Sully said to Nigel as they entered Durdle Door, a massive limestone arch.

"Drat," Sarah yelped, sitting up.

"What is it?" Marcus asked, trying unsuccessfully to
gather her back into his arms.

"It's something Marlowe said—before I shot him."
Her fists balled in her lap. "He told me to 'find Dixon.'
What do you think he meant by that?"

Marcus wasn't entirely sure. Obviously Marlowe had been keeping information concerning Dixon from him, but the extent of the man's involvement was still unclear.

However, there was no point in involving Sarah or Nigel any further in the case, on that point Marcus was clear. "Sarah, let us get ashore—"

Without warning, the stern of the boat was struck by something large, and the longboat turned over, throwing everyone out into the cold, dark water.

Marcus held tight to Sarah as they sank, the murky depths and dark night above obscuring his view of all but her slim hand in his.

Trained in freezing cold Scottish lochs, Marcus was an experienced swimmer, and he easily stopped their descent, reversing direction to propel them back to the surface. His head broke the water's surface first, Sarah's heavy wet curls following closely behind.

Bits of splintered wood from the boat floated about them, and a cask bobbed gently in the current—the very one that had destroyed the boat, presumably. Marcus looked up to where the outline of two men could be seen standing precariously atop the limestone arch.

He searched the beach and found several men waiting just at the water's edge in the moonlight, the tall form of Dixon clearly visible as he held a lantern aloft.

"Won't you join us?" Dixon asked, the men about him laughing.

Sully and Nigel appeared from around the cask. "What will it be?" Sully asked grimly, holding on to the barrel.

"Are you a strong swimmer?" Marcus whispered to Sarah, looking down the coastline.

Treading water, Sarah stared at the small group of men gathered on the beach. "Yes," she answered. "I'll make it in."

"Not to this beach, you won't," he directed, pulling

her back against his chest when she made as if to set out. "I want you to swim back through the arch and come ashore at Man o' War Bay."

"Come in, Weston—and bring the rest with you. I'll send my men out to fetch you, if necessary," Dixon threatened from the beach.

Sarah squeezed Marcus's hand tightly. "I'm safest when I'm with you, remember?" she said simply, shivers from the cold water in her voice.

"You are trying my patience," Dixon added, his tone becoming more irate.

"Let's not keep the man waiting any longer," Marcus said reluctantly to the other three.

The four swam the short distance to shallower waters, wading through the surf and plodding along the wet sand until reaching Dixon and his men.

"Marlowe suggested we find you," Sarah said fiercely, stopping just in front of Dixon. "And here you are. How kind of you to oblige."

The man struck Sarah across the face, knocking her to her knees. "Do not take that tone with me, Sarah."

Marcus lunged at Dixon but two burly smugglers made a grab for him and restrained him by the arms, one on each side of him.

"And to think I'd considered taking you with me," Dixon continued, sweeping Sarah with a disgusted look. "Hardly any chance of that now, you common whore."

Sarah rose slowly, squaring her shoulders, her spine ramrod straight. She looked Dixon in the eyes without flinching, even as a thick-bodied smuggler yanked her wrists behind her back. "I've already killed Marlowe tonight—don't give me a reason to kill you."

"Have you, now?" Dixon said snidely, reaching out to trace the neckline of Sarah's sodden shirt with insolent familiarity. "I suppose I must thank you, then. Sticky fingers, that one. He made off with one of the emeralds which would have severely lessened my bargaining power. Hardly a worthy partner in all of this, just as I predicted from the start. Good help who know their place are so hard to find."

"So you're a traitor," Sully interrupted with disdain, earning a punch to the stomach for his trouble.

Dixon continued to stroke Sarah's skin with his long, thin finger. "Hardly. I'd no choice in the matter. My brother's oldest brat will inherit the title, leaving me with hardly enough to live on," he explained. "Smuggling brandy was not going to save me, so I began to look for other, more lucrative, endeavors."

"And supporting Napoleon's quest for world domination seemed worthy of your time?" Marcus taunted. He twisted, testing the grip of the smugglers who restrained him. His only hope was to free himself long enough to get to the knife in his boot. But the men holding him didn't seem distracted by the conversation.

"Precisely," Dixon answered, scrubbing his hands together and wincing fastidiously at the damp seawater left on his fingertips by Sarah's shirt. He walked toward Marcus. "And do you know the best part? Hmmm?"

"Do tell me," Marcus ground out.

"It required very little effort from me. The robberies in London were hired out. The day-to-day interaction with the smugglers themselves? Hired out. Even the murdering was left to Charles." He looked over at Nigel, his lips twisting into a macabre caricature of a smile. "I must confess, though, I took it upon myself to do away with the Burroughs boy."

"Bastard," Nigel shouted, his eyes hot as he ran toward Dixon. One of the men intercepted the boy easily, pushing Nigel to the sand and planting his foot in the small of the boy's back.

"What has become of today's youth?" Dixon said

with an affected sigh. "I'll be doing society a service by ridding it of one more insolent pup."

"But you're short two stones, are you not?" Sarah pressed, attempting to draw Dixon's attention away from Nigel.

He turned back to her, pinning her with a lecherous gaze. "Right you are. One is due to arrive from London anytime now."

Marcus realized that Dixon knew nothing of the Corinthians being in possession of the seventh stone, which meant that Marlowe had failed to share a most vital piece of information with him.

"And the other?" Sarah pressed.

Dixon closed the distance between them, his head lowering to align with hers. "Come now, Sarah, don't play coy with me. If you did indeed murder Marlowe, then you're in possession of the last emerald."

"Funny," Sarah spat out, "I don't recall any emerald."

Dixon stood his ground. "That really would be too bad. You see, Napoleon's buyer must have all of the emeralds—nothing less." He closed one hand around Sarah's throat. "So, to be even one stone short is simply not acceptable."

He squeezed, lightly, but enough to make Sarah flinch.

"I have the emerald," Marcus drawled, tamping down his murderous rage. The bastard would pay for putting his hands on Sarah. "But you'll have to come and get it."

Dixon released Sarah and turned to Marcus. "Actually, I don't have to do anything. Black," he commanded, gesturing at one of the men holding Marcus "Relieve Lord Weston of the emerald."

The burly smuggler released Marcus's arm and shoved a heavy hand into his coat pocket.

It was just the opportunity Marcus had hoped for.

He staggered sideways as if pushed off balance by the

man's groping, slumped down, and reached into his
boot, palming the knife.

No one noticed. All eyes were trained on the smuggler
searching for the emerald.

"What do we have here?" the smuggler said, lifting
the small pouch from Marcus's pocket.

And with that, Marcus swung his weight around and
stabbed him in the stomach, pushing his body off with
his shoulder before rounding on the second smuggler
and slitting his throat with one quick slice of the razor-
sharp blade.

"Aye now, don't tell me we're late to the party."

Marcus's gaze flashed over Dixon's shoulder.

Thomas and a handful of local men stood on the
beach, just outside the mouth of the cave that led to
the tunnel at the Boot. Some were armed with spikes
and knives, others with only their scarred and well-
worn fists.

Thomas smiled.

Dixon made a break for it, running toward the cliffs
while a third smuggler attacked Marcus.

With the element of surprise no longer on his side, it
took longer to dispatch the man than Marcus would
have preferred, his rage growing until he stopped the
battle with a vicious left to the man's chin. The smuggler
toppled to the beach, bleeding and unconscious.

"Sarah!" Marcus yelled, searching for her as he
fought his way through the fray. He lunged and jabbed
as if set upon by wild animals, his heart pounding in his
ears.

At last he spotted her with Nigel, safely tucked inside
the mouth of the cave.

Assured that she was unharmed and a safe distance
from the fighting, he turned and ran in the direction he'd
seen Dixon head.

As he looked up the chalky hillside just beyond, he

caught sight of Dixon as the man labored hard to climb the crude path.

Marcus cut a swath across the melee and hit the path at full stride, his leg burning with every step.

"Dixon," he shouted.

The traitorous man looked back, his face contorting with anger and fear before he faced forward once again. Too late, he tried to avoid the exposed tree root that jutted up in the rocky trail.

He tripped, his lanky body lurching forward as he fell to his knees.

Marcus pushed harder, ignoring his leg as it threatened to give way beneath him. He reached Dixon just as the man was rising to move forward.

Marcus reached out and twisted his fingers into Dixon's hair, forcefully yanking him back. "You've the constable to answer to, you bastard."

Dixon shot back with his elbow, landing a painful hit to Marcus's leg wound. "Not if I have any say in the matter."

Marcus staggered, his leg collapsing beneath him.

Dixon jumped up and turned to face him. "Worthless half-blood," he spit out before waging a second attack, this time kicking at Marcus until his back brushed the cliff's edge.

Marcus endured one, then two kicks, the top half of his body coming to dangle precariously over the edge. Just as Dixon looked to be delivering the final blow, Marcus dug in and shifted his body to the left.

Marcus grabbed at the chalky cliff with both hands, but it was too late for Dixon. His forward momentum was too great, and when his kick failed to connect, it carried him over the cliff, his screams of terror filling Marcus's ears as the man fell to his death.

"For the record," Marcus said with grim satisfaction, lifting his battered body up the craggy cliff and back onto the rough path. "You do not, nor will you ever, have any say in the matter."

There was no reply.

Sarah had waited long enough.

"Take the tunnel back to the Boot," she told Nigel, clutching the boy's face in her hands. "Wait there for me. Do you understand?"

Her brother shook his head, the gaze he fixed on Sarah filled with all the fierceness and love he had left in him. "No, I won't leave you."

Frustrated, Sarah was torn. She needed to know that he was safe—and he needed to know the same of her. They were far too alike for Sarah to deny him. "Then promise you'll stay here in the tunnel."

Nigel's expression made it clear he wanted to object, but at last he nodded reluctantly. "You'll be careful, won't you?"

"Of course I will," she assured him, landing a kiss on his forehead. "I'm going to find Marcus."

Sarah left Nigel watching her from the tunnel and stepped out onto the beach.

Thomas and his men had taken control, and the smugglers who had not been killed were currently bound together and surrounded.

Sarah ran to where the men stood, searching the faces and not finding the one she sought. "Where is Marcus?" she asked Thomas anxiously.

The man landed a swift kick to the belly of one of the smugglers struggling to get up. "Last I saw of him, he was chasing after Dixon."

He turned to look at the cliff wall and Sarah's gaze followed. She gasped, her heart stopping at the sight of a body lying on the rocks several yards along the cliff from the foot of the path.

"I wouldn't waste a sigh on Mr. Dixon, if I was you,"

Thomas said by way of explanation, taking Sarah by the arm and shaking her gently.

Sarah looked again toward the body, and then burst into tears. "Where is Marcus?" she begged.

"I'd check near the top," Thomas replied, then turned her loose.

She hurried forward, tripping on the rough stones and catching herself with one hand splayed against the cliff rock.

"Have a care—he'll hardly want you if you're dead," Thomas warned, handing her a lantern then returning to the captives.

Sarah righted herself and ran, leaving the beach and climbing the path, dodging roots and loose rocks along the way.

She called his name over and over, until her lungs felt near to bursting.

Finally, around a narrow turn in the path, Sarah held the lamp aloft and found him.

He was stretched out flat on the rough track. Sarah could make out the soles of his Hessians and not much else.

"Marcus!" Terrified when he didn't respond, she ran, stumbling, to reach him.

She dropped to her knees beside him and held the lantern aloft, looking anxiously at his still form. When the light revealed no glisten of blood, Sarah abandoned the lantern altogether and set her frantic hands on him. She poked and prodded at his stomach, his chest, both arms, and finally his face.

"Please, Marcus, say something," Sarah pleaded, her heart threatening to break in two.

"Ach, woman," he replied hoarsely, then opened his eyes.

She leaned down and kissed him hard. "Bugger. I thought you'd . . . I was afraid . . ."

Sarah didn't bother to finish her sentence. She kissed him again, releasing all of her fears until nothing was left but relief and utter joy.

Marcus's arms wrapped around Sarah, pinning her to him. "You're happy, then, to see me alive?"

"How could you ask such a thing?"

Marcus gave her that small male smile that Sarah would never, ever tire of. "I know what you're thinking."

He sounded so annoyingly sure of himself she would have smacked him if she hadn't been so bloody glad he was alive.

"You'd almost hoped to prove me wrong about parting ways at the beach."

He *was* wrong, of course—except in a teeny little way, he wasn't. She'd have loved to have proven her point, so long as she could have done so without his dying. She couldn't say *that,* though, so instead she grabbed his face in her hands and said, "Kiss me."

Marcus smiled wider, almost triumphantly. "I'm right, aren't I?"

"Kiss me," Sarah demanded. "And never, *ever* stop."

And so he did.

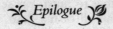

Epilogue

"It is not too late, dear," Lady Tisdale said hopefully while fussing with the drape of Sarah's bridal gown.

Sarah looked at her reflection in the full-length mirror, her gown simple in silk sarsenet, fine touches of bead-work interspersed with pearls edging the bodice and hemline. "The wedding is about to begin, Mother."

"Still." Lady Tisdale continued along the same path, "I am sure the vicar would be willing to accommodate us."

Sarah smiled. Although she'd never been a woman to dream of her wedding day, she had to admit that it was exactly as it should be.

The sun was shining gloriously in the clear blue sky. Her closest friends and family were in attendance—even Thomas, whom Lady Tisdale had been loath to invite, but whom Sarah could not imagine such a celebration without. The man had, in truth, saved her life and the lives of the ones she loved.

Sarah shivered at the thought. Nearly a month had passed, the days filled with emotion as Nigel had begun to heal from his ordeal, Sarah endured disconnected dreams of Marlowe, and Marcus had well and properly wooed Sarah as surely no other man had wooed a woman before.

She looked out the window of Lulworth Castle. In the spacious courtyard below, the guests were gathering for the short walk to the wedding site.

"Would you like me to fetch the vicar?" Lady Tisdale pressed.

Sarah turned to her mother, taking her hands. "Mother, I've explained to you why I wish for the ceremony to take place out-of-doors."

"Really, Sarah, it's unheard-of for a bride and groom to recite their vows in such a setting—"

"Mother," Sarah repeated, her tone more serious.

Sarah had very nearly not asked Marcus whether he would consider being married on the cliff top.

In truth, she knew that it sounded shockingly unconventional—never mind *sounding* unconventional, it most surely *was*.

But everything that had anything to do with this day—the most important of Sarah's life—was tied irrevocably to the cove.

Sarah and Marcus had discovered while walking one day that both had made it a habit over the years to stare out over the cove, in the black of night, and think. About life, love, and everything else that seemed so complicated despite the simple terms with which any of the issues could be—and should be—handled.

Many a night the two had looked out upon the same expanse of water, perhaps even passing each other without knowing.

Marcus had willingly and heartily agreed to exchanging their wedding vows in what was, truly, the place where they'd begun, their individual yearnings of the heart leading them to each other.

His only request was that she not race for the woods partway through the ceremony.

Sarah had laughingly assured him that she would

never run again. Not from him, not from life. Not from anything that came their way.

And besides, she'd thought to herself though she didn't say it aloud, she could just as easily run from the church.

With a small smile, Sarah came back to the present and her mother's concerns.

"You're missing the point," Sarah said gently, patting her mother's hands before turning back to the mirror. "All that matters is that Marcus and I want this—therefore, you should too."

Sarah observed her mother's reflection in the mirror, her mouth opening and closing like a trout's.

And then, for no apparent reason, Lady Tisdale drew in a determined breath and nodded. "I'll go fetch Claire for you. And Sarah," she added, reaching to pat her daughter's shoulder. "I love you."

She turned quickly and walked from the room, leaving Sarah quite thunderstruck.

"Bollocks! If I'd have known that all it would take was obstinance, I would have tried that years ago."

"I believe a bride is entitled to do whatever she likes on her wedding day," Claire called, sweeping into the room, resplendent in a gorgeous amethyst gown, "but I'd be careful with the profanities, dear. One never knows who might be listening."

She caught Sarah in her arms and hugged her, careful not to disturb her friend's hair. "You are the most beautiful bride I've ever seen."

"Thank you," Sarah replied, tears threatening. She brushed moisture from her eyelashes with her fingertips, and then fixed Claire with an excited gaze. "Now, you'll never guess what just happened."

Claire bent down awkwardly to remove a pale thread from Sarah's skirt. "Is it something to do with your mother? I passed her in the hall just now and she looked as though she'd been struck with something quite large—and hard."

"I told her exactly what I thought. *Exactly.*"

Claire looked confused at first, then her eyes grew round. "*Exactly?*"

"*Exactly.*"

"And she failed to spontaneously burst into flames?" Claire asked teasingly.

"Nary a flicker," Sarah answered, hardly believing it herself. "And she told me that she loves me," she added in a small voice.

Claire wiped at a tear slowly slipping down Sarah's cheek. "Well, truly it is a day for miracles," she said gently, "as you'll have to agree once you've seen the remainder of your wedding party."

Bones came into the room, his graceful gait in marked contrast to that of Titus, who bounded up behind.

Both dogs were elegantly turned out in ruffs about their necks, the purplish hue of their fashionable attire perfectly matching Claire's gown.

"Oh," Sarah sighed, dropping to her knees to accept a lick from each dog—Titus's decidedly sloppier than Bones's more delicate touch. "I shall dissolve into a puddle of tears now."

"Oh, no, you will not," Claire commanded, catching Sarah's hand and pulling her upright. "Your mother may have reached some sort of epiphany in regards to you, but I highly doubt we can hope the same as concerns me."

She straightened Sarah's gown and eyed it critically. "She'll never forgive me if you walk down the aisle in a wrinkled dress. Turn," she instructed, brushing here and there as Sarah obeyed.

"Ladies," Gregory's voice called from the hallway.

"Is it time?" Sarah's heart pounded.

"It is," Claire confirmed. "Now, gather your dogs and let's be off."

"Any news of Marlowe?"

Carmichael clasped his hands behind his back and looked solemnly out over the small gathering. "Really, Marcus, on your wedding day?"

"I feel responsible. If only I'd realized sooner—"

The Corinthian leader sighed. "We managed to retrieve all eight emeralds, which means Napoleon has been stopped for now. I could not have asked any more from you. As for Marlowe, I can only assume that he had his reasons. As should you.

"Now, are those dogs I see?" Carmichael asked, his tone indifferent as he hastily changed the subject. "In purple neck ruffs?"

Marcus made to argue, then found he could not help but smile as Bones and Titus proceeded down the flower-strewn ground between the aisles of chairs, their noses held high as they caught the scent of Cook's pheasant, which had been strategically placed just behind an arrangement of flowers near him. "Yes, amethyst, I believe that particular hue is called."

"Of course."

The dogs sped up as they sensed the nearness of their prize, Nigel retrieving the morsels and urging Titus and Bones into line next to him.

Marcus smiled at the boy, warmed by the kindness and acceptance in Nigel's responding grin. It had not been easy, the mending of their friendship.

But for all the talking they'd done, Marcus couldn't deny that what was truly drawing them closer was simply time spent in each other's company.

It did not seem to matter what they did, though fishing had quickly become a particular favorite. No, whether enduring Lady Tisdale's rant concerning the length of sleeves that season or trying—and, most of the time, failing—to entice Percival into the barn for the night, the activity hardly signified. They were comfortable in each other's company and grew closer by the day.

Claire walked slowly down the aisle, a jubilant smile lighting her pretty face. She took her place opposite Carmichael.

It was the talking and, more important, the listening that was bringing Nigel around, Marcus thought, his gaze moving from Claire and back to Nigel.

In Nigel, Marcus saw a bit of himself. Marcus could help the boy in a way that no one else could, because of Sarah.

And all of a sudden, as if he'd conjured her with his thoughts, she appeared.

She was a vision in silk, her auburn hair piled atop her head, the creamy expanse of her delicate neck and shoulders rising above the scooped neckline of her gown.

She'd made him see that he was so much more than what others allowed him to be.

"I read your letter," Carmichael whispered, pulling Marcus from his thoughts.

"The one I asked you to read tomorrow, after I'd left for my wedding trip?"

Carmichael cleared his throat. "Weston, you really should know by now that I'm an exceedingly efficient individual."

Marcus turned his head to meet Carmichael's gaze, his smile wry. "And?"

"You really mean to leave the Corinthians?" Carmichael asked, an uncharacteristic sadness in his tone.

"I do," Marcus replied confidently.

"I see," Carmichael began, turning his gaze back to the bride. "And what will you do?"

Marcus looked down the aisle at Sarah as she walked toward him with her father, a sense of euphoria filling his chest. "The possibilities are endless."

"I'd have to agree," Carmichael replied, and then fell silent.

Sir Arthur stopped in front of Marcus. He bent to press a tender kiss on Sarah's cheek and placed her hand in Marcus's.

"Dearly beloved, we are gathered together here in the sight of God . . ."

"You're beautiful," Marcus whispered, his eyes remaining fixed on the vicar as the man read from the Book of Common Prayer.

"I require and charge you both, as ye will answer on the dreadful day of judgment . . ."

"Thank you. I have to say, I've always loved a man in a kilt." Sarah glanced sideways through half-lowered lashes, a small wicked smile curving her lips.

Marcus's gaze snapped to her face.

"If no impediment be alleged, then shall the Curate say unto the Man . . ."

"Tell me, what does one wear under such a garment?" she murmured.

"Wilt thou have this Woman to be thy wedded Wife . . ."

"Nothing."

"I will," Sarah blurted, the small crowd gathered for the most joyous of occasions politely covering their mirth.

"*I* will," Marcus answered, turning to Sarah and mouthing "I love you. With all of my heart."

"Wilt thou have this Man to be thy wedded Husband . . ."

Sarah laughed and it caught on the mild breeze, the beautiful sound of it drifting over the wedding party and beyond, to the cove and the wide sea. "I will.

"I love you, Marcus, with all that I am, and all that I will ever be," she said loud enough for all to hear.

Marcus pulled the ring from his pocket and recited the words that would bind him to his beloved forever:

"With this Ring I thee wed, with my Body I thee worship, and with all my worldly Goods I thee endow: in the Name of the Father, and of the Son, and of the Holy Ghost. Amen."

"Are we married?" Sarah whispered excitedly.

"Not quite yet, child," the vicar responded, clearing his throat.

"Those whom God hath joined together let no man put asunder."

"Now?"

The vicar winked at Sarah. "Very nearly."

"For as Marcus and Sarah have consented together in holy Wedlock, and have witnessed the same before God and this company, and thereto have given and pledged their troth to each other, and have declared the same by giving and receiving of a Ring, and by joining of hands, I pronounce that they be Man and Wife together, In the Name of the Father, and of the Son, and of the Holy Ghost. Amen.

"You may kiss your groom," he said to Sarah. "Finally."

Sarah turned to Marcus and threw her arms around his neck. "Do you recall what I asked of you on the cliffs?"

"That I kiss you," Marcus answered, his arms coming around to encircle her waist. "And never, ever stop?"

"Precisely," she replied, then leaned in, ready for her husband to make her the happiest wife in the world.

Marcus kissed her with the promise of forever on his lips and she responded in kind.

The low tones of a fiddle began, drawing Marcus and Sarah's attention toward their family and friends.

I'll no more to the sea, my first love, for sure.
She's ruined for me by the one I love more,
A woman of substance, so fine and so fair,
Of uncommon beauty and long auburn hair.

Have mercy, Miss Sarah, and take me to wed,
I'll give you my heart and a warm gentle bed,
You'll nay lack for nothin', we'll live a good
life,
Have mercy, Miss Sarah, and become my wife.

Thomas stood in the very back row, accompanied by his young son, who played the fiddle, and his wife, who gently tapped a tambourine with the palm of her hand.

Marcus took Sarah's arm in his and escorted her down the aisle to the fine music, those in attendance standing.

Oh, the sea she is mighty and the sea she is
strong,
But Miss Sarah's the one to whom I belong.
And I'll not go a-sailin' upon the great waves,
With Miss Sarah I'll stay for the rest of my
days.

Thomas gestured for everyone to join in, Marcus and Sarah singing with particular gusto.

Miss Sarah had mercy and took him to wed.
He gave her his heart and a warm gentle bed.
They nay lacked for nothin' and lived a good
life.
Miss Sarah took mercy and became his wife.

Acknowledgements

Randall, whose generous offer to pose for the cover of this book I continue to appreciate to this day. You'll always be my favorite pinup.

The Girls. I am proud and humbled to be your mama. And occasionally irritated, but let's focus on the positives.

Lois Faye Dyer. You read this book until your eyes crossed from the effort. And then read it again. Your enthusiasm means everything to me.

Michael Dyer. You owe me a handmade Christmas present. Like, now.

Julie Pottinger. In all honesty, you wrote a few of the best lines in this book—fueled by your caramel macchiato without vanilla, of course.

Jennifer Schober. You know your schmidt, but always give me the room and support to learn it for myself.

Junessa Viloria. Working with you is a dream come true. Exclamation points to eternity!

Franzeca Drouin. I'm not sure which I appreciate more: your amazing research skills, or your baking abilities. Thank you for your friendship. And scones. Really, lovely scones.

Read on for an exciting sneak peek at

The Sinner Who Seduced Me

Stefanie Sloane's next Regency Rogues novel

Published by Ballantine Books
Available wherever books are sold

Late Summer 1811
PARIS, FRANCE

"Crimson?" the male voice drawled in disbelief. "*Vraiment?*"

Lady Clarissa Collins steadied her hand as she brushed the right hue onto the canvas. She stepped back and narrowed her violet eyes critically over the voluptuous female model draped across the blue damask divan. The elegant sofa was placed several yards away from her easel and angled toward the outer studio wall. The late morning sun poured through the elegant windows that made up the southern wall of the space, bathing the nearly naked woman in warm golden light.

Clarissa considered the canvas once again and used the tip of her little finger to barely smudge the fresh paint before nodding with satisfied decisiveness. "Now, Bernard, observe. Would you like to ask me again?"

Bernard St. Michelle, preeminent portrait painter of Paris and indeed all of Europe, frowned, lowered his thick black eyebrows into a forbidding vee, and turned toward the model. "You may go."

The woman lazily reached for her dressing gown and rose, nodding to both before disappearing down the hall toward a dressing room.

Bernard meticulously unrolled a white linen sleeve down one lean forearm and then the other. "Clarissa, how long have I been a painter?" he asked, his Gallic accent more pronounced.

Clarissa dipped her brush into a jug of turpentine and vigorously swished the bristles back and forth. She knew the answer to Bernard's question, of course. In fact, she knew the entire conversation that was about to take place, since they'd had it too many times to count.

"Longer than I," she answered, tapping the brush hard against the earthenware pitcher before dunking it a second time, resuming the swishing motions with more force.

Bernard adjusted his cuffs just so. "And while you were learning to dance and capture the attention of unsuspecting young men in London, what was I doing?"

Clarissa pulled the brush from the jar and rubbed the bristles with a paint-stained rag. Her grip was too tight, the pressure too fierce, and the slim wooden brush handle broke in two. "Destroying your tools?" she ventured, tossing the snapped end of the brush handle to the floor.

Bernard sighed deeply, ignoring the broken wood as he walked to where Clarissa stood. "I was working in London too, *chérie*, honing my craft during the Peace of Amiens. Even when the war broke out, I painted night and day—"

"Until returning to Paris—in the hull of a blockade runner, no less," Clarissa interrupted. "I know, Bernard. And I will remember if I live to be two hundred and two."

"Then you know that when I question your work, you listen? I believe that I've earned such respect. Don't you?"

He was right, of course. Since returning to Paris, Bernard's popularity with the ton had grown, his limited availability only making him more desirable. Sheer genius combined with the adoration of the elite was difficult to deny.

Clarissa eyed the other brushes in the pitcher, the urge to break wood calling to her like a siren. "But I was right, Bernard. The touch of crimson to define the subject's lip line is exactly what was needed."

"That is hardly the point, my dear—and you know it." Bernard pushed the table with the pitcher of brushes and the clutter of stained rags, paints, and palette knives beyond Clarissa's reach. "How can you expect to grow as an artist if you do not allow the world—and others with more experience—to inform your work?"

His midnight black hair had escaped its queue and feathered about his temples like so many brushstrokes, piled one atop another.

No matter how hard she tried, Clarissa could never stay angry at Bernard—especially when he was right. And since the day she'd met him, he'd been right about everything, unlike the long list of French painting masters who, despite her talent, had refused to take her as an apprentice because she was female.

Five years earlier, when their world in England had come crashing down, Clarissa had agreed to flee with her mother to Paris. The prospect of studying with François Gérard or Jacques-Louis David had held all her hope for the future. When both artists scoffed at her request simply because she was a woman, Clarissa dismissed them as the idiots they clearly were and moved on, working her way down a list of suitable teachers in Paris.

Despite her impressive portfolio of work, everyone she approached refused, until she was left with one: Bernard St. Michelle, the highly respected and, arguably, most talented painter on the European continent. She'd not placed St. Michelle higher on her list, having overheard that even male artists of her caliber could not secure a position with him.

But when she'd found herself with nothing to lose, she'd had her finest painting delivered to him—signed, "C. Collins"—and St. Michelle had granted her a personal interview. Clarissa had procured suitable men's clothing and made her way to his studio, intent on letting her art speak for itself rather than her sex doing all of the talking.

He'd agreed to take her on and with a handshake, the deal was sealed. Clarissa had taken particular pleasure in ripping the beaver hat from her head and revealing her topknot of glossy black curls.

Bernard had only sighed deeply and instructed her to arrive by eight in the morning—no earlier, no later—then told her to go.

Though he was her senior by only a handful of years, Bernard had become a mentor and friend, father and confidant. As trustworthy as he was endlessly talented. And he'd taught her more about her art and her life in the last five years than she'd learned in the previous nineteen.

The memory of just how much she owed this man had Clarissa sighing, her annoyance evaporating. She placed the flat of her palms on Bernard's cheeks, cupping his face, and gently squeezed. "At least I did not throw the brush this time, *oui?*"

He raised a thick black eyebrow in agreement. "Nor did you shout. Improvement, indeed, my dear. The fire in your heart is beginning to meld with the sense in your head. One day you will be the finest portrait painter the world has ever seen. Such self-possession will be of great value when working with the aristocracy."

"That, and my beaver hat," Clarissa replied teasingly, playfully pinching Bernard's face before turning to attend to the remaining brushes.

The sound of the front door slamming below followed by the heavy tread of feet on the stairs caught Clarissa's attention.

"Jean-Marc?" she asked, referring to Bernard's paramour.

"No." Bernard shook his head, waving her toward the dressing screen in the corner. "She weighs no more than a feather," he whispered. "Go."

Clarissa complied, leaving the brushes to the turpentine and tiptoeing quickly toward the colorful screen. She'd made use of the hiding place many times before when delivery boys or Bernard's friends had dropped in unexpectedly. A strategically placed peephole located in the upper corner of a painted butterfly's wing allowed her to see all that was happening without revealing her presence.

She'd barely whisked out of sight when three men entered the spacious studio.

"*Bonjour, Messieurs,*" Bernard greeted them in his native French.

"Bernard St. Michelle?" the tallest of the three men asked. He was perhaps Bernard's age, with small, glistening, black ratlike eyes and a balding head.

Bernard nodded. "Yes. And who might you be?"

The ratlike man stepped closer to view Clarissa's canvas, eyeing the painting with a lascivious gleam before turning back to Bernard. "I'm a man with a business proposition that I feel certain you will not refuse."

"If you're in need of my services, I'm afraid you will leave here disappointed. I am committed to the Comte de Claudel until next year," Bernard replied, his tone remaining even.

The Rat licked his thin lips. "Are you certain?" he inquired, gripping the carved silver top of his walking cane. With a quick twist, he pulled out a slim épée, the lethal fencing sword sliding silently from its hiding place. "Because, as I mentioned before, I'm quite certain you'll find this proposal impossible to refuse." He raised the blade and brought it down with force on the canvas. The painting ripped in two, a jagged cut appearing down the center of Chloe's reclining body. "And I am never wrong," he said, the words remarkable for their total lack of emotion.

Clarissa bit her hand to stifle the scream building in her throat. The men were more than common street ruffians and she was sensible enough, even when outraged by the wanton destruction of her canvas, to know when to keep quiet.

Bernard regarded the painting with quiet concern. "You have my attention, monsieur."

The two men positioned behind the Rat smirked in unison, their broad heads nodding with approval.

"You'll leave in three days' time for London to paint a portrait for a wealthy Canadian. There will be compensation, of course, as would be expected. And lodging . . ." the ratlike man paused and flicked a disdainful gaze about the cluttered studio, ". . . that will suit your needs."

Bernard folded his arms across his chest. "And the comte?"

With a swift, smooth flick of his wrist, the man slashed the blade at Bernard and a thin line of blood appeared on his face. "Tell the comte what you will. It makes no difference to me."

"And if I do not?"

"If you do not?" the Rat parroted disbelievingly. Without warning, he lunged at the dressing screen, the blade slashing the painted silk covering until all that stood was the wooden frame. "Then my employer, Durand, will kill the girl—and her mother, for good measure."

An instinctive survival response had sent Clarissa stepping back and away from the deadly tip of the weapon. Now she was exposed by the shredded silk screen and she lunged at the swordsman, raking her nails against his cheek. "Not if I kill you first," she spat out.

The Rat stood motionless, seemingly suspended by his utter surprise at Clarissa's attack. The neckless pair stared at the unexpected sight of the slender woman in blue dimity attacking their superior.

Of the four men, Bernard recovered first, grabbing Clarissa and shoving her protectively behind him. "Three days, gentlemen. I trust you'll stand by your word?"

The Rat touched his face, dabbing at the blood left by Clarissa's raking nails before licking the red stain clean from his fingertip. "Three days. No more, no less," he confirmed, his cold, menacing smile directed at Clarissa before he turned toward the hallway. The muscular pair of henchmen followed behind, their heavy footfalls growing more muted, until the outer door to the street below slammed and they were gone.

Bernard turned, his face set in stark lines.

"Do you remember what I said regarding the fire in your heart and the sense in your head?" he asked, clutching Clarissa's arms so tightly the skin beneath his hands turned white.

"Yes," she answered, wincing at the pressure of his fingers, a thousand unanswered questions threatening to spill from her lips.

"I was wrong."

Clarissa eased from beneath his hands and lifted the hem of her smock, pressing it firmly against the line of blood welling on Bernard's cheek. "Who were those men?" she asked, unable to control the tremble in her voice.

"Your guess is as good as mine," Bernard said grimly, his dark gaze meeting Clarissa's wide eyes. "But I may know someone who can tell us more."

James Marlowe detested salt water. Swimming was all well and good, but taking in repeated mouthfuls of the briny liquid was, in a word, hell. He dug his heels into the wet sand and looked out over the black water of the English Channel. A full moon rode high in the night sky, illuminating the crest and curl of the rolling waves.

He'd known from the beginning that penetrating Napoleon's darkest of organizations, Les Moines—The Monks— would be difficult. But when Henry Prescott, Viscount Carmichael, asked, one hardly thought in terms of ease.

He spat once, then twice, grimacing when the salty taste failed to disappear. James was an agent within the Young Corinthians, an elite British government spy organization that operated outside the bounds of normal channels.

Carmichael was the liaison between the spies and those in control of British government at the highest level—and those at the top were anxious to be rid of Bonaparte. When intelligence reports revealed Les Moines's troublesome strides toward securing Napoleon's dreams of adding Russia and Britain to his continental empire—Carmichael was tasked with putting an end to their efforts—once and for all—by fair means or foul.

James untucked his sodden linen shirt, pulling it free of his waistband, and rolled his aching shoulders. Carmichael had made it clear that no one but himself would know the true nature of James's assignment. He'd have very little in the way of resources other than his skill and wits. James was well aware that eventually all within the Young Corinthians would assume he had betrayed his compatriots and become a traitor to Crown and Country. It was not a role he relished, but he'd rather take it on himself than have Carmichael hand it off to one of his fellow Corinthians. Compared to others he had little to lose—and no one to care if he died while carrying out his assignment.

And so he'd agreed. It had taken over a year to secure his footing within the organization, and six months after that to prove his dedication to the cause, establishing a place in the despicable group.

Which had landed him squarely on the beach of St. Aldhelm's Isle where he'd done battle with his fellow Corinthians mere hours before. His most recent undertaking for Les Moines had him hunting for emeralds in the wilds of Dorset. He'd managed to ensure that the jewels would not fall into Napoleon's hands, but not without incident. The time had come to reveal himself as a traitor to his fellow Corinthian agents, and thus he'd been shot at by a baronet's daughter while trying to board a boat. Acting on instinct, he'd sunk below the waves and swum until his lungs nearly burst. When he'd surfaced, the Corinthians were gone, leaving the world to mourn the loss of James Marlowe, traitor.

He doubted anyone would spend more than a passing moment regretting his "death."

Out on the dark water, a light flickered, rising and falling on the swell of the waves.

He shoved himself up from the wet sand, standing as the light drew brighter with the approach of a boat that was scheduled to retrieve both James and the jewels.

There would be hell to pay for the loss of the emeralds, he thought, and his apparent untimely demise would be a nuisance. But James was well versed in the art of improvising.

"*Un beau soir pour aller nager, oui?*" one of the men called out, the other crewmen responding to his sally with hearty laughter as they shipped their oars.

Lovely evening for a swim, James silently repeated the man's words in English, grinding his teeth with the effort it took to keep from snarling a reply. He walked to the water's edge and stepped in, the wet sand sucking at his boots as he waded through the surf to the waiting boat.

"Merriment not from you, Marlowe?" the man asked in broken English as he offered James his hand.

James hauled himself up into the small skiff, the boat rocking as he took a seat near the bow. "The emeralds are gone," he growled in French, hardly having the patience for Morel's butchering of his mother tongue.

"Oh," Morel replied matter-of-factly in his sailors' patois. "They'll likely kill you, then. It was a pleasure knowing you."

A second rousing chorus of laughter broke out as the men lowered their oars and began to row. Morel pounded James on the back with a beefy hand. "I am joking, of course. Dixon and his men will see to the emeralds."

James knew Morel was wrong. There was no way the traitorous Dixon could retrieve the emeralds—now that they were in the possession of the Corinthians. Still, James saw no benefit in answering the man either way, so he simply nodded and looked out toward the waiting ship that would take him to France.

"Still, if I were you," Morel suggested, "I would give some thought to explaining yourself. Your aristocratic English face will get you only so far."

As if on cue, Morel's motley gang erupted in rough laughter once again.

"How long is the crossing to France?" James asked, ignoring Morel's comment.

"Twelve hours. Anxious to be rid of your country?"

James deducted twelve hours from the coming months it would take to bring down Les Moines. The sale of the emeralds had been intended to fund Napoleon's fight. With the jewels now in safe hands, James was that much closer to slapping the hell out of the organization.

"Something like that."

*   *   *

"Clarissa, do sit down." Isabelle Collins, daughter of the Comte de Tulaine, the estranged wife of Robert Collins, the Marquess of Westbridge, and Clarissa's beloved mother patted the space next to her on the gold settee.

"Mother, please," Clarissa groaned. She pressed her forehead to the cool glass panes of the window. Below, Parisian society strolled past 123 rue de la Fontaine, blissfully unaware of the tempest of emotion within Clarissa and Isabelle's home. "How you can sit still is beyond me."

"I am hungry and thirsty. Now, do come and sit, *chérie*."

Clarissa lifted her head and turned, taking in her mother's somber face. "We are in danger—Bernard is in danger," she began, sitting down and taking the offered cup of tea. "I've been to the studio, his home. He is nowhere to be found."

"Not even at the café?" Isabelle asked in a whisper.

Clarissa reached for a fourth sugar cube and pitched it into the cup. "No," she replied grimly, "not even the café."

"I feel sure Monsieur St. Michelle would not want to involve you further." Isabelle patted Clarissa's arm reassuringly, though her darkened eyes betrayed her concern.

Clarissa returned her cup to the silver tray with a snap, the sweetened brew sloshing over the sides and onto the plate of biscuits. "But I *am* involved—*we* are involved, Mother. Those horrible men threatened both of us. I've no idea how, but they knew I was there, as if they'd been watching Bernard's studio."

Isabelle traced the rim of her delicate cup with the tip of her forefinger, frowning in thought. "*Chérie,* could they not have heard your footsteps?"

"Even so, how did they know of you?" Clarissa countered.

"What young woman does not possess a mother?"

Unable to sit still, Clarissa rose from the settee and began to pace the plush carpet. Her muslin skirts swirled about her ankles, echoing her agitation. "Mother, this is all too coincidental. I cannot believe their knowledge can be explained so easily."

Isabelle gently set her cup and saucer on the tray, then cleared her throat. "Clarissa, *chérie*, there is no need to be so dramatic."

"On the contrary—this is hardly my emotions at play," Clarissa countered, clasping her hands behind her back as she stalked the length of the room and back.

She was afraid. Deep within her bones, she was terrified, and for good reason. Her mother's response, however, was hardly surprising. Before they had left London to live in France, Isabelle could not have been a more doting mother, loving wife, and caring friend. Her beauty and charm were matched only by the love she lavished on all those fortunate enough to be in her life.

And then her husband's flagrant affair came to light. The other woman was never identified, nor would Clarissa's father deny or confirm, but the damage was done all the same. Isabelle shut tight her heart and escaped into herself, choosing existence over emotion, the safety of distance over the danger of involvement.

Her father's betrayal had destroyed Clarissa as well, though her response could not have been more different from her mother's. She was enraged. She was embittered. She craved revenge.

For Clarissa, the betrayal was twofold, with the most important men in her life disappointing her in the worst way. For just as her father had set light to the happiness and security of her well-fashioned world, James had seen fit to burn it to the ground. James Marlowe, younger son of Baron Richmond, the love of Clarissa's life, had destroyed her world as surely as her father had set fire to Isabelle's.

"My dear," Isabelle said in a controlled tone, interrupting Clarissa's thoughts. "Let us not quarrel yet again on this point."

Clarissa stopped pacing and moved quickly to her mother, dropping to her knees next to Isabelle. "*Maman*, we are different, you and I—this you know all too well. You find weakness in love. I find my strength. I love Bernard, for he's been both mentor and dear friend to me here in Paris. I owe him far more than I can every repay. Therefore I must ensure his safety. I simply could not do anything else. Can you understand?"

Isabelle took Clarissa's hand and kissed it, holding it to her cheek as though it were the greatest of treasures. "I do, *chérie*, I do. But what is to be done? It seems that St. Michelle does not want your help. And do not forget: You are one woman against three ruffians. Hardly enviable odds."

"True enough," Clarissa agreed, "though perhaps not insurmountable."